What's Wrong with the Right Club?

Keith Edmondson

First published 2021
by Rowanvale Books Ltd
The Gate
Keppoch Street
Roath
Cardiff
CF24 3JW
www.rowanvalebooks.com

A CIP catalogue record for this book is available from the British Library.

Paperback ISBN: 978-1-913662-29-5

I dedicate this book to the extraordinary care and expertise I received from staff at both the Bradford Royal Infirmary and Marie Curie Hospice, Bradford. Without their input this novel would not have progressed beyond chapter five and would never have seen the light of day.

Contents

Fact: The Right Club – was a real organisation

In 1939 a secret political society called **the Right Club** was founded by British MP, Archibald Maule Ramsey. Its aim was to combat what Ramsay saw as the menace of 'International Jewry'. He recorded the names of the members, many of them MPs, peers, army officers and society hostesses, in a leather-bound ledger known as the **'Red Book'**. The members were a group of inter-war British pro-Nazis who attended meetings in South Kensington and were issued with a silver badge bearing the anti-Semitic motto 'Perish Judah'.

The society was short lived. Ramsay and many of his sympathisers were imprisoned for most of the Second World War under Defence Regulation 18b. The Red Book itself was seized by MI5 and Special Branch but 'disappeared' for many years, eventually being rediscovered in 1989 in a solicitor's safe. It was given to the British historian Richard Griffiths for purposes of research, and he in turn presented it to the Wiener Library in London.

The Red Book: The Membership List of The Right Club – 1939 by Robin Saikia (Foxley Books, June 2010) ISBN 978-1905742028

Praise for James Brittain
Series Novels

The 63 Steppes

Just finished reading your novel. I read it in about 4 days. It is great, fast paced, fun and I couldn't put it down! Interesting being set around Bradford....

— Peter Ingham

'A fast-moving thriller. Plenty of intrigue and action, twisting and turning to an exciting ending.'

— Penelope P

The puns made me laugh but did not detract from the tension and excitement as the story twisted and turned to its conclusion. The plot is clever and the detailed writing took me back to 1963 and the Cold War. I thoroughly enjoyed it and I would recommend it to anyone.

— Andrew Pullen

FROM CZECHOSLOVAKIA WITH LOVE

'Dear Keith, I did enjoy reading both books. I am now reading Len Deighton which bears a good comparison so that's all credit to you.'

— Edward Peel

'Much more than a sequel, this is a standalone beauty. Thrills, science, espionage and a tinge of humour are combined superbly. What makes this different however is the inclusion of some unique elements that are clearly familiar to the author: The Cold War, Leeds University, Textile Chemistry, 1960's life and politics of the day. Add some Northern locations and a distinctive but easily digestible writing style and you have a comfortable winner. Must re-read the 'prequel' now - and wait for the next (hopefully).'

— Phil Greaves

Acknowledgements

Grateful thanks are given to the following people for their encouragement, information, and valuable comments during the writing of this novel:

David Allen, David Dracup, Phil Greaves, Keith Hannay, Peter Ingham, Mike Lee, Mike Palin, Edward Peel, Liz Rice, Jennie Rowan and Colin Starkey.

A special thanks goes to Julie Partis for her expertise and diligence in proofreading the manuscript and her patience at putting up with my puns.

CHAPTER 1
JOBS FOR THE BOYS?

My feet on the flight of steps leading up to the Parkinson Building at Leeds University echoed in sync with my heartbeat, which was racing in anticipation of the meeting/job interview I was going to. Even I had to admit the venue was novel: an international conference on pesticides. What bugged me— *Oh God, pull yourself together, James*, I told myself. *We don't want flippant remarks like that to slip out on a stage like this—* was that in some respect the venue was a trip down memory lane as I'd studied chemistry at Leeds and knew the campus layout like the back of my hand. I had no problems locating the well-signposted room where the conference delegates were congregating to drink coffee and sign in.

'James Brittain,' I announced to a smartly dressed lady who was standing behind a small table, ticking off names on a form and supplying lapel name badges.

'Has Dr Gerry Engel of the wool institute arrived yet?' I enquired, as I struggled to force the blunt tip of the safety pin through the thick fabric of my Harris Tweed jacket.

'Here, let me help you.' She stepped out from behind the table, deftly removing the badge and re-attaching it, this time the correct way up and well positioned on my lapel. 'Yes—he's over there in the far corner, sir. He's the one with the smart blue suit.'

I thanked her and accepted a file of conference papers before taking a deep breath and heading for the man in the very smart blue suit.

The opportunity for this interview had cropped up unexpectedly as a result of my convalescence with Angela Jones' parents in their new home in Otley. Henry Jones was a long-standing member of MI6 and during our talks had suggested this interview for a job with a wool research organisation which had opportunities for foreign travel. Also, he could use a reliable undercover agent with impeccable credentials, so he'd wondered if this dual role would appeal to me. The idea sounded good to me, and things had been quiet for a few months after Nigel, Angela's and my boss in MI5, had decided I was expendable. I'd never really had a formal contract with them anyway, and Nigel and I had never seen eye to eye.

I was not sure whether Dr Gerry Engel was in on the undercover aspect of the job, but I was playing it straight and I wasn't taking anything for granted. Henry had told me the conference was an ideal opportunity to meet Dr Engel, as the wool research organisation was building a brand new facility in Ilkley and was interested in employing a German research chemist to work on wool mothproofing agents. This research chemist was also attending the pesticide conference, along with his boss, and Henry wanted me to keep an eye on them while at the conference and report back to him.

I wished I'd had time to read up on the international wool organisation, as it would have given me more background information and made me seem more professional. I would have to play it by ear and try to give a good impression.

Dr Engel was engaged in animated conversation with two other men when I approached, so I waited for an appropriate moment to catch his eye. He looked my way, glanced at my badge, immediately recognised my name and thrust out his hand in greeting.

'James, James Brittain, thanks for coming. Let me introduce you to Dr Heinrig Stein and Helmut Schultz. Helmut is considering coming to work at our new institute in Ilkley.'

We all shook hands. Dr Gerry Engel was American with a clipped accent which, I guessed, had been eroded by living for some time in London. His suit was a class above anybody else's in the room and could very well have been from Saville Row. Helmut was about my age with thick, horn-rimmed glasses, making him appear very studious. His English was limited, and he did not speak much. His boss, Dr Stein, was perhaps fiftyish and spoke good English, softly, with a strong German accent. His manner was condescending, as if it was a great honour for me to speak to him at all. Nevertheless, he did manage to shake my hand but avoided eye contact. Both Germans were dressed in rather shabby, almost identical, brown suits, which might have passed in this country as demob suits a few years ago.

'James is going to work in our international technical service department,' announced Dr Engel to my surprise, as I accepted a cup of coffee from a tray being offered by a waiter.

This form of work was obviously not deemed worthy of consideration by Dr Stein, who glanced at his watch and said, 'I think the first lecture is starting in five minutes. Come, Helmut; we find room.'

With that, they both bowed formally towards Dr Engel. I half expected them to click their heels as they left!

'Should we also be making a move, Dr Engel?' I ventured once the two Germans were out of earshot.

'Call me Gerry, James. We don't stand on ceremony in our organisation. Henry filled me in on your background, and the help you provided to MI5 last year during President Kennedy's visit was well appreciated by us Yanks.'

Dr Engel, or Gerry as I now should call him, omitted to mention the assassination of JFK in Dallas last November, which took the shine off any satisfaction I might have felt over my part in foiling a determined earlier attempt during his visit to the UK in June '63.

'I think we can give the first couple of lectures a miss as they are not really relevant to wool research. We can spend the time more usefully in getting you up to speed with our organisation and the part you might play in that.'

Gerry was the ultimate PR man and could probably have sold you anything from a fancy automobile to a washing machine you didn't think you needed; that's why he was overall research and technical service director for the wool research organisation. It was a fact that the wool-producing countries—Australia, New Zealand and South Africa—had joined forces to counteract the growing menace, as Gerry put it, of the man-made fibre market, which was making serious inroads into traditional wool areas, with trousers and suits with novel properties inherent to man-made fibres such as washable and easy-care written on them. The upshot was that the wool-producing countries had invested a phenomenal amount of money to fund a new research centre, the one now under construction in Ilkley, and there was to be a significant shift away from traditional marketing and towards technical marketing, which involved introducing new technologies into the marketplace, which would be to the advantage of wool products. All this was to be controlled and organised from the Ilkley institute, and it looked as if I could be part of this if I so wished. It seemed like a very good opportunity. Obviously I would need training up, which would take some time, but it was there for the taking—and on my doorstep too! Henry had been astute enough to realise the potential for undercover MI6 work carried out by wool experts travelling abroad on legitimate business—James Bond, watch out!

'It was opportune that you joined us when you did, James, since Stein and Schultz are the two German scientists Henry wants you to keep an eye on.' So Henry had already discussed my future role with Gerry, more than I would have expected. 'Stein is an expert on organophosphorus pesticides and knows all there is to know about them. He was actively involved in scaling up production of nerve agents during the war. Post-war he was offered a job at Porton Down but declined, preferring to work on agricultural pesticides instead, or so he'd like us to believe. He was lucky to avoid war crime charges since he actively helped the Nazi war effort, but fortunately, they didn't use their stockpile of nerve agents against us, or things might have been different.'

Things were starting to be a little clearer now. It was a pity Henry hadn't filled me in on more of the details before I'd jumped in, as usual, with my size tens.

'How does Schultz fit into this?' I asked.

'He wants to come and do a PhD with us on pesticide analysis. There's been an explosion of analytical work done recently, resulting in the detection of pesticides down to incredibly small levels. We need to be in on this, as mothproofing agents are important to us,' Gerry explained.

Gerry was clearly incredibly well connected; he might even have been a part-time CIA man as well, since he obviously moved in those circles, hence the Henry tie-up. I was keen to report back to Henry and hopefully prise more information out of him, since it looked as if it was going to be useful and I sensed there was more to Stein's visit than I'd been told so far.

'If you decide to join us, James—and I hope you will—I'd like you to meet our newly appointed R and D director, Dr Hamish Finlay, who's due to arrive in a couple of weeks' time. At the moment, the research staff are in temporary facilities in Bradford.'

'Why did you choose to build the new research institute in Ilkley?' I asked.

'We already fund a large amount of research carried out at Leeds University and Bradford Institute of Technology as well as WIRA—Wool Industries Research Association—just up the road from here, and Ilkley is closer to the major wool consuming and processing countries than the Southern hemisphere,' he answered.

Gerry then decided we ought to attend some lectures, and I sat through a number of interesting talks mainly concerned with new detection methods for analysing pesticide residues. I picked up on the growing environmental concerns regarding pesticide use and their persistence in the food chain, which were being discovered through these advances in analytical methods. We also attended a demonstration by one of the leading instrument makers, who showed how relatively straightforward it was to carry out the analytical procedures. I didn't find out how expensive the equipment was, but Gerry was straight in there doing some hard bargaining—I decided to ask him later for the details.

It was not difficult to keep an eye on both Schultz and Stein as they were present at all the lectures and demonstrations. At the finish, I waved to Gerry, who was deep in conversation with another delegate, as I left to follow the Germans out of the building.

For some reason or other, they decided to go into the Brotherton Library, which was attached to the Parkinson Building. I decided to leave them to it, mainly because I hadn't been instructed to tail them and there were another two days of the conference to go, so I made my way towards the main entrance, where I was stopped by a man I half recognised.

'What are you doing here?' he demanded.

'Why? What's it to you?' I replied, somewhat irritated.

'You're James Brittain, aren't you? They didn't tell me you'd be watching Stein.'

'Yes, I'm James Brittain. Who are you?'

'I'm with the security services. We've never met, but you were pointed out to me in London last year. I'm David Lithgow.'

We shook hands. I vaguely remembered seeing him when I'd been visiting Nigel with Angela. It turned out he worked for Nigel now. I commiserated with him!

'I've been interviewed for a job with an international wool research facility here in Yorkshire, as well as attending the conference,' I told him. 'It was by chance that I met Helmut Schultz and Heinrig Stein, who were talking to the research director I was meeting.'

'Oh, I see. What did you make of them?'

'Schultz didn't say much and Stein was rather arrogant; that was my first impression. They were in all the lectures I attended and have just gone into the library now. Maybe you should see what they are up to,' I suggested.

David Lithgow thought that was a good idea. He nodded and made his way towards the library entrance. I decided to see if Henry was still at home in Otley and hurried down the Parkinson steps towards a telephone box in Woodhouse Lane.

***

I drove over to Henry Jones' Otley house in Angela's minivan. Angela and I had cohabited for a while in her Leeds flat. It would probably have lasted longer but for Nigel wanting her back in London. However, I was allowed to stay on in the flat until I found out what I was going to do.

It was early October '64, about eighteen months since I'd attended my last interview in London, which had led me down a completely different career path than I'd intended. I just hoped my new venture would lead to a more stable way of life.

Henry's instructions seemed to be on a need-to-know basis. Perhaps he was testing me to see how I coped, or perhaps it was just his way of working, but I felt I should point out to him that I might do a better job if I was fully informed of all known facts right from the start.

Angela's parents had bought a house in Otley to retire to. Henry had about two years to go before he finally left MI6, but—in his words—he had a few loose ends to sort out first. One appeared to involve sticking his nose into MI5 business, and I was pretty sure David Lithgow would be reporting back on my presence at the pesticide conference to Nigel. I was interested to see how Henry wanted to play this from now on.

I drove through the centre of Otley to the main traffic lights, turned left at one of the many pubs strategically littering the main roads and soon came to a small road that led to a series of large stone-built houses backing on to the River Wharfe. I drove down the drive and parked in a substantial hard-surface area at the back of the house, overlooking the bend in the river. Grace Jones immediately greeted me at the back door with a beaming smile.

'Ha-ha, James—lovely to see you. You'll have a bite to eat with us the noo?'

As if you hadn't guessed, Grace was Scottish and was known to one and all as Amazin' Grace. She could talk the hind legs off a donkey, but tonight was not going to be one of those occasions as Henry butted in and, for once, put his foot down.

'Yes, Grace, but later. James and I have things to discuss first.'

'Come into the front parlour, James, where there's a nice fire. Want a drink?'

I accepted a straight Glenfiddich whisky and settled myself in a comfortable armchair. Henry wasn't Scottish but he'd acquired, possibly through marriage, an admirable taste for the single malt Scotch of which I highly approved.

'Well, how did it go?' said Henry.

'The interview, if it could be called an interview, went very well. It seems that Gerry Engel was well primed by you, and the job should be mine if I don't dirty my ticket over the next couple of days. Thanks very much for the introduction. Is Dr Engel connected to the CIA by any chance? He seems very well-up on security matters.'

'Excellent, I thought you'd get on well with Gerry. He's very perceptive and makes decisions quickly. I thought it best to let you handle it your way so you can decide whether the day-to-day job will be interesting enough for you. Since Gerry travels extensively worldwide, he keeps his ears open and passes on any useful information he comes across both to the Americans and to us. I don't think he has any formal arrangement with the CIA.'

'I met Heinrig Stein and Helmut Schultz. They happened to be talking to Gerry when I arrived, and he introduced me to them. They were both in the lectures we attended, and Schultz wants to do a PhD with the organisation.'

'Fantastic. I just wanted you to know who Stein was and to keep an eye on him. He's been a slippery customer, and I was interested to hear if he was in contact with anybody he shouldn't be.'

'Not from what I could see; he was with Schultz the whole time. But there's a fly, or more appropriately, a bug in the ointment! I was confronted by David Lithgow, MI5, who recognised me from last year and wanted to know why I was at the conference. I'm pretty sure he's swallowed my cover story, but he's going to report back that he's seen me. Is there anything I should know about Stein, for instance?'

'Right. Pity Lithgow recognised you, but it looks as if MI5 have put one of their more inexperienced laddies on watch duty. I'm not concerned if they connect me with your presence there. The worry is that Stein may still have connections to ultra-right-wing factions in this country. His nerve agent knowledge makes him a valuable asset, to both east and west, and he knows it!'

'Yes, Gerry hinted as much and said Stein was fortunate to have avoided war crime charges, since he assisted in the full-scale production of nerve agents for the Nazis. I found him somewhat arrogant and full of his own self-importance. Am I overreacting?'

'Not at all. He was a key man for them, and we're still not sure exactly where his loyalties lie; that's why I want to see if he makes any unusual contacts at the conference. Just keep tabs on him for the next couple days like you've done today, and that will enable us to get a better picture of him while he's in the UK.'

I was incredibly grateful to Henry for this job, but I decided that now was the time to press him further for more background on Stein.

'Is there anything you could tell me about Stein which would help me know what I'm looking for? After all, if I'm going to be any use to MI6 in the future, I'd need to be properly briefed before I jumped in at the deep end—or do I have to sign the Official Secrets Act again?' I said, rather undiplomatically.

'All right, James, point taken. I was one of the intelligence officers who debriefed Stein when he'd been captured after the war and we realised he was a key member of the group responsible for nerve agent production by the Nazis. When we discovered that the Germans had stockpiles of the wretched stuff, it became imperative to learn what we could from Stein. He was offered a job at Porton Down because we were worried that the Soviets would get hold of him. He refused the work but cooperated with us, reluctantly I thought, and he now works for Bayer on pesticides for agricultural use.'

'Do you keep tabs on him in Germany?' I queried.

'Of course. He's kept his nose clean so far, but these international conferences increase the risk of him coming into contact with Soviet agents or far-right sympathisers who don't accept that the war is over. MI5 is watching some known Soviet agents and a far-right group.'

'Don't you trust MI5 to do the job?' I ventured provocatively.

'It's not as simple as that; the political situation in this country is delicate at the moment. Should the socialists get in under Harold Wilson, which is a distinct possibility, there's a right-wing element within MI5 who would find it difficult to accept.'

'So, you're covering all options?' I mused.

'Yes, it just seemed a good opportunity to see things from a different unofficial angle as you were meeting Gerry Engel anyway.'

I wasn't sure Henry was telling me everything but I now had a clearer picture of Heinrig Stein's background, and from my brief encounter with him I, too, had got the impression he should be watched carefully. Henry was due to go back to London in the morning, so I was to ring him at his London office if there was anything important to report over the next couple of days.

After another Glenfiddich snifter, Henry and I surrendered to a very satisfying meal and endless local gossip from Amazin' Grace.

***

The following day, I trotted up the Parkinson steps once again, with more confidence than yesterday. At least I knew what was in store for me, and a job was on the cards at the new wool institute in Ilkley.

Sure enough, David Lithgow was on duty again, loitering close to the entrance of the Brotherton Library.

'Hello, David. I hope the two Germans haven't been in the library all night?'

'No, James, I've just arrived. Thanks for the library tip-off yesterday. Stein appeared to be looking at books on London, but we didn't think he was going there—that is, apart from the airport on his way home.'

I nodded and made my way to the lecture theatre, where I spotted Stein and Schultz in the same seats they had occupied yesterday. Gerry was, as usual, deep in animated conversation with another delegate near the door. We all sat through a couple of lectures which weren't very interesting to me—they were too theoretical and required a level of mathematical knowledge beyond my comprehension. I was relieved when it was time for coffee, which gave me a chance to stretch my legs again. I followed Stein and Schultz out of the lecture theatre and into the coffee hall.

'James.' Gerry dashed over to me, wearing yet another smart suit with pin-sharp trouser creases. *Who said wool science is not at the cutting edge?* I thought to myself. 'I was going to introduce you to Archer Martin, who worked at WIRA and invented the method of partition chromatography; he won the Nobel Prize for Chemistry for it in 1952, along with Richard Synge. I don't seem to be able to see him, but he said he was going to attend. He was also responsible for developing the gas-liquid chromatography technique, which is at the forefront of analytical methods in many different scientific disciplines today,' he added.

I didn't know this and was disappointed that Martin hadn't shown up yet. I was mightily impressed and realised I was very lucky to be invited to join this outfit; maybe the science part of my job would be more interesting than the MI6 work, which could turn out to be an unwelcome distraction. I decided it would be better not to mention this to Henry just yet.

Stein left the coffee room without Schultz, so I followed him out and saw he was heading for the library again. I noticed David Lithgow making a move to follow Stein, so I headed back to the lecture theatre.

Stein joined Schultz about an hour later after missing a lecture; I made a mental note to ask Lithgow on the way out what Stein had been doing. The day passed quite uneventfully, and we all trooped out of the lecture theatre into the main Parkinson Hall. Gerry kept me talking for a short while by mentioning there was a conference dinner in the evening at the university and I was very welcome to attend. I wasn't sure if it was a good idea as I didn't have a smart suit, but Gerry insisted and said he was sure Archer Martin would be there. I wilted and accepted.

I looked for Stein and Schultz, who had been ahead of me but had now left the building; I caught sight of Lithgow's back going through the door, so I followed him. As I left the Parkinson Building and stood at the top of the steps, looking down, I saw Stein and Schultz approach a waiting taxi. Lithgow had just reached the bottom of the steps and was watching them closely. A large Rover screeched to a halt in front of the taxi before they could get in. Two men in balaclavas jumped out and manhandled

Stein into the back seat. As Lithgow dashed towards them, shouting, one of the masked men pulled out a silenced gun and shot him neatly through the forehead, before jumping into the car and driving off.

It all happened so quickly, I didn't have time to react, but when I reached Lithgow he didn't look good at all. And then all hell broke loose!

CHAPTER 2
'CONSIDER YOURSELF...'

'Dammit, Angela, why the hell was Brittain at the conference?' seethed Nigel. 'And what was he doing with Stein?'

'I don't know exactly, but I believe he was trying to expand his contacts with a view to getting a job, since you let him go,' lied Angela, with as much conviction as she could muster.

Nigel knew that much, since David Lithgow had told him last night that Brittain was at the conference and had met Stein and his student companion. Now Lithgow was dead and Brittain had been at the scene. It all seemed too much of a coincidence, and he wasn't sure Angela was levelling with him either. He wasn't entirely stupid, and he'd realised immediately, much against his better judgment, that he was going to have to involve Brittain again, who he still believed didn't fit in or conform to his high standards.

Nigel, although he probably wouldn't have admitted it, was ultra-conservative with both a large and small C. He was one of the ill-defined number of senior staff at MI5 who dreaded the thought of the socialists gaining power, and now, with Harold Wilson at the helm, this was a real possibility in the next couple of weeks. He knew Brittain had socialist leanings—he'd seen the file MI5 had on him when he was at university—and under normal circumstances he would never have employed anybody like that.

Then there was Brittain's irritating, flippant sense of humour, which grated on him. At their first meeting Brittain had said he lived just outside the rhubarb triangle, which had thrown him completely. He hadn't understood it, and annoyingly, Angela seemed to find it amusing. Rhubarb, he hated the stuff. Working class stodge, to his mind. He stuck to the odd Garibaldi biscuit and, at a pinch, fig Newtons.

Nevertheless, he was now in a hole and was responsible for clearing up Lithgow's murder and finding out who had abducted Stein. This was serious and could blow up into a major incident if it wasn't handled carefully, and he had his own reputation to think of as well.

'You'd better get Brittain down here as fast as possible; we need to find out what he knows. I'm under a lot of pressure to get moving on this as soon as possible.'

Angela nodded, hastily left Nigel's office, made her way down the corridor to her own office and picked up the phone.

Eventually, about three hours later, she managed to contact James at her Leeds flat.

***

'Where have you been?' Angela said, irritated.

'Well, mainly trying to help the police with their enquiries,' I said, somewhat taken aback by her abrupt tone.

'Nigel wants you back in London as soon as you can make it. Can you get here tonight?'

'I don't work for Nigel now, Angela—remember?' I said, very sarcastically, still doubly sore at being dumped last year after taking a slug in the leg for Queen and country!

'OK, we need your help again, James. How about it?'

I'd anticipated I was going to be involved with the MI5 crowd again and had spent the last forty-five minutes on the phone to Henry in London, discussing the situation with him. He'd instructed me to cooperate fully but refrain from telling them anything about my connection with him or any of my future plans as an undercover MI6 agent. The fewer people who knew about that, the better. In a way I was looking forward to it. It could be very satisfying to see Nigel eating humble (rhubarb) pie, with or without custard. I spared a thought for the unfortunate David Lithgow who had paid the ultimate price, which nobody could have foreseen.

***

I travelled in unaccustomed luxury to London by the early morning train, which gave me time to go over the events of the past twenty-four hours. The main conclusion I came to was that I should have persuaded Angela to have the meeting in Leeds. Time was of the essence, and the trail could well have gone cold by the time I returned to Yorkshire. I had, at least, been able to supply the police with part of the registration number of the big black Rover car: AHD 5… I wasn't totally sure of the last two digits, but it gave them something to go on, as did the red upholstery I'd glimpsed in the interior. From the sound and performance of the engine, it could have been a souped-up Rover model 90 or 100. The thickset men with black balaclavas and jumpers had known exactly where to find Stein, but why had they only shot David Lithgow when Helmut Schultz was closer to them? Helmut was still helping the police with their enquiries. For once, the police had treated me with respect, as they probably believed I was still working for the security services. It was too complicated to explain the nuances to them, so I didn't try. All I could say, which was true, was Stein's abduction was totally unforeseen and we should pool our resources in order to find him.

I drew a deep breath as I knocked on Nigel's door and walked in. Angela was already present, a serious expression on her face.

'Sit down, Brittain. Good of you to uproot yourself from the rhubarb patch at such short notice,' said Nigel, rather jovially. I think I preferred him when he was in one of his normal moods and not attempting light banter; he should stick to the day job.

'What else can you tell us which might shed some light on the debacle yesterday?' he said, reverting to type.

I went over the details I'd told the police yesterday, including my couple of encounters with David Lithgow; then I remembered one thing I'd meant to ask Lithgow.

'Heinrig Stein kept going into the library, and David had found out that he was looking at books on London, which surprised him since he didn't think Stein was going to visit London. Also, Stein had missed a lecture and been in the library on his own. I think David saw this and had checked up on him.'

'Why were you interested in that?' asked Nigel sternly.

'Well, only because I'd been introduced to Stein and Schultz by Dr Engel and David had confronted me about my presence there. It aroused my curiosity,' I answered truthfully. 'It would be interesting to know what Stein was looking at in the library the morning he was abducted; it may or may not have anything to do with his abduction.'

'Yes, good point—perhaps you could follow it up?' said Angela, speaking for the first time.

'I don't think we should leave any stone unturned in the search for Stein,' agreed Nigel enthusiastically. Angela and I couldn't supress a giggle at Nigel's unintended pun, *Stein* being the German word for stone. Nigel appeared not to notice and continued, 'Consider yourself temporarily back in the MI5 fold again, Brittain. I think you're best suited to handle things in your neck of the woods.'

'I've been offered a job at The Wool Research Institute but no starting date has been discussed yet,' I pointed out, much to the surprise of both Nigel and Angela.

'Yes, yes, but this must take priority. I'll have a word with Dr Engel if you think there's going to be a problem?' countered Nigel.

'No, I don't think it will be a problem to Dr Engel, but it might have implications for Helmut Schultz, who was Stein's student and hopes to do a PhD in mothproofing research at the wool institute. I can liaise with Engel over this and perhaps find out more about Stein that way?' I suggested.

'Do it,' said Nigel decisively.

'You'd better get back to Leeds as soon as possible,' added Angela, reinforcing my original thoughts that we had wasted some time by my coming down to London, but it had served a useful purpose by gaining me employment again, and I was now even more sure I was ready and willing to get stuck into a new project.

Angela and I scurried down the corridor from Nigel's office, armed with the official go-ahead to carry out further investigations. To my surprise I realised I was humming:

'Consider yourself at home,
Consider yourself one of the family.
We've taken to you so strong.
It's clear we're going to get along.'

'You sound pleased with yourself, James,' said Angela with a disapproving air. 'But you know it's not going to be easy and it could be dangerous.'

'I know—there could be a *Twist* or two in it before we get to the end!'

Angela gave a groan and one of those exasperated looks which women are so good at when they want to silently express displeasure. I left to return to Yorkshire.

***

When I arrived back in Leeds, it was too late to go to the university library, so I called in at the police station to get an update on Helmut Schultz.

'He's still helping us with our enquiries,' I was told by the desk sergeant.

Just then, the inspector who had interviewed me appeared and shook his head, as if to say, 'Don't ask; I haven't got time to see you at the moment.' But I was wrong.

'His English isn't bloody good enough; we're getting nowhere,' fumed the inspector.

'I speak some German. Maybe I could help?' I offered.

'Really? Follow me.'

The inspector ushered me through the door and into the interview room where a dejected and worried-looking Helmut Schultz sat behind a table on which there was an ashtray full of cigarette butts. We exchanged a few pleasantries in English before I switched into German in an attempt to get Helmut to open up. It worked. The pent-up frustration from not being able to communicate effectively with the inspector and his colleagues spilled out in a torrent of rapid, colourful German. I didn't catch all of it, but after I'd queried certain points, the gist of it was that Helmut was as much in the dark as the rest of us. He didn't really know Dr Stein very well, as he'd worked in another department prior to learning he had been selected for transfer to the wool institute and would be accompanying Dr Stein to the conference in Leeds. All the details had been arranged between Dr Stein and Dr Engel, and the visit was being paid for by the wool institute. Stein hadn't communicated very much with Helmut on the journey to Britain; he'd been too preoccupied with reading papers to make any small talk.

My guess, from the brief encounter I'd had with Stein, was that he didn't do small talk with people he deemed to be insignificant or of lower status, such as students. There was definitely a touch of the master race about him, thinly masked under a veneer of scientific respectability.

Helmut was seriously worried that events might now affect his chances of studying for his PhD; this was his opportunity to make something of himself. I felt that we had something in common, since he was the breadwinner for his widowed mother in Germany, who relied on his financial support to get by. I believed his story, said I would liaise with Dr Engel and assured him that I didn't think that he was to blame and would put in a good word for him. He thanked me profusely and we shook hands again.

I then brought up the subject of his and Stein's visits to the Brotherton Library; what had they been looking up?

Helmut had been told, by Stein, to look up as much on wool research as possible. Stein had deposited him in a first-floor section of the library where the relevant references were situated and then gone back to quiz one of the librarians—he didn't know what about. They met up later at a prearranged time to go back to the lectures or to the Queens Hotel in the centre of Leeds. Trust Gerry Engel to choose one of the best city-centre hotels for his guests; he obviously believed in doing things in style, which seemed to bode well for me as a future employee.

Helmut also confirmed that after the conference he was returning directly to Germany via London Airport and not going into the city of London itself. He'd assumed Stein was doing the same, although he was not certain.

The more I learned about Stein, the more I began to distrust him. He obviously played his cards very close to his chest, and I now fully appreciated Henry's comment about not knowing exactly where Stein's loyalties lay. Helmut couldn't remember seeing Stein talking to anybody unusual; they had kept a fairly low profile both at the conference and in the hotel. He had only seen Stein once in the hotel, talking to Dr Engel in the bar. I realised the number Gerry Engel had written on the back of the card he'd given me at the conference was probably the Queens Hotel number. I would have to check it out later on.

Helmut was in need of some other relief, and he was let out of the room to visit the gents. I took the opportunity, in his absence, to update the inspector with my findings. It was not totally to his liking, but he accepted it when I volunteered my thoughts on Stein's character saying that, if he didn't believe me he should talk to Dr Gerry Engel, who'd obviously had more dealings with Stein than any of us. Helmut was going to be allowed back to the hotel to attend the final day at the conference; it was likely he would be allowed to return to Germany unless there were significant developments in the next twenty-four hours. I told Helmut all this when he came back into the room and said if he needed any support from me in liaising with Gerry Engel, he'd just to ask.

I took my leave and headed back to Angela's flat with the intention of ringing both Gerry at the Queens Hotel and Henry in London. The number on the back of Gerry's card was for the hotel, but he wasn't in; I was informed I would have to wait until tomorrow before I spoke to him at the university on what would be the final day of the conference. Surprisingly, since it was early evening, Henry was still in his London office and was keen to speak to me. I updated him on my meeting with Nigel and Angela in London and told him about my role as police liaison officer-cum-interpreter for Helmut Schultz. Henry informed me he'd be travelling back from London tomorrow morning—could we meet up at the Black Bull in Otley for lunch? I thought this odd, but Henry quickly explained that he didn't want to compromise Angela's position with Nigel, as his wife, Amazin' Grace, would be sure to tell her about my visit to their house when they next spoke. It was all getting a bit complicated for me, but I had no choice but to comply.

***

I'd had an unexpected phone call from Angela late last night informing me she was coming up to Leeds the following day, asking me to leave her van at the Mill. Nigel had thought it useful for her to be at the sharp end in order to keep him fully informed. I'd mixed feelings over this complication. It would be nice to have her around again, but it might seriously cramp my style in liaising with Henry, her father. I'd told her I was going to be at the university all day with Gerry—so how was I going to see Gerry then flash over to Otley for my lunchtime meeting with Henry without Angela's van? These were my immediate thoughts as I jumped off the bus in front of the Parkinson Building after having dropped Angela's van off at the Mill.

'Ah, there you are, James,' said Gerry Engel, who had obviously been hovering about just inside the main entrance, waiting for me to arrive. 'Terrible business over the guy who was shot and the abduction of Dr Stein. What can you tell me?'

'David Lithgow worked for MI5 and was also keeping an eye on Stein. He'd introduced himself to me on the first day of the conference. I was in London yesterday updating his boss on events and trying to help the police with Helmut Schultz, who they had detained for questioning. Helmut's worried that it could jeopardise his chances of doing his PhD at the institute. I said I would put in a word in with you, as he knows nothing about what happened,' I volunteered, as it was prudent to keep Gerry on side and I had been given the nod by Nigel to liaise with him. 'I've also been seconded by MI5 to look into things here—to take over from David Lithgow, you might say—so I won't be able to attend any lectures today, if that's OK by you?' I added.

'You'd better be careful; we don't want you shot before you have the chance to become 'Our Man in Ilkley' do we?' said Gerry, wittily but deadly serious. 'Don't worry about Helmut,' he continued. 'I'll have a talk with him and reassure him things will be OK. What are you going to do today?'

'I'm just going into the Brotherton Library to see what Stein was looking up. David Lithgow told me he'd been looking at books about London.'

'Interesting. Oh, by the way, James, Hamish Finlay is coming up to Yorkshire next week to see how the new institute's building is progressing and to meet his senior managers in Bradford. I've told him about you and our special arrangement, and he would like to meet you. How about Wednesday morning?'

'In Bradford?'

Gerry nodded, adding he would be there and would introduce me.

Just then, Helmut appeared as if on cue, Gerry nodded to me, took him by the arm and led him away for a confidential chat, giving me the chance to enter the Brotherton Library and buttonhole a librarian.

'Excuse me, miss, I wonder if you could help me. I'm helping the police with their enquiries, and I'm interested in finding out what the German gentleman who was abducted the day before yesterday was looking at?'

The librarian, a very attractive young lady, nodded and begged me to wait a minute. She swiftly disappeared and returned with the head librarian, a formidable Miss Frobisher, probably forty years wiser, who listened intently to my questions.

'I'm sorry, Mr Brittain, the person who could help you is Miss Havisham, but she only works afternoons. Could you come back later?'

Disappointed, I toyed briefly with commenting that I shouldn't build my hopes up for any 'great expectations' from Miss Havisham, but Miss Frobisher's piercing gaze quickly dampened my thoughts of a witty aside, so I lamely agreed to do as she suggested.

Nevertheless, I quickly realised I would now have more time to get to Otley for my meeting with Henry, so I left the university and jumped on the first bus heading into Leeds city centre, where I made my way to the bus depot and consulted the timetables on the waiting room wall. In thirty minutes, I was on my way to Otley, relieved to have a minor distraction and looking forward to seeing Henry. Perhaps he could suggest what I should/ shouldn't tell Angela, as it was going to be tricky.

***

The Black Bull was easy to find, only a couple of minutes away from the Otley bus station on Vicar Lane and right next to the small, cobbled marketplace. My eye was caught by a prominent sign on the outside whitewashed wall, which announced that the pub had been drunk dry by Cromwell's troops on the eve of the battle of Marston Moor in July 1644. I was relieved to find the bar was now fully stocked with Tetley beers; I selected a pint of mild for a change. It was expertly pulled by the talkative, mutton-chopped landlord, who in addition to informing me that the Black Bull was the oldest pub in Otley was also keen to find out as much about my business as he could. I was somewhat economical with my answers, preferring to concentrate on my meeting with Henry.

I settled myself comfortably in the empty snug bar and was on my second pint when Henry finally arrived and, after ordering an identical pint to mine, sat down with a smile.

'Great, James, we shouldn't be disturbed much today as it's not market day. They do a very good pie and peas here—shall we order?'

I nodded, just realising I was getting decidedly peckish.

'Angela's arriving in Leeds today to keep a close eye on developments so she can report to Nigel, which might make things a bit awkward for us. You'd better brief me as to how I should handle this.'

'Oh, I see, I hadn't anticipated that. We'll worry about that in due course. Are there any more developments to report since we last talked?'

'No, not really. I won't be able to find out until later on this afternoon what Stein was looking at in the library, since the librarian who dealt with him only works afternoons.'

'I thought I might find you here, Dad, but not you, James!' said a puzzled Angela, who suddenly appeared in front of us in a somewhat aggressive stance.

'Sit down, luv; it's nothing sinister,' said Henry, who was obviously well versed in handling tricky situations and family confrontations. 'I asked James here last night as I was keen for an update on how his meeting with Gerry Engel had gone, and obviously James' first-hand account of the shooting and abduction as well. What you probably aren't aware of is I was one of the officers who debriefed Stein after the war and I've kept an interest in his career since, so I may be able to fill in some background which could come in handy. It would appear you could use all the help you can get, wouldn't you say?'

Henry had taken the wind completely out of Angela's sails, and she meekly acquiesced, sitting down at our table and accepting my offer of a drink plus pie and peas. I slid away thankfully to the bar to place the order, marvelling at Henry's handling of the situation and leaving him to complete the job. At this stage, it was not necessary for Angela to be in on my potential MI6 future career—after all, nothing had been formally agreed yet. If Henry was happy to handle it this way, I could go along with it.

'So you see, Angela, it was opportune for us all for James to be aware of Stein's nerve gas history with the Third Reich, and it was your unfortunate MI5 laddie who confronted James at the university, which focused our attention on Stein's activities. Now all we've got to find out is what Stein was really up to,' said Henry, just as the pie and peas arrived.

We demolished our food in silence, each preoccupied with their own thoughts. Henry waited until we'd all finished and put our knives and forks safely down before announcing:

'Oh, and by the way, we've just had word yesterday that Stein gave notice on his flat and handed in his keys. As far as we know he's not rented another flat anywhere else in Germany. This is what I specifically wanted to tell James today. Call it MI6/MI5 interdepartmental cooperation, if you like.'

This time both Angela and I were speechless. The implications were obvious—Stein was definitely up to no good.

CHAPTER 3
CETTE SAUCE DE HAUTE QUALITÉ...

I managed to persuade Angela to give me a lift back to Leeds since she was as keen as me to find out what Stein had been looking at in the Brotherton Library. We presented a combined front to the formidable Miss Frobisher, who wished to see our credentials before allowing us to talk to the elusive Miss Havisham.

Having satisfied her on this score, Miss Havisham was wheeled out. She didn't fit my mental picture at all. Instead, she was a well-groomed, thirty-fiveish stunner, who quietly and efficiently placed a series of books in front of us, explaining that Dr Stein had specifically asked for anything they had on the Houses of Parliament and the Palace of Westminster. She had also been asked to provide a copy of this page—a layout of the Palace of Westminster building. Angela asked if she could do the same for us whilst we thumbed through the contents of the pile of books. The first book I examined outlined the composition and function of both Houses of Parliament, Lords and Commons, together with the sitting members of Parliament at the time of writing and the timetable of major events throughout the parliamentary year. Everything, in fact, you'd need if you were a modern trainee Guy Fawkes!

'Are you thinking what I'm thinking, Angela?'

'Too right I am. We need to inform Nigel right away.'

We quickly arranged to borrow the books, which required Miss Frobisher's permission, then headed for the Mill.

'Shouldn't we bring Henry in on this?' I suggested.

'Nigel wouldn't like it. Better to let him come up with that,' Angela replied.

***

Nigel didn't like his routine disrupting, especially when it meant travelling up to Yorkshire by the early morning train. Nevertheless, this was an emergency and even he could see the logic of making the trip. His intuition had told him there was more to Brittain's involvement than he'd been told, and he was going to get to the bottom of it. He'd keep Henry Jones out of it of course, but it was good of the old boy to be so helpful.

Naturally, Nigel knew of Angela's dalliance with James—that was all he could seriously believe it was. Angela was good at her job, for a woman, and she had all the right connections too. He interpreted her involvement with James mainly as sympathy for a colleague after he had been shot in the leg during the JFK incident last year. Nigel was well aware of her father's position within MI6 and believed he was in the winding-down phase of his career, with only about two years to serve before retirement. Like Henry, Nigel had similarly been introduced into the security services by serving with military intelligence during the war and had been involved in screening potential ex-Nazi war criminals post-war. He'd admired Henry, but was jealous of him, since he'd reaped the rewards Nigel knew *he* deserved. Nigel had his eye on Henry Jones's job and intended to make the most of any potentially useful opportunities which may come along. He sensed the Stein case might fit the bill. He found it interesting that Henry had apparently pulled a few strings to get Brittain a job with a wool institute, a type of employment which, in Nigel's opinion, would be a much more suitable position for him, given his training and class background, than MI5 work. Angela would soon come to her senses and forget him when he started his new career—good for Henry for spotting this.

Nigel was feeling a little more relaxed now, as the train approached Leeds. The first-class travel to which he was entitled, together with a very appetising early morning breakfast, had put him in a really good mood.

***

Angela and I were all ready and waiting when Nigel made his appearance. He shuffled into the meeting room in his smart, blue, pin-striped suit, which had developed some unseemly creases, probably due to the train journey. I no longer viewed Nigel's infirmity lightly, as I too had suffered some side effects from being shot in the calf. Even though more than twelve months had passed, I still had some stiffness and aching, which was worse on a Monday morning if I'd been less active over the weekend. The doctor had said it would lessen with time. I just hoped he was right.

In the past I'd judged Nigel to be the pinnacle of smartness, but Gerry Engel was streets ahead to my mind. Maybe I should arrange for them to meet up and observe Nigel's reaction? Mavis, Angela's highly efficient secretary at the Mill, had prepared coffee and biscuits and was hovering around in case there was anything else she could assist with. There wasn't, so she went into her office and closed the door, leaving us free to start the meeting. To my delight, Mavis had provided, amongst others, four-fingered KitKat chocolate biscuits, one of my favourites, which I readily sampled.

Angela took the lead and started the meeting off summarising our latest findings.

'I think we now have enough info to go on to be sure that Stein is involved in some plot which threatens the fabric of our nation,' she finished. 'The police have just informed me this morning that they have found the car which was used to abduct him.'

Nigel looked suitably pleased and was in a far better mood than I ever would have expected, especially as he'd been up since the early hours of the morning. Angela laid out the floor plan of the Houses of Parliament directly in front of him.

'You think he's planning an attack on the government?' said Nigel sharply.

'At least. He's got all the information he needs to plan something centred at Westminster,' I added, showing Nigel the reference books we'd borrowed from the delightful Miss Havisham. I'd made a mental note to return them personally to her one afternoon.

'Don't you think we need to put more resources into this now, Nigel?' queried Angela.

'He could have just been abducted. Have there been any sightings of him at airports or cross-Channel terminals? What's the police take on this? They're involved in a major manhunt; I don't want to just duplicate what they're doing.'

'There's one thing that doesn't add up,' I said. 'Stein's obviously pretty smart and has managed to keep his nose clean since the war, yet he makes the obvious mistake of cancelling his flat rental, which he'd have known we'd pick up on. Seems out of character for one of the master race. Maybe we need to ask Henry Jones for more on Stein's background?'

Angela looked uncomfortable about this, and I remembered too late that she'd previously requested that we'd leave involving Henry to Nigel.

'It could be useful,' conceded Nigel, much to Angela's and my surprise.

'He's actually in Yorkshire at the moment,' said Angela, before I was tempted to put my foot in it again.

'Ah well; might be worth having a word with him, since he's been helpful so far.'

This seemed totally out of character for Nigel, and I could see Angela thought the same. There was no doubt in my mind that he had an ulterior motive behind this.

'Do you think we could see him this afternoon? I could fit it in before I return to London this evening,' said Nigel.

Angela jumped up, went into Mavis' office and rang her father at home.

She returned a few minutes later. 'Yes, he can see us. Since it's a busy market day in Otley, he's offered to come here around one p.m., OK?'

'Fine. James could probably follow up the lead on the car while we see Henry, yes?' said Nigel, to my annoyance. I was not happy about this; it was my idea to research Stein's background, and now Nigel wanted to muscle in on it.

'Stein's nerve gas expertise makes him especially dangerous,' I said. 'You know he oversaw the scaling up of the manufacture and stockpiling of certain nerve agents, such as tabun, for the Third Reich during the war, don't you?'

'How do *you* know?' said Nigel sharply.

'Gerry Engel told me. He's been liaising with him since Helmut Schultz is supposed to be coming to do a PhD on mothproofing at the institute.'

'Did you manage to quiz Dr Engel on Stein yet, like we agreed in London?' Nigel asked irritatingly.

'No, he was tied up in lectures, so I concentrated on getting the library angle first,' I replied evasively. I sensed Nigel was getting a little out of his depth, as he didn't appear to see the link between mothproofing chemicals and nerve agents.

'Best you quiz Dr Engel while we talk to Henry, OK?' he concluded.

'It probably won't be until next Wednesday, since Gerry's gone back to London now the conference has finished. He's invited me to meet the new director of the institute next week,' I parried, angling to be included in the Henry talks.

'OK. Since you're closer to the chemistry side of nerve agents, we'll all see Henry,' agreed Nigel.

***

The time passed quickly until Henry Jones tapped on the door and walked in with a nod to us all.

'So good of you to come and see us at such short notice, Henry,' fawned Nigel, embarrassingly to my mind.

'Not at all, Nigel. Would have preferred the Black Bull in Otley to here, but with it being market day, holding a private conversation might have been difficult,' responded Henry, putting Nigel at ease effortlessly. 'I think I should come clean with you all, since the Stein events have taken a turn for the worse,' he continued to our surprise. 'As you know, I got James an interview with Gerry Engel, and from what James has told me, he has secured a job with the institute, which is having a new research centre built in Ilkley. It should be a good opportunity for James as he has the right scientific background they are looking for. What I also asked James to do, while he was at the conference, was to keep an eye on Stein and his student and report back to me.'

Nigel looked ecstatic. He'd clearly suspected there was more to my involvement, and he'd been proven right. I could read his mind; it was so obvious. I noted that Henry hadn't divulged his future plans for me as an undercover MI6 agent, so I left it up to him to inform the others if he wanted them to know. I was impressed, watching a master at work.

'Before I go on, I'd like your assurances that what I'm going to tell you remains between the four of us,' said Henry pointedly.

Angela and I immediately nodded in agreement, but Nigel's expression changed from one of extreme benevolence to apprehension.

'I'll have to keep my DG informed of course,' he said uncomfortably, well aware that he needed to put a positive spin on his trip to Leeds.

'At this stage we need to keep both our DGs out of it; it's as sensitive as that,' insisted Henry, referring to the Director Generals of both MI5 and MI6.

I could see where he was coming from, since he'd previously told me that one of his major concerns was the right-wing bias of certain sections of MI5, which may or may not include the DG himself. Nigel, faced with a rather embarrassing outcome if he didn't agree, caved and accepted Henry's conditions, desperate to learn what he knew.

'Like you, Nigel, just after the war, we screened technical experts and ex-Nazis with special knowledge to see if we could make use of them,' Henry said. 'Stein claimed he'd been forced to work on nerve gas development, which involved scaling up production for future use. We subsequently found they had manufactured 12,500 tonnes of tabun, which was loaded into munitions such as shells and bombs. We offered Stein a job at Porton Down to work on nerve gases, but he refused, saying he only wished to work on insecticide research. The trouble is the chemistry of insecticides and nerve gases is so similar, it's difficult to monitor what the scientists are doing unless you are in the laboratory with them.'

'So how is Stein a threat to us here in the short term?' Nigel asked, looking puzzled.

'Well, if you take tabun as an example, it is extremely toxic to mammals, working by destroying the functioning of the nervous system. Once tabun is absorbed, it prevents the action of a key enzyme that regulates all nerve transmission processes. Victims suffer blindness, lose control of bodily functions and suffocate. Death follows in a matter of minutes. It can be absorbed though the lungs, skin and eyes; as little as one millilitre absorbed through the skin could be fatal. This means you could potentially kill all sitting members of the House of Commons with less than one litre of tabun, if correctly administered!'

We all sat there in stunned silence.

'Stein was researching all aspects of the Houses of Parliament, Palace of Westminster, et cetera,' I quickly added.

'Yes, but where would he get this stuff from?' asked Nigel naïvely.

'Nigel,' said Henry, matter-of-factly. 'Stein is more than capable of making tabun himself if he has access to the chemicals and suitable laboratory facilities. It's a distinct possibility that he's involved in a plot to strike at the heart of our government. I've been told, at the highest level, to cooperate with you to find Stein and his abductors and neutralise them.'

I remembered Gerry Engel mentioning to me that Stein had managed to avoid being charged with war crimes due to a lack of substantial evidence of his knowledge of the inhumane use of concentration camp labour to carry out tabun production at the Monowitz-Buna (or Auschwitz III) factory in Southern Poland. How he could distance himself from the human suffering when he was on site beggared belief—the nerve of the man.

'Does Stein have family in Germany? Wife, children?' asked Angela.

'Yes—good point, Angela,' said Henry. 'He's married, second wife, and she appears to have disappeared. We haven't been able to trace her as yet.'

'But he's cancelled the rent on his flat, which looks as though he's not intending to go back.' I said.

'Correct,' said Henry.

'Isn't that rather a basic mistake to make? He must have known he was under surveillance.'

'Correct again.'

'OK, Henry, what's the worst scenario we're looking at here?' said Nigel, focussing all our attention on where we were going from here.

'My guess, it's a nerve gas attack on the Houses of Parliament at some important occasion in the near future. My bet, since we're in the middle of a general election, is that it's the State Opening of Parliament, which will be three to four weeks after the election, sometime early November. Which means we've got about six weeks to sort it out,' said Henry solemnly.

'Of course—a Guy Fawkes-style assassination attack to paralyse our democracy,' said Nigel, finally getting the point. 'James was just about to go and see what the police could tell us about the getaway car they've found when we realised you were in Yorkshire.'

'Ah, a further development, good,' said Henry. 'This could be a very important lead; perhaps you should follow this up immediately, James?'

I felt very much the junior partner, being summarily dispatched to follow up the lead. In reality, that was exactly what I was, and in some respects I preferred it to be this way as it was my chance to move things on and really contribute to the inquiry. I duly nodded, slyly palmed the last remaining KitKat, picked up Angela's minivan keys from Mavis' office and headed for the police station in the centre of Leeds.

***

To my annoyance, I learnt that Inspector Broadley, with whom I had dealt previously, was on site close to where the getaway car had been found. Apparently, he had set up his operation room in the Rodley Barge pub, about five miles away from the police station—*Very convenient*, I thought—so I set off immediately to find him.

'Oh, they've sent you, have they? About time,' said Inspector Broadley from behind a large plateful of ham and eggs with a generous helping of chips, which had just been placed in front of him in a small room reserved for small public functions. It was now turning half past two, and I quickly realised that my present irritability, despite the KitKat hors d'oeuvres, was probably influenced by a lack of sustenance. It was immediately obvious that I was not likely to get anything sensible out of the inspector until he had dealt with the task in front of him, so I enquired at the bar if they were still serving food, and could I have something similar? They were, so I settled for just ham and eggs, which was likely to be the quickest option.

The inspector was aptly named, being virtually as broad as long. He was seemingly oblivious to my presence as he attacked his ham with a surgical dexterity honed to perfection by years of practice, no doubt. I tried, unsuccessfully, not to stare, but was transfixed as he dolloped his chips with a generous helping of HP sauce. It was strangely appropriate, I thought, since we were no doubt trying to avert an attack on the Houses of Parliament. In a moment of distraction, I was transported back to my schooldays when the HP label gave me my first lesson in French: *Cette sauce de haute qualité est un mélange de fruits orientaux, d'épices et de vinaigre. Elle est absolument pur et ne contient aucune matiere colouratif ni preservatif.* See, I could still remember it word for word, and fancied I could do a passable impression of Maurice Chevalier saying it, although now was not the time to try. I didn't want to give Inspector Broadley indigestion through laughing.

'There, that's better. I was ready for that,' said the inspector with a satisfied sigh.

Broadley speaking, I thought to myself indulgently.

'You know we've found car? Down by t' canal.'

I nodded.

'Clean as a whistle, apart from Kraut's prints,' added the inspector. 'Rover was stolen day afore abduction in Rotherham; nowt really to go on there.'

I was not liking what I was hearing so far. 'Did anybody see the car being left by the canal?' I queried.

'No, you'll see later, it's a deserted spot near t' canal, not overlooked,' said the inspector, almost enjoying seeing me squirm with the as yet negative findings. 'But, taxi driver who was waiting to pick Krauts up at university is sure he heard bloke shot shout, "STOP, COLIN!"' said the inspector triumphantly.

'So; David Lithgow recognised one of the men wearing balaclavas?' I said excitedly.

'Exactly. There's summat to go on there.'

I was trying to remember what I'd seen from the top of the Parkinson steps, looking down on events. I'd been too far away to hear anything clearly, but it would have made sense if David Lithgow had been shot because he had recognised one of the abductors.

Chapter 4
Barging Around Yorkshire

Heinrig Stein had been expecting to be picked up by associates of the people he'd been dealing with in Germany, but he hadn't expected anybody to be shot. Things had gone horribly wrong.

Stein was acutely aware of his value to both the east and west. Some might interpret this smug self-confidence as arrogance, but he didn't care what people thought. He held all the cards, and for the immediate present, he was going to make the most of it. Terrified of being abducted into the Soviet Union, he had allowed himself to be seduced into cooperating with a far-right political group in Germany, the National Democratic Party (NPD). Alright, they were Neo-Nazis, if you like, but they were ruthless and had kidnapped his wife a week before he was due to fly to England. They'd suddenly upped the stakes and demanded that he prepare a quantity of tabun nerve agent while he was in England, since they were worried the socialists were going to win the British general election.

Stein was not overly political, but he had sympathies with the new right wing in Germany, and as a pragmatist he did what he had to do to further his career and survive. He'd been lucky to avoid being prosecuted for war crimes. To be honest, he'd been well aware of the atrocious conditions the labour force had endured in the work camps but had justified it to himself in terms of the bigger picture—there are always casualties in total war;

they were just collateral damage. He'd overseen the scaling up of tabun production from laboratory to factory for the Third Reich, a significant technical achievement in very difficult conditions, of which he was justly proud and for which he had been rewarded. It was this knowledge that had shielded him, and he had eventually managed to return to Germany to continue basic research on pesticides, which he believed would better further his career and achieve international scientific recognition.

He'd known before he left Germany that what he was being blackmailed into doing was a step too far. All his plans would be destroyed. So, he had subtly cancelled the lease on his flat just before he left, knowing this would be noticed by those who kept him under surveillance. Nothing had happened—he'd not even been questioned—and he began to wonder how good the security services were nowadays. During the war, the SS would have pulled him in like a shot over a stunt like this. He'd noticed a man hanging around the university building who could have been watching him; this was almost certainly the case, as the man had attempted to intervene when he was abducted, resulting in his being shot.

Stein had specifically made a trip into the university library to look up details on the Houses of Parliament; he was familiar enough with the British political system to know it would be a key target for any terrorist attack. He had no specific knowledge that this was the intended target but hoped somebody might put two and two together. Unfortunately, the man who might have noticed had been eliminated.

For a short time before he'd left Germany, Stein had toyed with the idea of calling his captors' bluff. His marriage was on the rocks anyway and they might do him a favour by disposing of his wife—she was becoming a liability. He'd decided against it, as the trip to the Leeds conference was vitally important to him and he needed to develop his new contact, Dr Gerry Engel, the wool research director who seemed to have unlimited funds at his disposal. In the short term he had no option but to go along with his abductors, a decision he was now regretting, and right now self-preservation was paramount.

All these thoughts flashed through his mind. He had had plenty of time to think. He was being held captive on a canal boat somewhere in the north of England. After being bundled into the car outside the university, a sack had been placed over his head then he had been driven quickly, and somewhat erratically, for no more than fifteen minutes before stopping just after crossing a short, creaking bridge. He had been half dragged at a run by his two abductors back over the bridge and onto a boat, which began to move shortly afterwards. The sack was removed after about two hours, but by then it was dark outside, and he was told to remain inside the cabin until they were ready to move him again.

Two days passed. All he could see through gaps in drawn curtains during the daylight hours was that they were on a canal system, as they moved through a series of locks and moored up for short periods of time. It was peaceful and obviously they had escaped the attention of the police, who were no doubt concentrating on roadblocks and searches at airports and ferry terminals. He was singularly impressed by their getaway plan, which appeared to be working so far. He turned his attention to thinking how he might extricate himself from this situation but decided he would have a better chance when they gave him access to laboratory facilities. He could think of a few nasty tricks he could use when he could 'try out' the effectiveness of tabun; he'd witnessed first-hand its devastating effects on selected workers deemed expendable during the war. Yes, he could easily pipette a few millilitres into small phials for emergency use when necessary. He was likely to be alone in the restricted area during preparation, when he could virtually do whatever he wanted. In Germany, he'd given them a list of the chemicals he needed, also the facilities and equipment necessary for the safe preparation and storage of tabun. His main worry was that he might be required to assist in advising on administering the tabun, but he would have to wait and see.

***

Henry Jones had specifically dispatched James to find out about the abductors' getaway car, knowing he was probably a bit miffed at being left out of the talks. Henry had been angling to meet up with Nigel in the sticks, not in London. He'd primed Angela to set up the meeting, but he needn't have worried. James had unwittingly done the job for them; good for James. Henry wanted to find out what Nigel was really about, in order to see how much he could trust him. Apart from Angela, he needed somebody at a higher level to lift the veil on any right-wing bias within MI5. He judged that Nigel was susceptible to flattery, and he was going to butter him up something rotten!

'Nigel, since we've been thrown together unexpectedly—by chance you might say—I thought I would sound you out as to my current thinking,' he said rather chummily once Angela had left the room to see Mavis.

Nigel preened himself, absolutely delighted to be taken into Henry's confidence, swallowing the bait hook, line and sinker.

'I guess you're aware I've only about two years to serve now and have bought a house close by in Otley?'

Nigel nodded appreciatively.

'Well, I've been asked to give some thought as to who my successor should be—get my drift?'

Nigel couldn't believe his ears. This trip up to the fringes of the rhubarb triangle had suddenly taken on a rosier and sweeter taste.

'You're asking me if I'm interested? Of course I am. I've admired your work ever since we worked briefly together during the war,' said Nigel, almost beside himself.

'Of course, we'll have to keep this hush-hush, as we used to say—even from Angela and James.' Henry fixed Nigel with a very serious look.

'Naturally; anything you say, Henry. Is there anything I can help you with?'

'I've heard rumours that certain people within MI5 have very strong feelings about Wilson's socialists getting into power and might try to influence the outcome of the election. Do you think there's anything in these rumours?' said Henry pointedly.

'Do you mean is anybody going to leak another Zinoviev-style letter to the press, just before polling day?' responded Nigel, somewhat flippantly.

'Well, that would definitely come into the category of interference.'

'No, I've no knowledge that anything like that is going on,' said Nigel seriously.

Nigel was referring to a controversial letter printed by the *Daily Mail* four days before the 1924 election. The *Mail*'s front-page headline claimed: '*Civil War Plot by Socialists' Masters: Moscow Orders to Our Reds; Great Plot Disclosed.*' The letter, purporting to be from Grigori Zinoviev, president of the Comintern, the internal communist organisation, called on British communists to mobilise "sympathetic forces" within the Labour Party. It had come into the hands of the security services, who thought it could be genuine, and was leaked to the press, probably by somebody in the service. Subsequent information showed the letter was fake and had almost certainly originated from a faction within the security services hell-bent on preventing the re-election of the socialist government. Ramsay MacDonald's Labour lost by a landslide.

'I was actually thinking of ultra-right-wing sympathisers willing to go even further if Harold Wilson won the election,' said Henry pointedly.

'Wow—you mean like a Guy Fawkes plot? Definitely not. None of us really relish the thought of a socialist government, but if it's democratically elected, we've got to accept it,' said Nigel, giving vent to his true feelings for once.

Henry was satisfied that Nigel was probably on the level and he could trust him. Nigel was a snob and a product of his elitist background and education, but basically honest.

'Good. Just thought I'd ask since there's recently been trouble with the National Socialist Movement in Smethwick supporting the right-wing Conservative candidate against Labour on a racial issue, who are vehemently against Labour's immigration policy.'

Henry was referring to the controversial campaign against the Labour candidate, the shadow foreign secretary Patrick Gordon Walker, who supported the current government's policies including immigration from the Commonwealth. The Conservative candidate was accused of exploiting the slogan, '*If you want a nigger neighbour, vote Labour.'* The NSM was a blatant British Neo-Nazi group formed in 1962 by Colin Jordan.

Just then, Angela returned into the room, preventing Henry from developing his theme further.

***

I finished off my ham and eggs and followed the inspector out of the pub, which I'd learned was formerly called the Three Horseshoes, to look at the abandoned car.

'T' pub used to be a smithy serving canal 'osses afore it was converted,' confided the inspector knowledgeably, as if he was a tour guide. I'd guessed that, as there were some faded photos on the snug's wall showing large horses in front of a building which I took to be the pub in former times. I'd always wondered why pubs get called 'Three Horseshoes', since most horses have four legs.

The inspector's words took on significance as we soon diverted off the causeway outside the pub onto a cobbled path that led us directly to the canal and a mooring point just in front of a wooden bridge. The black Rover was parked at the other side of the bridge, just off the towpath, guarded by a policeman who, on seeing us, quickly flicked a cigarette onto the ground, expertly extinguishing it with a size eleven boot.

'As I told thee, it's a good spot to ditch it as it's out-o'-way like,' the inspector reported. 'There's a farm over there, and a boat repair yard opposite, but nobody saw nowt. Well, not quite right—a lass walkin' dog saw a moored barge but nobody saw it leave.'

'Are you checking further along the canal?' I asked.

The inspector gave me one of those exasperated looks which gave me the answer. 'Time they've had, they could've almost reached Liverpool by now, tha naws,' he snorted.

I'd seen all I needed for now: the black Rover car with the AHD registration and red upholstery was now firmly etched in my mind. I relived the violent episode over again in my mind as I walked back to where I'd parked the minivan in front of the Rodley Barge pub. The inspector said they were finalising interviews with people they'd missed first time round and would extend the search as and when they received further useful information.

I was keen to head back to the Mill. I wondered if Nigel and Henry were still there. It would be useful if they were, as I'd something positive to report.

'Ah, James; I was just on my way out,' said Nigel, who had, at the second I walked through the door, put his overcoat on.

'You might want to hear what I've got to say before you leave, as we've got a lead on the fugitives,' I said forcefully.

Nigel, who already seemed to be in a good mood, perked up even more and sat down quickly.

'Go on, I've got about thirty minutes before my train leaves. Shoot.'

'The police found the abandoned Rover about five miles away beside the canal in Rodley. It had been stolen, and the only fingerprints found in it were Stein's; it was clean otherwise. It looks like they escaped on a canal barge. The inspector said the taxi driver who had stopped to pick up Stein and Schultz heard David Lithgow shout 'Colin', so he'd recognised one of the abductors even though he was wearing a balaclava. This would seem to be the reason why he was shot,' I added.

'What was your laddie's background, Nigel?' said Henry sharply.

'Well, he was originally from Special Branch,' said Nigel uncomfortably.

'You must know more about him than that, or else why would you give him the job of keeping tabs on Stein and Schultz?' probed Henry.

It was obvious Nigel didn't want to cooperate but seemed afraid of upsetting Henry. I couldn't put my finger on why, but Nigel was acting very oddly and out of character.

'I can ask around when I get back to London. I really should go, or I'll miss my train.'

'We do know more about David Lithgow,' said Angela, much to Nigel's embarrassment.

'As I said, I'll check when—'

At this point Angela interrupted. 'Don't you remember, Nigel? I vetted a number of candidates' files, and you specifically liked David because he had experience of far-right organisations—from the inside!'

'Ah yes, I believe you're right. I'd forgotten that. You can provide the details, Angela; I must go—I've got a meeting later on in London.'

Nigel's attempt at saving face failed miserably. He stood up stiffly, nodded and self-consciously made an inelegant, shuffling exit.

I was pleased to see the back of him and keen, as I could see Henry was, to listen to what Angela had to say. Angela, for her part, was anxious to contribute what she knew.

'From memory, David Lithgow had been in Special Branch and had got close to Colin Jordan's far-right Neo-Nazi National Socialist Movement group. He'd watched their paramilitary force, called "Spearhead", performing military drills at weekends in '62. The evidence David and another colleague gathered contributed to the conviction of Jordan and others for an offence under the Public Order Act of 1936, for which they went to prison. I can check the files again when I get back to London.'

'So, it looks as if this NSM group is upping the ante and preparing to go to extreme measures to damage democracy,' I said.

Henry had been unusually quiet but now nodded and added, 'It ties in, to some extent, with our information sources in Germany. We, MI6 that is, have a contact who has been telling us for some time that Neo-Nazis in Germany are infiltrating the British far-right groups. This could be evidence of a direct link to Stein.'

'Why don't we ask David Lithgow's old Special Branch colleague what else he knows about the NSM?' said Angela.

'Excellent—better get right on it,' said Henry.

'It means I'll have to return to London today,' Angela said, somewhat crestfallen.

I knew exactly what she was implying. I'd half-expected her to stay in Leeds over the weekend, and I'd thought we might have a bit of time together.

'Never mind—your mother won't mind, especially as she doesn't know you're up in Yorkshire at the minute anyway,' said Henry, totally misreading the signals Angela was giving.

Angela smiled weakly and gave me a glance which said 'sorry'.

'There's one thing that worries me about all this: who is behind it?' said Henry. 'You're right, James—I don't believe the current NSM leaders have the intelligence and organisational skills to pull this off. They're more used to disrupting meetings and petty disturbances.'

'You're not suggesting that this might be linked to the security services, are you?' I said, thinking of Nigel's peculiar behaviour this afternoon.

'Well, I suppose we shouldn't rule anything out, but I think it's unlikely,' said Henry.

Nevertheless, Nigel had acted strangely and was certainly holding something back. I was under the distinct impression Henry was now running the show and Nigel was taking a back seat. It wasn't my place to question things, but I would ask Angela when the time was more appropriate, which wouldn't be for a few days now.

'Are we completely ruling out the possibility of communist involvement here?' I queried.

'No, but the evidence we have so far points towards a far-right plot to destroy democracy as we know it if the socialists under Harold Wilson win the general election,' said Henry firmly. 'The plot is almost worthy of your Bishop Brennan, James—although in this case, I don't believe he's had time to regroup since last year.'

I hadn't thought of that, but readily agreed that Brennan would have been proud to be associated with this scheme. Nevertheless, the mention of Bishop Brennan sent a chill up my spine and a twinge of pain in my calf where I had been shot last year.

Since it was Friday afternoon, I said I would prepare for meeting with Gerry Engel and Helmut Schultz next week and keep in touch with the police in case they turned up any more information on the whereabouts of Stein. Henry was spending the weekend in Otley and said if I needed to contact him he was always available and we could meet up again in the Bull. The one advantage of Angela going to London was that I would have the use of the minivan, which was very convenient.

With that, we all went our separate ways.

***

After a period of relative inactivity on the canal boat, things significantly livened up for Stein on the morning of the third day. He was told to prepare to leave by one of the two men who had abducted him. They had moored overnight close to some locks they had navigated the previous day. It was just becoming daylight when he heard a car approach and stop just outside, motor running. He was hastily bundled through the door, up onto the canal bank and pushed unceremoniously into the back of the car. He caught a brief glimpse of the lock gates and a bridge about fifty yards in the other direction as the car did a five-point turn and headed towards the bridge on a dirt track alongside the towpath. He spotted a sign: *Dowley Gap Locks*. It meant nothing to him, but at the end of the track they reached a tarmac road and turned right directly over the canal bridge, where he saw, to the left and just across the road, a large inn: the Fisherman's. They were on a small, winding country road which started to rise up through a couple of sparsely populated villages and then into open countryside. They reached a T-junction close to another large inn, Dick Hudson's, turned right and then left about a couple of miles further on. Stein was completely lost and only conscious of the road becoming even narrower and then passing another inn, the Hermit—a name whose meaning he couldn't understand—before descending into a large village and heading on an even smaller road into a dilapidated, deserted mill complex with a bumpy cobbled road. They pulled up after about twenty-five to thirty minutes, in front of a large warehouse. The driver got out and pulled the doors wide open, allowing him to drive inside.

Once inside, Stein was instructed to get out of the car and he looked around the large, mainly empty warehouse, which he adjudged to be part of an old textile mill. Once the outside doors were closed again, it was rather dingy and the only light was that from high sky-light windows. He was taken towards the back of the warehouse, where parked against a wall were two caravans and a blue, medium-sized van with 'Thompson Laboratories' written on the side. A nervous-looking young man stood in front of one of the caravans waiting to meet them.

'Hello, I'm Julian Thompson. I've been asked to liaise with you and show you our laboratory facilities.'

Stein had guessed what was coming, but couldn't work out if the man was a willing or captive collaborator. Apart from his rather untidy appearance, Stein got the impression Thompson was a chemist of some sort, as he had what Stein judged to be yellow nitric acid stains on his hands. Stein was not impressed— Thompson wouldn't last long in a pesticide or nerve agent laboratory if he allowed his skin to be in contact with chemicals.

Stein and one of his abductors followed Thompson through a door behind the caravan into an office and then into a laboratory which was split into two. One half had benches either side of two side-by-side fume cupboards. The fume cupboards looked suitable, and he noticed three or four cardboard boxes containing chemicals and bottles of solvents. Thompson showed him a sheet of paper which Stein recognised as the one he had supplied to his contacts in Germany before he set off.

'Since I understand time is short, perhaps you could check that we've got everything you need?' Thompson said, again rather nervously.

Stein went through the list of chemicals in the boxes and ticked them off, one by one, against the list, confirming everything was in order. He noted on the bench a brand new Büchi rotary evaporator, which needed to be set up in one of the fume cupboards and coupled up to a water pump, as he pointed out to Thompson. Stein glanced at the other half of the laboratory, which was obviously for larger-scale preparations. Instead of a fume cupboard, a transparent plastic screened-off area with ventilation extraction was evident. It contained, on the red-brick tiled floor, a number of 2 ½ litre Winchester bottles labelled 'Concentrated nitric acid 98%', confirming the nature of the staining on Thompson's hands.

'What about protective clothing, gloves and glassware, et cetera?' asked Stein sharply.

'No problem, sir. We keep them over here.' Thompson indicated another area. Stein critically examined a cupboard full of glassware, all of the most modern type fitted with ground-glass connections, of which he approved.

'When do you want to start work?' said Thompson, a little less nervously now, probably because he was relieved that Stein was satisfied with the facilities and he had obtained all the correct chemicals and materials.

'I start tomorrow when things set up. I have need to clean clothes; where I staying?' said Stein.

'You're staying in one of the caravans outside,' said the accompanying abductor authoritatively from the doorway. He was a tall, thickset man, not the one who'd shot David Lithgow, but he'd done the driving and piloted the barge. It was the first time Stein had really heard him speak.

'I need clean clothes,' said Stein, angry now.

'The sooner you do your stuff, the sooner you'll get out of here,' was the terse reply.

Stein was not happy. He was desperately thinking of ways he could escape, but his abductors seemed to have everything covered. The only way he could see was to prepare some tabun and use it to disable his two abductors. He wasn't sure about Thompson, although it might be better to include him since he might contact other people.

Unlike the barge, the laboratory and caravan were cold. The barge's coal-fired stove had made the inside of the cabin cosy, but no such luxury was available here. Stein, therefore, had no option but to knuckle down.

He set about setting things up, with Thompson acting as his lab assistant. The watching abductor positioned himself in an adjoining office, listening to the radio. The second abductor had been delegated to preparing meals and providing drinks, which were taken in the office. A hot stew with crusty bread was provided, which went some way to combating the cold. At the end of the first day, Stein and Thompson had more or less organised everything for starting tabun preparation the following day. Thompson hadn't a clue what was being prepared, and Stein was very sure now he wasn't in on the plot; he wondered what hold the abductors had over him.

The catering abductor called him into the office, and the watching abductor left, closing the door and motioning to Thompson to follow him out of the lab.

'Right, Dr Stein. You know what we want, don't you? I've been instructed to oversee the preparation work and offer you the chance to join us. This could be your contribution to a new Anglo-German alliance,' said the abductor seriously. 'Another question: the student you were with, he's a chemist too, and quite capable of preparing tabun. I'm right, aren't I?'

It was no use denying it; they'd obviously done their homework. This put a different complexion on things.

'I know how dangerous tabun is if it's prepared correctly,' said the abductor, menacingly. 'Do you want to volunteer to prove to us that you've been successful?'

CHAPTER 5
HELMUT WOULD MAKE A GOOD NERVE AGENT?

After Angela and Henry had left the Mill, I rang Gerry in London to see if there was any possibility of bringing forward my meeting in Bradford with the institute's new director to Monday instead of Wednesday. There wasn't, as he was in London with Dr Finlay until Tuesday, when they were travelling up to Bradford together in the evening. I explained there'd been some developments that might have less impact on our enquiries if the meeting were held sooner rather than later, but there was nothing that could be done. Gerry did, however, suggest I call on Helmut Schultz, who was still in Leeds, and transfer him over to the Midland Hotel in Bradford on Tuesday so he could be ready for an early start in the Bradford offices on Wednesday. This would save some time, and I agreed to do it.

I had, therefore, the best part of three and a bit days to myself and wondered how I should best spend the time. Optimistic that I would get the job at the wool institute, I decided to make a start on looking for alternative accommodation closer to my place of work.

I duly set out early on Saturday morning in Angela's minivan from her Leeds flat to drive to Bradford, initially to locate the institute's offices there and then to review location options which might suit me. Finding the institute's building was easier than I had anticipated, as it was just off Forster Square, close to the general post office and the cathedral. I didn't stop but noted that parking nearby might be a problem unless I was early enough to get a parking spot on one of the side streets in Little Germany. I headed out of the city centre towards Father O'Reilly's old rectory, stopping just after the traffic lights at Bolton Junction, where I bought a *Telegraph and Argus* from the nearby newsagents in order to study the property section. My eyes were immediately drawn to an advert for a property for sale or rent within half a mile of where I was parked. I set off and located the house, a pre-war semi-detached house on an estate close to the trolleybus route into Bradford. The location was perfect. There and then I decided to ring the estate agent in charge of the property for more details. I was in luck. The agent, a chatty Mr Green, would meet me at the house within the hour and show me around.

To cut to the chase, as my American ex-associate Rod Trask would have said, the house was almost ideal. I said I was more interested in renting it for a limited period of time than purchasing, and Mr Green was very flexible on the rental terms. I was pleasantly surprised to find out that the house was still furnished and could be lived in right away. This would be very convenient, as I had sold my mother's house and contents on her death thinking I would have no need of them as a priest in London.

The only downside was a five-foot-high privet hedge some thirty yards in length which separated the property from next door. Mr Green thought it was the responsibility of the next-door neighbour, but he would check. I decided to take the house and agreed on a six-month rental period. We arranged to finalise things at his Bradford office the following Wednesday, when I was meeting up with Gerry and Dr Hamish Finlay. With that, I shook hands with Mr Green, and he drove away.

I sat for a few moments in the minivan thinking on what I had done. An elderly couple walked past me and opened the gate next door.

I jumped out and said, 'Excuse me—do you live here, and is this hedge yours?'

'Yes it is, lad. Wot's it to you?' said the man.

'I'm James Brittain and will be your next-door neighbour very shortly,' I said with what I hoped was a pleasant smile, trying to mend any misunderstanding, and holding out my hand.

'Oh, right. Pleased to meet yer. Got any children?' said the man directly, probably concerned about potential noise problems in the future.

'No, it's just me; I'm not married,' I volunteered helpfully.

'Why don't you come in for a cuppa? We're ready for one, aren't we, Stan?' said the lady.

'Aye, good idea,' said Stan, shaking my hand.

Since I had time, I thought it sensible to accept and attempt to build bridges with my new neighbours—hedging my bets, as you might say. That thought concentrated my mind on the very substantial privet shrubbery which separated our two properties.

Stanley and Edna Robinson were the neighbours. Stan had just retired from the Inland Revenue as a tax inspector and, as I'd already observed, had a very inquiring manner.

'Stan likes a chocolate biscuit with his tea; do you?' said Edna, taking the lid off a substantial tin, revealing both KitKats and Mars bars.

I nodded in approval and selected a Mars bar, which I hadn't sampled for a while. Stan was already tearing the foil off a four-fingered KitKat as we sat down. In the space of about forty-five minutes, I learned that Stan's pride and joy was his privet hedges and, to my relief, only he was allowed to cut them; it required an expert precision of which only he was capable. He was the secretary of the local allotment society and a long-standing member and supporter of Yorkshire cricket. Now he had retired, he planned to follow the team to every ground in the country where they played. I'm not sure Edna was as enthusiastic, but as it probably meant he wouldn't be under her feet all the time now he was retired, it might be appreciated. In amongst the information he provided, he also expertly wheedled out of me in a fashion reminiscent of Wilfred Pickles' popular long-running radio programme *Have a Go*, who I was, where I was going to work, what religion I was, whether I was courtin', and did I have transport? I was able to satisfy his curiosity as much as I could, the only disappointment I observed was when I said I didn't have transport, as I think he would have been lining me up for taxi duties in the future, if I had.

***

Pleased with my day's work so far, I travelled back to Leeds, intending to contact Helmut Schultz at the Queens Hotel to arrange to take him over to the Bradford offices on Wednesday. I rang the hotel from Angela's flat and was informed that he wasn't in but had left instructions that should anyone need to contact him, he'd be in the library at Leeds University. *Interesting*, I thought. *Either very conscientious or trying to take his mind off recent events by keeping busy.* The latter was probably nearer to the mark.

I decided, since it was a reasonable day, to walk there as it was only about a mile away and the exercise would do me good. I found Helmut in the Brotherton Library on the second floor, deep in concentration reading a wool textile journal, *Melliand Textileberichte*; he'd found the German edition, which I thought was good thinking. His pens and notebook were arranged very neatly on his desk. I'd observed before that he liked everything to be 'just-so'. When I'd talked to him at the police station, his cigarette butts had been carefully arranged in a pyramid structure in the ashtray, an odd mannerism which perhaps had some deep psychological meaning beyond my comprehension. He wasn't allowed to smoke in the library, so I wondered how long his reading sessions lasted before needing the next nicotine fix.

'Hello, Helmut—the hotel said I might find you here. Catching up on some interesting wool research, are we?'

The comment was a bit too subtle for Helmut, who thought I required an in-depth description of the article he was reading, triggering a simultaneous rearrangement of his pens on the desk. To avoid further misunderstandings, I switched into German to get my main message across, that I was to arrange to take him over to Bradford. I'd originally planned to do it tomorrow, Sunday, but as Helmut wanted to spend Monday and Tuesday in the library, we compromised on travelling on Tuesday afternoon, much to my disappointment as I wanted to sort him out ASAP.

'Fancy a coffee?' I said, trying to get Helmut to stop fiddling with his pens, which was beginning to irritate me.

There was no chair for me to sit on since Helmut was in a bookshelf bay with just a single desk and chair situated at the end next to the outside window. I was very familiar with the layout, as it brought back not-so-fond memories of revising for my finals. These nooks offered ideally secluded revising conditions, but there were only a limited number in the library. The trick was to get there early enough to bag a desk and deposit your folders on it to reserve it, as periodic breaks were necessary, even for a non-smoker like myself, to maximise concentration.

There was a coffee bar almost directly opposite the Parkinson Building, which a group of us used to haunt at regular intervals to compare notes. It would be good to see if it was still the same.

'Two expressos please.'

The coffee bar's layout was exactly the same as far as I could remember, but the staff were different. A couple of espressos were rapidly prepared at the counter using the noisy steam injection machine. I paid for them and we sat down at a table close to the door. Helmut was already halfway through smoking a Capstan full-strength cigarette, which he had ignited as soon as we left the university buildings. It was clear he was in need of a nicotine break and my appearance was probably a convenient diversion.

'Is there news of Dr Stein? I worry he in danger,' said Helmut, flexing his English. 'Why they no take me too?' he said, surprisingly.

'How do you mean?' I said, puzzled.

'They want Dr Stein for his organophosphorus knowledge. I have same knowledge.'

'You told me you didn't work for Dr Stein and were in another department in Germany, didn't you?' I said, rather confused.

'*Ja*, but I make chemicals and analyse them for Dr Stein.'

I was beginning to understand now. Stein, with his elevated ivory-tower status, formulated the pesticides he wanted to investigate, and Helmut synthesised and characterised them for him. It was a case of my misunderstanding how Stein and his subordinates worked.

I borrowed a pencil and a piece of paper from the counter and got Helmut to draw out the organisational structure of the departments Stein was involved in. Helmut took his instructions from a laboratory supervisor who liaised directly with Stein.

'So you would know exactly which chemicals, equipment and methods would be required to synthesise nerve agents, wouldn't you?' I said directly.

Helmut looked uneasy but nodded in agreement. He said it was general knowledge that Dr Stein had been involved in nerve agent manufacture during the war and some of the experimental chemicals they produced had been eliminated from further examination as they were too toxic.

No wonder Gerry Engel wanted Helmut to come and work at the institute; he could contribute some essential chemical knowledge to combat moth damage done to wool materials. It was also becoming clear to me that Helmut's knowledge might give us some clues with regard to finding Stein, if he was going to be forced into synthesising a nerve agent. Angela, Henry and Nigel should be quickly made aware of this.

**

Angela hadn't been idle since returning to London. She'd seriously considered arranging everything by the phone from Leeds but needed to consult files from the archive as she didn't want to miss a trick. On Saturday morning, before she contacted Special Branch, she scanned through the files on David Lithgow and Tom Hardy, who had both been shortlisted for transference to MI5. All things being equal, Tom Hardy should have been the favourite as, unlike David Lithgow, he was from a well-to-do family and had been to a public school—normally Nigel's preferred choice. So why had Nigel changed his mind and chosen David?

Her earlier recollection was correct. David had been chosen because he had infiltrated the National Socialist Movement and liaised with Tom who, because of his background, reportedly hobnobbed with aristos who were sympathetic to the NSM's cause but wouldn't have dirtied their hands with some of their strong-arm activities. She hadn't met either of them previously, only done the research for Nigel, so she needed to meet Tom to see how he ticked. She was in luck when she contacted Special Branch; Tom Hardy was on duty and could meet up with Angela at her office in the early afternoon.

Tom was a good looking, tall, thirty something, with an in-built self-confidence that characterised many public-school men. On the surface he was affable enough and was naturally shocked that David had been killed but appeared to have misinterpreted the reason for Angela wanting to speak to him. He thought he was being lined up as David's replacement in MI5 and a bit miffed when she explained she just wanted background information. Nevertheless, he readily agreed to help out all he could.

'Did you meet any of the NSM's gang that David dealt with?' Angela asked, getting straight to the point.

'Not many. I was David's contact on the outside, feeding back information as to when the next disturbance was being planned,' said Tom.

'Did you know anybody called Colin?'

'I knew Colin Jordan. Everybody knew Colin; he was our main focus in the operation. I don't think there was anybody else. Why?'

Angela considered for a moment whether it was wise to share this vital bit of information with Tom, but Tom and David had been a team, so she went for it.

'Well, we believe David recognised the man who shot him. A taxi driver heard David shout "Colin" immediately before he was killed. It could have been somebody from the NSM who didn't want to be identified.'

'I see what you mean, but it wouldn't be Jordan, as he didn't get involved in the strong-armed stuff. I don't think I can help you. It must be pretty serious for them to resort to shooting?' said Tom, angling for further information.

'Yes, we believe it is. Who were your contacts in the NSM, and was anybody else from Special Branch involved?' Angela probed.

Tom shook his head, reiterating that only two of them had been allocated to the operation and he was just the go-between, but he had observed one of the military-style operations from a distance and taken some photos as evidence. David had taken an active part in this one. The 'officer' directing the manoeuvre was an ex-army man whose name escaped him for the moment, but he could easily check. Angela agreed this would be useful.

Tom did not come up with any significantly useful information, and she half wondered if he was being deliberately unhelpful—surely he must have formed some opinions from working with David. Angela let him go, asking him to phone in the name of the ex-army officer whose name he'd forgotten.

On reflection, she remembered that Colin Jordan had been convicted under the Public Order Act for attempting to set up a paramilitary force and had spent some time in prison, so there must be some useful information to be had in the court transcripts. Since it was Saturday, she quickly penned a note to Nigel's secretary to do this first thing Monday morning.

She returned to her earlier thought that she could have easily obtained what she'd learned from Tom Hardy over the telephone and had a weekend in Leeds with James. C'est la vie!

***

'Hello James, ha-ha,' said Amazin' Grace, when I called on Sunday morning. 'You want to speak to Henry? He's in the garden at the minute; I'll just go and fetch him.'

She put the phone down.

'Yes, James?' said Henry, after what seemed like an eternity.

'Hello, Henry. Helmut's research background is more interesting than we first imagined. He synthesised and characterised pesticide compounds for Stein to order, so he could be very useful to us in trying to find Stein,' I blurted out.

'Not only that, but he could be a back-up nerve agent scientist for our foes as well,' emphasised Henry.

'Exactly! He wondered why he hadn't been abducted along with Stein, which alerted me to probe into his research activities in Germany.'

'Might be that they hadn't done their homework properly, but it probably won't take them long to cotton on—Helmut could be in danger. Have you moved him yet?'

'No. I've arranged with Gerry to take him over on Tuesday afternoon for the meeting with the new research director, Dr Finlay, but Helmut wants to spend the interim period in the library.'

'I think you've got to move him today, don't you? said Henry emphatically.

'Agreed. Have you heard anything from Angela or Nigel yet?' I asked.

'No, but it could take a day or two to interview your unfortunate laddie's colleague, depending on what he's doing.'

With that, we agreed to keep in touch and I prepared to go and visit Helmut at the Queens. On the way, I decided it wouldn't do any harm to call in at the police station to see if Inspector Broadley was on duty and if there'd been any developments there. I was in luck: Inspector Broadley was in his office and having his elevenses supplemented with a hot Cornish pasty, which smelled very appetising. Unfortunately there wasn't a spare.

'Got to keep me strength up,' volunteered the inspector with a grin as he interpreted my expression correctly.

'Just wondered if there'd been any further developments in the search for Stein, owt or nowt?' I inquired, lapsing into his vernacular.

After a short pause to finish off the pasty and wash it down with a swig of tea, he gave me his full attention. 'Haven't found him, but we think we've got t' barge he was on. Abandoned.'

'Where?'

'Dowley Gap—close to Bingley. Stein's fingerprints all over t' barge but nobody else's; must have worn gloves.' And as always, Inspector Broadley left the best till last. 'Cleanin' lass in t' Fisherman's pub opposite saw a large car go in and out've canal towpath and head ovver t' bridge t'wards moor,'

'When was this exactly?' I asked excitedly.

''Bout nine thirty a Friday.'

So, the abductors hadn't travelled too far from Leeds, about fifteen to twenty miles as the crow flies, before they abandoned the barge. Perhaps this indicated that they were holed up not far away.

'There's summat else. Car left good set of tyre marks in t' mud where it turned round.' The inspector beamed.

'Blimey, you have been busy. Why didn't you let us know about this before?' I chided him, still slightly miffed over the Cornish pasty.

'I did. Yon lass in your office said head woman was in London and she didn't know where you were but she would pass it on.'

'Any clues from the tyres?' I asked.

'Dunlop, type used by many models, but looks like it's had a recent puncture as offside front is brand new, spare like. Oh, and it could be a big car since wheelbase is long—similar to abandoned Rover,' added the inspector.

'So, two days ago they left the barge and headed in the direction of Ilkley Moor—not a promising place to find a laboratory set up, is it?' I said dejectedly. 'We're going to move Helmut Schultz nearer to the institute's Bradford offices since he might be a target now as well. In fact, I'm just on my way to pick him up now.'

With that, I took my leave, headed the short distance into City Square and parked close to the station. I walked past the main entrance and entered the Queens Hotel. I went up to the desk and asked the receptionist if he could give Helmut a ring.

'He's not in at the moment, sir, as I told the other two gentlemen. I think he said he'd gone out for a walk.'

My nerves were immediately on edge. I hoped I wasn't too late.

'Where are the two men now?' I said sharply.

'They said they'd wait in the lobby and catch him as he came in,' said the receptionist, motioning with his head in the direction of the entrance. I must have walked right past them.

I thanked him and slowly made as if to walk out again when a door at the side of the reception desk opened and Helmut walked through it. He spotted me.

'James? What you want?'

'There are two men looking for you. We need to get out of here ASAP—can you get your things from your room now?' I urged him.

He nodded, understanding the implications immediately. As he quickly made his way via a nearby staircase to his room, I noticed he had a newspaper tucked under his arm.

I gestured to the door to the side of the desk. 'Where does that lead to?' I asked the receptionist, who was taking an interest in us.

'That's the hotel's private passageway direct to the station, sir. Excuse me—I said I'd let those gentlemen know if I'd seen Mr Schultz.'

'Don't do that. They are reporters who want to buttonhole him, and he doesn't need that right now—understand?'

The receptionist looked a bit dubious but understood fully after I deftly inserted a folded-up pound note in his top pocket!

'Fine, sir. I'll tell them I haven't seen him if they ask. I'm off duty in quarter of an hour anyway.'

I was tempted to try and have a look at them but decided against it. Instead, I asked if I could use the telephone. I rang Inspector Broadley, informing him of the situation and suggesting he get down here pronto. He said he was on his way.

Helmut seemed to be taking ages, and I was on tenterhooks every time somebody approached the reception desk. Finally he appeared with a case, and I ushered him through the door into the corridor which led to the train station; I didn't think we were seen. The short passageway led to the station's other entrance from Wellington Street, with which I was familiar, and I realised we could reach the minivan by going out of the station's main entrance and turning right.

So far so good. I started up the van, pulled away and on the spur of the moment, decided to drive past the hotel's main entrance. As we approached, two men were standing outside.

'Get your head down!' I yelled to Helmut, and he buried his head in his paper as we drove by the two men, who were taking an unusual interest in anybody or anything that passed. One of them stared at me and the other made to run back into the hotel. I was sure we'd been rumbled as I saw him staring after us in my rear-view mirror. Damn!

Chapter 6
Stein Tries, Unsuccessfully, to Pull Out All the Stops!

Stein's confidence had been seriously shaken by the veiled threat to use him as a guinea pig to test the effectiveness of the tabun he was tasked with preparing. The offer to join this so-called new Anglo-German alliance sounded risky in the extreme, but if he refused and then successfully prepared sufficient quantities of tabun for their scheme, he could see that he might be deemed expendable. There was also the young Helmut Schultz factor, which he had completely overlooked. They had questioned him in the barge about his colleague, and he'd been somewhat dismissive of Schultz's relevance, explaining that he was merely a post-grad student who worked for him in the lab. They'd obviously put two and two together and perhaps also done some checking up and found that Schultz was a very competent chemist, capable of taking Stein's place if necessary. It looked as if he was going to have to agree to join them in the short term.

He angled for more information about how they intended to use the tabun, arguing that he may be able to advise on the most effective ways of administering it. He was attempting to make himself indispensable again, and it appeared to be working as he was going to be taken to meet the organisers before he started the tabun synthesis proper. He got Julian Thompson to set up most of the glassware and re-sited the single pan weighing balance in one of the fume cupboards, as well as testing the efficiency of the water pump. He was a bit rusty over certain things as it had been quite a few years since he'd been at the sharp end in the lab. It was, he told himself, just like riding a bike.

The phone rang, and the man with whom he had been negotiating answered it, saying that Mr Thompson was away on business and they would need to ring back in a couple of days to find out when they might receive their order. He explained he was just a contractor carrying out some repair work at the premises. Obviously, Thompson's business was on hold now. The man made a call and took instructions, then ordered Stein out of the room towards the large warehouse and into the car. They were on the move again.

***

Things were beginning to develop quickly now on a couple of fronts, Henry thought. Probably a bit too quickly, if he was honest, for the resources he currently had available. His original brief, of which only he and MI6's Director General were aware, had been to discretely investigate MI5's DG, as a potential KGB mole. During the 1950s and up to the present day, a large number of MI5 operations had failed in circumstances that suggested the Soviets had been tipped off. In Henry's opinion, there had been far too many leakages and defections recently for it to be a coincidence, and rumours of a mole at the top of MI5 were rife. Two recent cases came readily to mind: Kim Philby's flight last year from Beirut to Moscow strongly suggested he had been tipped off as to his impending arrest, and MI5's DG was in the frame. The same official had also been strongly criticised for not warning John Profumo, the War Secretary in Prime Minister Harold Macmillan's Conservative government, that through his friendship with Stephen Ward, he could have become entangled with a Soviet spy ring through his affair with showgirl Christine Keeler. Keeler was also involved with Soviet Naval Attaché Eugene Ivanov, who sought to learn from Profumo via Keeler the date of American plans to arm nuclear warheads in West Germany. Profumo had been forced to resign in mid-1963, and there were still repercussions from the scandal which could have an impact on the coming general election.

MI5 were carrying out their own investigations but progress was slow, so Henry had pressed the flesh in the Westminster corridors of power and listened to some extraordinary gossip, some of it very unsavoury. One of the main gossips, and a potential double agent, was Tom Driberg MP, who prior to becoming an MP, wrote the William Hickey column in the *Daily Express* and knew virtually all the smut there was to know about anybody of influence. He was brazen in flaunting his own illegal homosexual activities to the full by continually getting caught but, due to his connections in high places, always managed to escape prosecution and embarrassing publicity. Henry couldn't seriously believe that MI5 were silly enough to use him—he would be constantly open to blackmail; if he was a double agent then he was incredibly clever at getting out of the scrapes he effortlessly found himself in. The salient thing that Henry picked up on was that Driberg seemed to be constantly strapped for funds, which could also make him open to bribery.

The zeal with which the police pursued homosexual activities of men without powerful protectors was fuelled by the British government, which was under American pressure to demonstrate that it was being tough on subversive networks. Sir Alec Guinness had a gay side to him and had been arrested in his early career for importuning but had been advised by a sympathetic policeman to give a false name. He had astutely given his name as Herbert Pocket, the character he was playing in Dickens' *Great Expectations*, a ploy which went unnoticed and enabled him to escape embarrassing publicity. Henry was also aware of Driberg's association with Lord Boothby, a popular TV presenter and former MP for East Aberdeenshire, and the dubious connections of both with the gangster Ronnie Kray, plus their shared taste for young men. The matter had come to a head in July when a bombshell *Sunday Mirror*'s front-page story announced: '*Peer and a Gangster. Yard Inquiry.*' Neither

Boothby nor Ronnie Kray were mentioned by name but simply identified as '*a peer who is a household name*' and '*a leading thug in the London underworld, involved in protection rackets*'. The police were said to be investigating an alleged homosexual relationship between them. Most people in the country could put two and two together, and the *Mirror*'s proprietor had personally authorised the article's publication, obviously believing it would be to the advantage of the Labour party in the forthcoming general election.

Henry knew that MI5's DG and the Metropolitan Police Commissioner had been summoned by the Home Secretary, Henry Brooke, who feared that the sordid link between Westminster and the Krays could cause an even greater scandal than the Profumo–Keeler one last year. Henry was perhaps more concerned with the fact that Boothby had been flying out to Moscow for a briefing with Soviet leader Nikita Khrushchev and had been on several trips to Russia over the past decade.

Now, purely by chance, he and James had uncovered something in a completely different ballpark, as their American cousins might describe it. James seemed to have the happy knack of stumbling upon things, an arguable talent which Henry believed James himself didn't quite understand. Perhaps it was just luck, which reminded Henry of a saying, attributed to Napoleon: 'I would rather have a general who was lucky than one who was good.' This issue, which had blown up out of nothing, was almost certainly ultra-right-wing in origin and poles apart from the Cold War Soviet threat. Yet Henry believed they were both inextricably linked to the up-and-coming general election and aimed at destabilising the fabric of the incumbent ruling party. At the moment, the Conservatives were fighting a rearguard battle to stay in power and were desperate to avoid, at all costs, another scandal that might tip the balance in favour of the socialists, as both parties were neck and neck in the latest opinion polls. If the socialists did win the election and Angela and James were right in their assessment of the use of Stein's nerve gas expertise to wipe out the ruling classes in one fell swoop at Westminster, then democracy was at stake.

Henry hadn't yet spelt this out to MI6's DG, as he hoped James and the police might be able to find Stein and his abductors and nip things in the bud before they went too far. It seemed to Henry that he was between a rock and a hard place and didn't know which way to turn, but soon he would have to make some difficult decisions.

Just then, the phone rang. It was Nigel wanting a word in his shell-like, with some news that Henry found truly astounding. Henry was pleased that Nigel wanted to confide in him; it was clear Nigel was keen to keep on his good side after their recent meeting at the Mill in Leeds.

***

Stein was pushed unceremoniously into the back of the large car in which he had arrived. Thompson opened the shutter doors of the warehouse and the car quickly drove out of the deserted mill complex onto a small village road. Stein hadn't a clue where he was but surmised he couldn't be too far from Leeds, as they had meandered their way on the canal and the trip to the laboratory had taken less than half an hour, so they were still in the north of England.

They drove for about an hour. Stein was not able to gain much information as to where they were, as he was belatedly asked to lie face down on the back seat when they left the village, and he could feel he was being intensely watched. He was conscious of the car turning left off the main road and stopping. The man in the front passenger seat got out, and Stein heard a gate swing open to let the car through, after which they continued for a short distance further before he was ordered out of the car.

'Dr Stein, I presume?' said the cultured voice of a man behind a large desk, in a large office.

The implication at Stanley's greeting to Dr Livingstone on their first meeting in Africa was lost on Stein, who nodded in agreement without a hint of understanding the subtleties.

'Colin tells me you're willing to cooperate with us regarding the most effective way of distributing the chemical to the best effect?' the man said, getting straight to the point.

'My knowledge and experience of working with these chemicals is good. You need to create an aerosol of the chemical in air which is breathed in by the victim; the toxic effect is greater and faster by breathing than by skin absorption,' said Stein authoritatively.

'I didn't know that,' said the man earnestly, obviously realising that Stein could be key to the success of this project, not only from the synthesis of tabun but also the administration of it. 'Since time is getting short, we thought your colleague Helmut Schultz could prepare the chemical and you could test it and work on the effectiveness of the application? What do you say, Dr Stein?'

'You have catched Helmut?'

'No, not yet. Who is helping him? A young man who I think you've met—is he with the security services?'

Stein knew exactly who he was referring to—Dr Gerry Engel's technical service new employee at The Wool Research Institute, who hadn't impressed Stein, and whose name he couldn't for the life of him remember.

'He was seen driving Helmut away from his Leeds hotel in a hurry but we lost him. Do you know where he might be going?'

Stein didn't know but replied that Helmut could have been taken to the institute's offices. He wasn't sure where that was, but it shouldn't be too difficult to find out. The man nodded, and Colin, who was hovering in the background of the large office, left the room to investigate this new information.

Stein and the man were now alone. He didn't know who the man was, but he was obviously somebody with influence and authority. Stein's self-preservation instinct told him to be as helpful as necessary—he'd had plenty of similar experiences during the war with Nazi officials whom he'd had to placate to survive.

'You'd been given previous instructions in Germany to investigate how the chemicals could be used, for example, in the Houses of Parliament?'

Stein nodded.

'We'd originally thought that glass phials of the stuff could be thrown from the spectators' gallery into the chamber, but from what you've just told me it might not be the most effective method, right?' the man continued.

'I think that might only affect a small number of people close to where the glass phials break—better to spray chemicals into the air from above to contaminate a wider area, yes?' Stein said, matter-of-factly. 'I notice the big room where the Lords might have a pipe organ. Air is blown into pipes to make music; this could be used to atomise chemical, which would be blown into the air and fill the room, yes?'

'Very clever—I like it—but no, the Lords' chamber doesn't have a pipe organ. But it does have air conditioning—maybe that could be useful?'

Stein was deflated. He'd pinned a lot of hope on there being a pipe organ in the Lords' Chamber, as he thought he'd seen pictures of such an instrument in Leeds University library, but obviously not. The man seemed very well informed, and Stein was now intensely interested to know who he was and how he knew so much about the House of Lords.

The man now seemed to decide he could trust Stein, as he had shown a willingness to cooperate and was more likely to do so if put in the picture. He was virtually under house arrest, so they had full control over him.

'I know quite a bit about the Lords' Chamber, as I sit in it,' said the man. 'I'm Lord Sketchley and am well acquainted with its procedures.'

Stein didn't quite understand what *sitting in the chamber* had to do with it but realised the man was very important and could probably provide sufficient information for him to suggest suitable methods.

'The air-conditioning ducts are a possibility, but it depends on the design and accessibility,' continued Stein. 'Maybe you know that at the Nüremberg trials, Albert Speer said he intended to kill Hitler in 1945 by introducing tabun into the ventilation shafts of the Führerbunker? The air-intake position and the availability of tabun prevented him carrying it out.'

Albert Speer had been the Minister of Armaments and War Production for the Third Reich; he was found guilty of war crimes and crimes against humanity, principally for the use of slave labour and forced labour. He claimed he was unaware of Nazi extermination plans, which probably saved him from hanging, but he served twenty years in jail. He'd become known as 'the good Nazi', claiming he was unaware of the atrocities carried out in the concentration camps. Stein was sceptical, since Speer had been one of the elite in charge of many departments; he himself remembered him visiting the tabun production plant, so it was unlikely he wasn't aware of what was happening.

'I see. No, I wasn't aware of that,' said Lord Sketchley.

Stein tried to get more information about the air-conditioning ducts, but Lord Sketchley's knowledge didn't run to a detailed layout, apart from the principle that 'fresh' air was introduced at low levels and 'hot' air was extracted from above. Unless the system was shut off, it might remove any vapours, thus nullifying the toxic effects.

One piece of useful information Lord Sketchley provided was that the opening of Parliament was going to be televised again, as had been previously done in 1958. The chamber would be disrupted by engineers for up to a week beforehand, fitting lights, sound equipment and extensive cables, etc. They both realised this could be an opportunity to introduce their stuff in the confusion.

Lord Sketchley was tempted to fill Stein in further regarding the new Anglo-German Alliance and the National Democratic Party (NPD), which had primed and blackmailed Stein into cooperating in Germany. This was very much his pet subject, but he decided it was probably a bit too ideological for a technical man who was more into playing with test tubes and Bunsen burners—little did he know! Instead, he suggested to Stein that the extensive estate they were in at present could be used to test out the effectiveness of the chemical. It was secluded and had sheep, which could perhaps be used as guinea pigs. An unfortunate metaphor, which was also lost on Stein. He got the message later.

Lord Sketchley decided to show Stein round part of the large country estate. He told Stein it wasn't his but that he had the run of it from a fellow colleague who also sat in the House of Lords. Stein began to realise that the estate was massive and had its own extensive grounds, woods and walled vegetable garden with greenhouses. The main building had its own chapel, where Stein pointed out that the pipe organ could be used to atomise the chemical and work out the best dosage to achieve the maximum effect on sheep tethered in different positions around the chapel. Lord Sketchley agreed, and Stein was somewhat relieved testing on humans was not envisaged at this stage—especially himself!

Lord Sketchley was quite satisfied with Stein's attitude and approach to the task in hand and suggested he return to the lab; at least until Helmut was found, he might as well start preparing some of the chemical to be going on with. Stein would have preferred to stay at the new, more comfortable premises but had little option but to agree. They nodded to one another, and Colin ushered Stein into the back of the car for an uncomfortable return journey.

CHAPTER 7
WHAT'S WRONG WITH THE
RIGHT CLUB?

I'd driven hell-for-leather out of Leeds from the Queens Hotel along the main Kirkstall road towards Bradford, one eye on the road and the other in my rear-view mirror to make sure we weren't being followed. I was pretty sure we were OK, so I turned off onto a side road I was familiar with, slowing down dramatically to avoid any unwelcome attention. I breathed a sigh of relief and allowed one eye to focus on Helmut, who was still crouched down in the passenger seat with a terrified look on his face.

'Get up. They're not following us,' I said sharply, somewhat annoyed at his lack of awareness.

He obeyed and immediately fumbled with a new packet of Piccadilly king size cigarettes, lighting up before I could stop him. He inhaled deeply and breathed the smoke out onto the windscreen. Angela would be furious when she found out, as smoking in her minivan was one of her pet hates. Henry had been correct in his reading of the situation: another few minutes and Helmut would have been caught; we'd been very lucky. It's a pity I hadn't thought things through a little better, as I was not sure exactly where I was taking Helmut. Bradford, yes, but which hotel? I didn't think Gerry Engel had mentioned one... then I remembered he had—the Midland Hotel in Forster Square, within a few minutes' walking distance of the institute's offices.

I pulled into Forster Square and found the entrance to the hotel's small car park. Luckily there was a free space, and I motioned to Helmut that we had arrived. He could kick his heels here for a couple of days until the meeting with Gerry Engel and the new research director, Dr Finlay. At the reception desk I confirmed that Helmut was expected, and they could check him in immediately. I told him to stay mainly around the hotel until I picked him up about 9:00 a.m. on Wednesday morning. He nodded that he understood, and we shook hands. I realised it would be best to remove the minivan, as the two men had seen it and no doubt noted its number plate. Very inconvenient, as being without transport would cramp my style. I decided the Mill would be the best place for it, so I set off for Leeds after leaving Helmut to sort out his registration details.

Now I'd got Helmut safely out of the way, I needed to regroup and touch base again with Henry and Angela to see if anything had emerged which would give us a lead on Stein's whereabouts. I began to wonder how the two men had located Helmut so quickly and had been waiting for him at the Queens Hotel. They seemed to be one step ahead of us, which was disconcerting.

I called in again at the police station. Unfortunately, Inspector Broadley had gone off duty, but the duty sergeant didn't think anything had come of their dash to the hotel earlier, except that they'd got a description of the two men from the desk clerk, which might be useful—something at least. Before I left the police station to drop the minivan off at the Mill, I rang Henry to mention that Helmut was safe for now but we'd escaped in the nick of time. Henry informed me that Angela had told him David Lithgow's sidekick, Tom Hardy, was not being too helpful; however, Nigel had told him there was an informer who was tipping off the NSM that their military training events were being targeted, so Tom could well be in the frame. Angela may have said something to Tom that tipped them off. Angela was on her way back to Yorkshire, so I mentioned to Henry that neither she nor I should use the minivan again since it was known to them; Henry said he would tell her if he spoke to her first.

I dropped the minivan off at the Mill. There was only the 'back agin, lad?' gateman on duty. Didn't he have a home to go to? I told him that, for the present, the minivan should stay at the Mill and I would leave a message in it to explain why. He logged it down in immaculate copperplate black ink; it reminded me of my father, who had been taught the 'three Rs' properly! Sad to say, my writing is atrocious. I put it down to the introduction of the biro. Being left-handed didn't help either, but I'd managed to get through my exams. One lecturer had drily commented that with handwriting like mine, medicine would be a good profession as the only people who could normally read it would be pharmacists.

On my somewhat lengthy journey back to Angela's flat in Hyde Park, I realised that we might have the luxury of a couple of days together, unless her parents were expecting her. It had been quite a while since Angela and I had had time to get re-acquainted; what an old-fashioned phrase, I thought. While peering through the bus window at the uninteresting Leeds city architecture I realised that *absence really does make the heart grow fonder* and wondered if I was any different from the thousands of servicemen and women who, not too long ago, during the war, wrote letters to each other and put suggestive acronyms on their envelopes. It was still quite common to use S.W.A.L.K. (sealed with a loving kiss), and I had just learned fairly recently that N.O.R.W.I.C.H. stood for knickers off and ready when I come home. I smiled inwardly as I faintly remembered a group of us at uni researching some of the more vulgar acronyms; at the time it seemed more interesting than getting to grips with the molecular orbital theory! I half remembered L.O.W.E.S.T.O.F.T., E.D.I.N.B.U.R.G. and E.N.G.L.A.N.D. getting great guffaws but didn't now remember why. The one that might be viewed with consternation, depending on whether the marital knot had been tied, was, C.H.I.P. (come home I'm pregnant!). It must have been very interesting to be a postman at the time!

I reached the door of Angela's flat and realised the light was on in the kitchen. Angela had arrived before me and was sitting on the sofa, drinking a cup of tea.

'Hello, Angela. Henry said you were on your way back. Bit of a wasted journey, I understand?' I said in anticipation of warm welcome and looking forward to a cosy chat—know what I mean?

'No, not exactly. In the end it was worth going, as it may influence the way we go from here,' said Angela in an unexpectedly reserved manner.

Sometimes you get a sixth sense of something not right. She was in a completely different mood from when I last saw her at the Mill. When you know somebody so well, you instinctively know by their body language and phrases used that something important is on their mind.

'What's up, luv? Got a crush on Nigel, 'ave you? Get it off your chest,' I said, lapsing into a poor impersonation of Inspector Broadley, which I immediately realised was wasted on Angela, since she hadn't met him.

I got a fleeting smile in acknowledgement, which quickly reverted to her original serious expression. 'After I'd seen Tom Hardy, I contacted Nigel to see if he remembered anything else. He hadn't. He wants me to be based mainly in London permanently now; it's a sort of promotion,' she said, completely taking the wind out of my sails.

'How do you mean, *sort of promotion?* Is it or isn't it?' I said, puzzled.

'Yes, it is a promotion. There's more money in it and he wants me to handle the Mill as well, mainly from a distance. Obviously, it'll mean we'll see one another a bit less often since it looks like you'll be working for this wool organisation in Bradford, won't you?' she added, trying to soften the blow a bit.

'I see. Congratulations are in order then—well done. Are we going to celebrate tonight?' I persevered, still hoping to change her mood. No luck, I'm afraid.

'Mother found out I was coming up to Yorkshire and is expecting me tonight. It's her birthday. I'm sorry.'

'Shit!' I said with as much feeling as I could muster to vent my frustration, getting up and going into the kitchen to make myself a cup of tea. This coincided with an audible double-toot from outside.

'That'll be my taxi, James. I have to go. No doubt we'll have a catch up with Henry shortly. Oh, and don't you think you might get your hair cut before your meeting with the wool institute's directors next week?'

With that, Angela quickly donned her coat, picked up her case, gave me a very unsatisfactory peck on the cheek and disappeared out of the door before I could say *Jack Robinson*. When the outside door had closed, I murmured 'shit' again but quietly under my breath as there was nobody else around to appreciate it.

***

Stein was now under no illusion that he had to cooperate with Lord Sketchley, but his thoughts remained firmly on escape, though—short of poisoning all his captors with tabun—he could see no clear route. He hadn't a clue where he was, and despite being taken somewhat into their confidence, he got the distinct impression that he was expendable. It was something about Sketchley's manner that was reminiscent of the SS officers he'd had experience of during the war, who knew they had all the power and would use it ruthlessly, if necessary. Only one of the captors was at the laboratory, apart from the owner, Julian Thompson. The one Sketchley had called Colin hadn't travelled back with him.

Stein sat down and immediately started to work out what quantity of tabun he was going to prepare first. In theory its synthesis should be relatively straightforward—he'd previously chosen to work with it as it was the easiest nerve agent to prepare. The main consideration was safety. He'd witnessed first-hand the devastating effects it could have on people if they became contaminated. He'd had a narrow escape himself in his early research days, when he was unaware of just how toxic it was, and he'd spent a week recovering from its effects.

He checked again for reassurance that the antidote, atropine, was included in the box of chemicals he'd ordered. The fume cupboard was also checked by carrying out a preliminary test with a smoking match and candle to see if the fumes were effectively pulled from where he was standing into the cabinet with the sash fully open; they were. Ideally, he would have liked to measure the air velocity with a vane anemometer or the like, to see if it was at least 0.5m/sec., but from experience he judged the draught into the cabinet was adequate for the task in hand. He inspected the protective equipment—rubber gloves, respirator, etc.—which would be needed when he handled the tabun outside. Both he and Thompson went outside to look at the exhaust vent from the fume cupboard, and he satisfied himself that the fumes were not likely to be introduced back into the laboratory. One concern he had was that it was just a simple extraction system without any kind of scrubber or filter to remove the tabun from the air stream; on the other hand, the laboratory was in an old, disused textile mill with open fields on the other side of the river, so the fumes were unlikely to cause a problem to the general public. Anyway, this was all that was available, so unless he was prepared to cause a major objection, he had to make do—it was Hobson's Choice. The handler followed them outside to watch where they went and make sure he didn't attempt a runner; this was noted by Stein, who was acutely aware of everything now.

Stein found that occupying himself with the tabun synthesis took his mind off his worries, and he began to think clearly about what he was going to do. Assuming that Helmut was found and persuaded to take over what he had started, he realised he'd need some suitable, unbreakable, spill-proof bottles in which to transport the tabun to the estate in order to carry out the tests on sheep in the chapel; he also needed a remotely controlled delivery device to introduce the tabun into the pipe organ air supply. He'd probably need another visit to the estate to familiarise himself with the system. He discussed the bottles with Thompson, as he thought it was urgent. Thompson said he could get some delivered in a few days' time. For his own good and Thompson's, Stein intentionally kept what he was about to prepare secret, but realised that if Thompson was any sort of informed chemist, he would probably have guessed what was going on anyway.

It was already late afternoon, too late to start the preparation, so Stein told his minder he'd start first thing in the morning and at some stage, probably in a couple of days, he would need to visit the estate again to examine the pipe organ. This information was immediately relayed by the minder presumably to Sketchley, and a nod to Stein indicated that it was acceptable.

He retired, somewhat exhausted, to his cold caravan sleeping quarters for another fitful night's sleep.

***

Since talking to Nigel on the phone, Henry was keen to have a face-to-face meeting with both Angela and James to share with them his thoughts and the latest information. Under normal circumstances he might have suggested that James join them for the birthday celebration meal Grace was planning now she'd learnt Angela was back in Yorkshire, but he preferred to keep work and home life separate, so he'd told Grace that James was busy and not to invite him. Grace had never been interested in Henry's work; she told people he did something in the City, not really knowing what that meant. Henry was well aware of this and joked in company that he and Grace had the ideal arrangement: he earned the money, she spent it! He'd lost count now of how many times he'd used that one to good effect. In truth, Grace knew where Henry worked, but it suited them both for her to act dumb, so they made a good double act.

Henry mulled over what Nigel had told him and decided to share it with Angela and James, even though Nigel had wanted it to be kept confidential. Part of it involved a secret society which had originally been set up by Archibald Ramsey, the Conservative MP for Peebles and Southern Midlothian, in 1939: the Right Club. The aim of the Right Club, according to Ramsey's autobiography, *The Nameless War*, was '... *to oppose and expose the activities of Organized Jewry, in the light of the evidence which came into my possession in 1938. Our first objective was to clear the Conservative Party of Jewish influence, and the character of our membership and meetings were strictly in keeping with this objective.*'

Since talking to Nigel, Henry had immersed himself in Ramsey's autobiography and was convinced that the paranoia of far-right groups was fanning the flames again against the Jews and communism, in fear of the election of a socialist government, which would lead to communism. History was in danger of repeating itself, with many similarities to the late thirties, when fears of communism were rife. It was, after all, barely twenty years since the war in Europe had ended.

Nigel had been keen to point out to Henry that, in the early part of the war, it was down to MI5's success in infiltrating three women into the Right Club that many of its members, including Ramsey, were rounded up and interned with other right-wing extremists under the Defence Regulation 18B, which was designed to root out people likely to '*endanger the safety of the realm*'. Henry did wonder if MI5's standards had slipped somewhat since then, but nevertheless, Nigel was being very helpful, and surviving ex-Right Club members might be worth looking into.

Henry had been well aware of the Right Club's existence but had been abroad during the war, involved in military intelligence. The thing that had stuck in his mind about them was the Tyler Kent affair. Tyler Kent was a cypher clerk at the American Embassy in London and was concerned that America might join the war against Germany. He had been copying correspondence between Roosevelt and Churchill which supported this. Kent had met Anna Wolkoff at the Russian Tea Room, which she ran in South Kensington and was the main meeting place for members of the Right Club. Kent showed the documents to Wolkoff and Ramsey, and copies found their way to Germany, where they were seen by Admiral Canares, head of the Abwehr (military intelligence). Wolkoff also tried, unsuccessfully, to get sensitive material to William Joyce (Lord Haw-Haw), via one of the MI5 lady plants, for broadcasting on Radio Hamburg. Both Wolkoff and Kent were arrested and charged under the Official Secrets Act; in Kent's case, his diplomatic immunity was waived by Joseph Kennedy, the American ambassador, and at a secret trial, Wolkoff was given ten years and Kent seven. Surprisingly, Ramsey was not charged with breaching the Official Secrets Act but just interned.

Henry also remembered that Anna Wolkoff, daughter of Admiral Nikolai Wolkoff, the former aide-de-camp to Nicholas II in London, had been watched by MI5 as early as 1935 and suspected of passing state secrets to Germany. She had developed a close relationship with Wallis Simpson, the future wife of Edward VIII.

Henry couldn't understand why Nigel wanted this to be kept under wraps. Angela and James worked for him, and it might prove useful background information in the long run. He would explain his findings when he could get both of them together, which was likely to be Wednesday at the earliest now. He would arrange it with Angela when she arrived for Grace's birthday meal.

***

'I thought both you and Henry knew I was meeting the new research institute's director in Bradford on Wednesday morning?' I said tetchily to Angela when she rang early Monday morning.

Apparently, it had slipped both their minds after a rather good celebratory dinner last night. We provisionally arranged for early Wednesday afternoon at the Mill, as I believed that I would be free by then.

I'd been up and moving earlier and had strolled down to the newsagents at Hyde Park, close to the traffic lights, to pick up a *Yorkshire Post* and the latest edition of the weekly *Exchange and Mart*. Since I had the best part of two days before the meeting with Gerry Engel and Dr Finlay, I'd decided to investigate the acquisition of some transport. The minivan was now out of commission and I wasn't sure of the procedures for hiring a vehicle, but I realised I was going to need some personal transport shortly for when I started work at the research institute. My initial thought was that something two-wheeled might be good since parking near the Bradford offices seemed difficult, and I needed to watch my expenditure carefully as I'd just taken on the expense of renting a house. I quickly thumbed my way through the 'used' columns in both papers and spotted a relatively new Lambretta scooter which I thought I could afford. By chance it was in the Kirkstall district of Leeds, very close to Angela's flat. A phone call established that the owner was looking for a quick cash sale, and I headed out of the flat to call in at the bank to cash a cheque. Rightly or wrongly, I parted with the money for a 1961 150cc Lambretta scooter after establishing that it would start and all the lights were in good working order.

On Tuesday morning, I decided to make a trial run to Bradford to call in at the estate agents and finalise the details of my house. The Lambretta brought back memories of my flight from London last year on the AA motorbike, which I'd enjoyed. The Lambretta wasn't as powerful, but it was nippy and agile in traffic compared to a car. I decided to worry about the technicalities of whether I needed L-plates later, as I had a full driving licence. I got my business sorted with Mr Green at the estate agents and picked up the keys for the house.

I started to give some thought to tomorrow's meeting with Gerry Engel and Dr Finlay at the research institute and remembered Angela's advice to get a haircut just as I was approaching the road which led to my new house. There was a barber's shop on the opposite side, so I pulled up. There were two barbers, clipping away at a couple of older men with very receding hairlines. Both barbers nodded at me as I sat down to wait and picked up a *Dandy* comic, which took me back to my youth when I used to catch up on the exploits of the characters in both the *Beano* and *Dandy* at my local barber's, which was not far away from this one. I'd just established the fact that Desperate Dan's appetite hadn't waned over the years and was getting on to Dennis the Menace when I heard the older barber say, 'There you are, Jack, young and handsome again. Want any Brylcreem on?'

Jack shook his head and said, 'Nowt; can't stand B-b-b-brylcreem.'

By the time Jack had got his words out, the barber had niftily taken the cotton drape off from around his neck, shaken it, helped him out of the chair, accepted half a crown and sat me in his place.

'Thanks very much, Jack. See you next month,' he said whilst ushering the man out of the door with a kindly smile, with Jack now mumbling, 'OK, thanks Ber-Ber-Ber—'

'Now then, sir, how do you want it? Short back and sides or a moderate trim? Haven't seen you before—just passing through, are we?'

We settled on a moderate trim as it was getting late in the season and I'd seen Jack's ultra-short 'trim' as he'd departed and seriously wondered where the barber would have smeared the Brylcreem if Jack had taken a shine to it. The two barbers were father and son, Bernard and Peter Ackroyd, and were both identically kitted out in smart knee-length smocks which reminded me of dentists'. Bernard quickly combed my hair into place and set about removing the hair on my neck with an electric trimmer, which buzzed soothingly while he expertly directed the conversation on to a topic from which he could extract the maximum amount of information about me. I'd often admired the depth of knowledge barbers seemed to have about virtually any topic you could mention, from the latest football teams' news, political events of the day and personal gripes, usually about illnesses and partners in older clients. This was done diplomatically and sympathetically. It struck me they provided a public service akin to a psychiatrist, with the added benefit of getting your hair trimmed at the same time, and for a fraction of the price.

I fell for the trick, volunteering, 'Well, I'm moving to the area shortly to work in Bradford. I'm renting a house just off Idle Road, next to Stanley Robinson and his wife Edna—do you know them?'

Through the looking glass in front of me, both Bernard and Peter's faces lit up.

'Stan's been coming here for donkey's years. He's a big Yorkshire cricket fan; has he sold you a ticket for an autographed cricket bat yet?' asked Peter Ackroyd.

'No, not yet. What's it for?' I asked.

'For the benefit of a Yorkshire cricketer. Stan does it every year, rain or shine,' said Peter.

By the time my haircut was finished, they knew virtually everything about me, apart from my government work and inside leg measurement. It had been an entertaining fifteen minutes, and I even got my jacket brushed down before I was ushered out of the door by Bernard, promising to see them in a month's time. It put me in a good mood to travel home on my Lambretta and look reasonably smart for my meeting in the morning with the research institute directors.

On Wednesday morning, I was still in a good mood until I'd almost reached the Midland Hotel on my Lambretta, when it started to drizzle heavily. I was going to have to invest in some waterproof biking gear, especially as winter was fast approaching. I managed to park in the hotel's carpark and dashed quickly into the foyer and up to the reception desk, where the same man was on duty as when I had delivered Helmut on Sunday. He acknowledged me as I asked him if Helmut Schultz was around.

'Are you James Brittain, sir?' he said.

I nodded.

'Herr Schultz has left sir, with two men who said you had sent them. He kept saying he must wait for you, but they insisted. No—forced him, actually, to accompany them out of the hotel. I was uncertain what to do, and now you are here.'

It was clear Helmut had been snatched from right under our noses.

Chapter 8

Losing One German is Unfortunate, Gerry, but to Lose Both Seems Careless!

My meeting with Gerry Engel and Dr Finlay did not exactly go to plan. I had to shake their hands hastily and introduce myself while explaining that Helmut Schultz had just been abducted. It was a case of 'hello, goodbye, I needed to dash back to Leeds as soon as possible.'

I'd already tried, unsuccessfully, to ring Inspector Broadley from the hotel, and after taking my leave of the now worried-looking directors, I jumped on my Lambretta and set off towards Leeds as fast as it would go. Dr Finlay had seemed a nice enough guy, for an Australian, and I just had to hope he'd formed a reasonable opinion of me. Only time would tell. He'd made a pointed comment to Gerry Engel about losing both Germans, and on the spur of the moment, I'd quipped: It was a misfortune to lose one but to lose both appeared careless! An aside I wasn't Wilde about now, as I was hopefully going to be employed in a serious technical role at the institute, not as a witty second-rate music hall turn taking liberties with *The Importance of Being Earnest*!

It was turning out to be a day to forget. Inspector Broadley was out on another case, and even though the desk sergeant was helpful, I really needed to speak to the inspector, so I left word for him to ring me at the Mill. Nor was I in any mood to appreciate the good-natured query from the Mill's gateman as to whether I was intending to enter my Lambretta in the lower-class race in the Isle of Man TT next year.

When I reached the office, Mavis informed me that neither Henry nor Angela would be in until around lunchtime, which was something I hadn't anticipated. Apparently, Henry had to run his wife somewhere and Angela was cadging a lift with him since she didn't have the minivan; as they weren't expecting me until the afternoon, that made sense.

I was therefore stymied on all fronts. I could have rung Nigel but thought the bad news should be relayed by Angela, who was best placed to do it. Mavis commiserated with me and alleviated things as best she could by conjuring up a fine cup of tea and some chocolate biscuits. I set about them as if my job depended on it, which of course was true—in fact, two jobs for that matter. I was midway through a chocolate marshmallow when the phone rang. Mavis passed it to me with a laconic, 'Inspector B.'

'Nah then, James. Lost another one 'as ta?' asked the inspector in his droll way.

'Well, that's about what it amounts to,' I agreed.

I filled him in on the details and asked what he'd learned about the two men from the receptionist at the Queens Hotel.

'Nowt much. Two thickset men, thirty-five to forty-ish, probably not local-like. One who did talkin' had dark hair and sideburns, Elvis-like.'

This didn't tell us a lot. They could have been the ones involved in Stein's kidnapping, but they'd had balaclavas on when I'd seen them, so it wasn't much help.

Just then, the door opened and Angela walked in briskly, followed more slowly by Henry.

'It sounds as if it's probably the ones who were at the Queens. OK, thanks for that, Inspector. We'll be in touch if anything else comes to mind,' I said as Angela and Henry took their coats off and sat down at the table.

'Anything interesting to report?' asked Angela.

'Well, it's not good news, I'm afraid,' I said, deciding it was best to get the bad news off my chest and out in the open as soon as possible. 'Just before I arrived to pick him up this morning, Helmut was lifted and virtually frogmarched out of the Midland.'

'How did they know he was there?' asked Henry incredulously.

'Don't know. I'm sure I wasn't followed on Sunday when I picked him up, as I told you before,' I said defensively.

'Have you spoken to Nigel?' asked Angela.

'No, I wanted to speak to Inspector Broadley first to see if he'd learned anything from the staff at the Queens on Sunday. I've just spoken to him and got a superficial description of the two men, which matches those at the Midland; it doesn't help too much.'

Angela took a deep breath, which distracted me somewhat by drawing attention to her heaving, well-formed bosoms.

'I'm afraid I've got some further bad news for you, James,' she said seriously. 'Nigel told me there's been a change in policy and that you're no longer required to carry out any further investigations for MI5.'

I was stunned—no wonder Angela's attitude had changed since going to London.

'Great timing—I've just rented a house in Bradford and bought a Lambretta. All I need now is for Gerry Engel to tell me he doesn't think I'm suitable for working at The Wool Research Institute,' I said, thinking of my major gaffe this morning.

'Did you discuss your starting date with Gerry this morning?' said Henry.

'No. Basically all I had time to do was shake their hands, tell them about Helmut and come back to Leeds; very unsatisfactory.' I deliberately missed out the Oscar Wilde quip in case it made things worse.

'I'll have a word with Gerry to see if I can get an idea of when they want you to start,' said Henry, helpfully. 'I've got access to a fund which should tide you over in the short term.'

I breathed a sigh of relief and thanked him profusely. At least now we could concentrate on finding Helmut and Stein.

'I'm going to let you both in on some extremely confidential information Nigel told me the other day,' said Henry. 'It might go some way to explaining why MI5 doesn't need you at the moment, James, but this must stay within these four walls. OK?'

He first described the ideology behind the Right Club and the possibility that some surviving members could be the brains behind the right-wing extremist group we were looking for.

The second, and frankly equally disturbing, piece of information supplied by Nigel was the confirmation of MI5's distrust of Harold Wilson's Labour party. This went back to the Attlee government, when Wilson had been a junior minister for trade attempting to increase exports to the USSR. This was strongly opposed by the United States and MI5, who almost went hysterical when Wilson was sent to the USSR to successfully negotiate the sale of twenty advanced jet engines. From this point on, Wilson had been viewed with great suspicion by MI5.

It got worse. The unexpected death of the Labour leader Hugh Gaitskell in 1963 led to Wilson's election as leader later that year, compounding MI5's worries. The FBI had recently told MI5 that it had discovered a KGB mole who had been operating inside MI5 in the key post-war period. Embarrassingly, in addition, was the fact that Sir Anthony Blunt, who had close connections to the Queen and was now known to be a KGB agent, was certain to create a spy scandal as damaging as that of Kim Philby. Even worse for MI5 was the knowledge that they had been tipped off about Blunt's spying a decade earlier but had failed to take any action. The fear now was that if Wilson won the general election, he would use the excuse of a potential scandal to decimate its organisation. For MI5's DG, it was definitely a case of self-preservation, which had led to an on-going cover-up to avoid Blunt going public.

Angela was the first to react. 'Where the hell does this leave me?'

'There's nothing you can do, other than do your normal job,' said Henry. 'But even though Nigel wants you to spend more time in London, it might be prudent, in the short term, to delay your move whilst we're dealing with the missing two Germans.'

My initial feelings towards Nigel mellowed, as I could see he was in a difficult position and it was nothing personal this time—

though I still frequently found him difficult to deal with and, quite often, as irritating as Izal toilet paper. He obviously had immense respect for and confidence in Henry, otherwise he wouldn't have divulged such sensitive information as this. Cynically though, I did wonder if he was looking to the future in case MI5 was disbanded; he could be angling for a job in MI6 through Henry.

I was searching for a suitable response to Henry's revelations when the phone rang and I answered it. It was Mavis, saying that Nigel wanted to speak to Angela, urgently. I passed the receiver over to her.

'Yes, Nigel. I'm with James and Henry in a meeting at the moment. Helmut Schultz, the other German, has just been abducted from the Bradford hotel this morning… Yes, unfortunate.'

There was then a long pause while Angela listened intently to what Nigel had to say before putting the receiver down with a worried expression on her face.

'Nigel's just told me that Tom Hardy, David Lithgow's Special Branch colleague, has just been murdered.'

***

Stein had just finished his first successful synthesis of tabun in the laboratory. He was told he was needed immediately at the country estate, so he started to prepare a special glass phial to transport the nerve gas sample safely, but his minder told him to forget it this time, they'd do it later. The now-familiar uncomfortable journey in the back of the car followed.

'Good of you to come, Dr Stein,' announced Lord Sketchley as Stein was ushered into his study. As if he'd had any choice.

Stein sat down and was waiting to hear why he had been summoned when in walked his handler, accompanied by a terrified Helmut Schultz.

'Herr Schultz doesn't seem to appreciate the situation clearly, Dr Stein. Perhaps you could explain it to him on the way back to the laboratory?' said Sketchley menacingly.

'I've prepared the first sample for testing,' said Stein, hoping it might alleviate some of the tension.

'Good, I was expecting that. Do we have sufficient to carry out the first trial?'

'Yes, but I need to examine the *Kirche* first,' stuttered Stein, struggling to find the right English word for chapel or church.

'OK, we can go now to look at the chapel,' said Sketchley, getting up from his chair and motioning to the handler for Stein and Schultz to follow him.

The chapel was positioned just off the main entrance to the hall. It was a small family chapel with probably about a dozen pews, and a pipe organ at the side of the pulpit. Stein immediately went over to examine the electric fan that supplied air for the organ pipes. He could see it had been converted from a hand pump to electric some time in the past. He asked permission for it to be switched on, which resulted in a low background hum. He pressed a few notes and observed, with Helmut's help, which pipe the sound/air was coming from. This was an easy task as the organ was small and the pipes were just behind the keyboards.

Stein outlined his plan for the atomisation of tabun to Sketchley. It involved simply tethering a few sheep, three in the first instance, to pews in different positions in the chapel and coupling a glass separating funnel with its tube to introduce the liquid tabun into the organ pipe. To avoid contaminating himself, he suggested placing a weight on the correct keyboard key to hold it down, with the power supply switched off, and then turning it on again from outside the chapel. The tap on the separating funnel would have to be turned on just before he left the chapel to drip the liquid tabun into the pipe. The effects of the tabun on the sheep could be viewed through a window on the chapel door. From knowing the quantity of tabun used and the volume of air in the chapel, he could scale up the quantity required for the Lords' Chamber.

'Excellent, Dr Stein. Very impressive. When do you want to carry out the first trial?' asked Sketchley.

'Perhaps in the next day or two. I need to check that the laboratory has a suitable separating funnel,' replied Stein. He might also need a few days to get Helmut up to speed, and he was not yet sure of his willingness to fully cooperate.

'Good, let's make it Saturday. I'll get the farmer to supply the sheep,' said Sketchley, indicating to the minder that the audience was over and he should take the Germans back to the laboratory. 'Incidentally, some official has been asking questions about our organisation. We have dealt with this matter successfully, so it's very unlikely that your work at the laboratory will be interrupted.'

Helmut didn't understand any of this, but Stein got the message loud and clear.

The journey back to the laboratory was even less comfortable for Stein as he and Helmut were both cramped into the same space he had previously occupied alone. It was not possible for him to speak to Helmut due to the noise and the fact they were both covered by blankets. He wondered what fate the nosy official had suffered; he had no doubt that Sketchley's organisation was deadly serious and ruthless in dealing with people who might interfere with them. He decided he must impress on Helmut the importance of carrying out their wishes in the short term. He was sure the survival of them both depended on it.

***

As a result of Nigel's chilling news of Tom Hardy's murder, the meeting at the Mill was adjourned, since Henry decided the time was now ripe to put his DG fully in the picture and find out if there were any political activities he ought to be aware of. He made a rapid exit in order to catch the next London train.

My initial thought, which was a touchy one, was to wonder if Angela's meeting with Tom had somehow contributed to his elimination. Had Tom been playing a double game? I was thinking hard about how to approach the subject without upsetting the applecart, since Angela had admitted previously that she might have told Tom more than she'd intended. They often say, *Great minds think alike but fools…*

My train of thought was broken when Angela said, 'Tom promised to get back to me with the name of the ex-army man who organised and directed the military-style operations for the NSM, but he didn't.'

'What else did you tell him that you later thought better of?' I asked.

'Well, I told him we believed that David had recognised the man who shot him.'

'Did you mention that David had called out, "Colin"?' I said sharply.

'Yes, I believe I did, because I asked him if there was anybody he'd been dealing with called Colin. He said no, apart from Colin Jordan, but that he wouldn't be involved in the strong-arm stuff,' Angela admitted, taking a deep breath.

'Henry told me that, according to Nigel, an informer was tipping the NSM off about the military training exercises. Do you think it could have been Tom?' I probed.

'Nigel never mentioned anything to me,' said Angela angrily.

'What was Tom's background?'

'Public school, parents with a bob or two, right up Nigel's street you'd think, but in this case David had infiltrated the NSM, so Tom missed out on joining MI5—for all the good it did them both,' said Angela ruefully.

'I think your meeting with Tom was very revealing and worth the journey after all. Well done,' I said, thinking it was a pity we hadn't had a review meeting earlier.

Angela nodded and appeared pleased to have got things off her chest.

'Does this mean I'll be working undercover again?' I said provocatively. 'We could continue the discussions at your flat?'

'Over a bottle?' Angela suggested.

'Good idea. We could have an early night?'

Without saying a word, Angela got up, went into Mavis's office and told her we were going out and wouldn't be back until the morning. It was a quarter to four.

***

When they got back to the lab, Stein showed Helmut around the sparse accommodation in the caravan and the equipment set up at Thompson's Laboratories. The look on Helmut's face said he wasn't impressed. They could now converse in German, making it easier for Stein to get Sketchley's message across. Helmut was no fool and quickly took on board that they were in a big hole and expendable if they didn't cooperate. He brought up the important question, to which Stein had no answer, of what would happen to them when they were no longer useful. It was obvious to both of them that they were likely to be a big embarrassment to the organisation in the future, if they talked. Nevertheless, they agreed that for the present they should cooperate fully and take the Mr Micawber approach—*something would turn up*!

So, for now, they channelled their thoughts towards the practicalities of making tabun. Helmut was able to contribute significantly to the preparation side, both from a practical and a safety point of view, leaving Stein appreciative and impressed. Helmut was taken with the ingenuity of using the pipe organ to generate the nerve agent in aerosol form for the sheep trials. It had been pointed out to them that they'd about two to three weeks to sort out the tabun synthesis and quantify the optimum dosage for the Lords' Chamber, so they had their work cut out.

Stein was worried about the fact that the Lords' Chamber didn't have a pipe organ in it. Sketchley had been very sure about this, and as Stein had based his original plans on one being present, it was a huge blow. Sooner or later he would have to find an alternative way to create an aerosol. He decided to wait and see how the first sheep trial went before looking at alternative methods. He'd estimated the amount of tabun required and asked Helmut to prepare two more same-sized samples, which would take a couple of days. In the meantime, he asked Julian Thompson if he had any small separating funnels, which he would need to introduce the tabun into the pipe organ. Unfortunately, the only one he had was too big, but Thompson assured him that he could get a smaller one in the next day or so. Stein impressed on him that it must have a ground glass stopper and a good tap; Thompson understood exactly what he wanted.

Helmut got to work in earnest the following day, Thursday, and prepared another sample to the satisfaction of Stein, who was looking on. Thompson turned up towards the end of the day with a separating funnel, which Stein was happy with. He set about fixing it in a stand and clamp for the sheep trial on Saturday.

Initially, Stein had intended that only he would carry out the sheep trial, but with Helmut's valuable practical expertise, Stein thought it right that he should be present, as he could be useful. On Saturday they packed everything they needed very carefully in an air-tight container and placed it in the boot of the car, not forgetting the atropine antidote, and set off on the uncomfortable journey to the estate.

On arrival there were three sheep tethered nervously outside the entrance, oblivious to their impending fate. Lord Sketchley came out to meet them with the farmer, who ushered the now restless sheep into the chapel and re-tethered them in the positions Stein indicated. They registered their displeasure by depositing droppings on the tiled floor. Sketchley made some aside about taking lambs to the slaughter, which was totally lost on Stein and Helmut—and inaccurate, since these sheep were fully grown ewes, which demonstrated Sketchley's poor grasp of normal day-to-day activities.

Stein took charge of the trial and first of all suggested a dummy run. They were shown where the power supply switch was located, and Helmut, who was in charge of this, switched it off. Stein set up the empty separating funnel with its outlet in the organ pipe, placed a small piece of lead pipe on middle C and turned the tap on, then dashed out of the chapel and yelled to Helmut to switch the electricity on. A monotonous sound came from the chapel, at which Stein went back into the chapel—since it was only a dummy run—and inspected everything. He realised he could increase the sound, and the airflow into the pipe with it, by depressing the loud pedal. It all seemed to work well, apart from for the sheep, who were irritated by the noise. Now for the real thing.

Stein donned a protective mask and gloves and carefully took the top off the tabun container. He poured the contents into the separating funnel and switched the tap on to allow the tabun to drip relatively slowly into the organ pipe. He left the chapel rapidly and shouted to Helmut to switch on the power. The organ responded as before, and Stein, Sketchley and Helmut peered expectantly through the window in the door into the chapel.

Stein had started a stopwatch as he dashed from the chapel. Five minutes went by with little movement of the three sheep, but shortly afterwards, the one nearest the organ became agitated and collapsed, followed shortly afterwards by the other two. The trial had worked.

Sketchley was obviously pleased and invited Stein and Helmut back to his study for a stiff drink. 'Excellent, gentlemen; you obviously know your stuff. Since the Lords' Chamber doesn't have a pipe organ, how do you intend to disperse the nerve agent into the air?'

Stein was almost completely stumped. All he could say was, 'We're working on it.'

But Helmut piped up, 'Small hairdryer would work. Gives hot air, which is good.'

'Yes, I see what you mean. As long as you are on to it,' said Sketchley, apparently satisfied.

Chapter 9
Would James Make a
Good Butlin Boy?

Henry wasn't able to see his DG until mid-morning Thursday. He came away from the meeting disappointed that he wasn't going to get any additional help to find the two German scientists. He was told to leave it up to MI5, Special Branch and the police. The DG didn't share his fears that an ultra-right extremist group was planning an imminent attack on democracy, aided perhaps, inadvertently, by MI5's distrust of Harold Wilson. He just didn't think there was enough evidence for it, and he was more interested in discovering MI5's mole. He then added on a reminder that, unlike Henry, he'd been transferred from MI5 to MI6 so he knew how they ticked.

Henry didn't divulge Nigel's latest piece of information—the feeling within MI5 that if a Wilson Labour government got into power they might be disbanded. Obviously his DG didn't have his ear as close to the ground as he thought he did!

The DG did approve of Henry taking on James Brittain as a future undercover agent. MI6 were always on the lookout for suitable people who would make regular trips behind the Iron Curtain. One businessman in particular, Greville Wynne, an electrical engineer who had established a profitable export business, had proved extraordinarily successful until his capture in 1962. He had been in the news recently, having been released from prison in April 1964, in exchange for the Soviet agent Gordon Lonsdale. Wynne had originally been approached by MI6 and asked if he could make contact in Moscow with a senior Russian military intelligence officer, Colonel Oleg Penkovsky. He had obliged and was handed some highly secret documents on microfilm, which he'd managed to bring back safely to London. Over a period of time, it became evident that Penkovsky had access to thousands of secrets, not least those concerning Soviet missile developments, nuclear plans, locations of military headquarters and identities of KGB officers. Penkovsky had also told Wynne that the USSR was not willing to start World War Three over Cuba, information which was of immense value to President Kennedy during the Cuban Missile Crisis in October 1962, and it is for this reason that Penkovsky was often referred to as the 'spy who saved the world'. None of this would have seen the light of day in the West but for Wynne, who facilitated it at great personal risk. Wynne was lucky to be released early, but Penkovsky was executed.

Henry had argued that a highly trained wool technical scientist would be an ideal cover. OK, it would take some time and some investment to him get up and running, both as a wool scientist and useful agent, but it would be worth the gamble; the DG agreed. Henry also thought Wynne and James had a similar sense of humour; Wynne was reported as saying after being arrested that he was not expecting prison to be 'a Butlin's holiday camp'.

After the meeting, Henry began to wonder if they had got it all wrong and were reading too much into the ultra-right-wing conspiracy theory. He began to imagine 'what-if' scenarios. The one he kept coming back to was: what if the monarchy, government and leading politicians were all wiped out—who would take over? Whoever was behind this must have somebody in mind for the country to rally around, or else it would be chaos.

Oswald Mosley came briefly to mind. He was a British politician who had risen to fame in the 1920s as a Member of Parliament and later, in the 1930s, founded the British Union of Fascists (BUF). He was a charismatic speaker and tipped for stardom. After the outbreak of war, Mosley had led the campaign for a negotiated peace, but after the invasion of France and the commencement of the London Blitz, support for him waned and turned to hostility. The government considered him too dangerous and interned him under the Defence Regulation 18B, along with other most active fascists including members of the Right Club. This resulted in the BUF's practical removal at an organised level from the United Kingdom's political scene.

If the invasion of Britain (Nazi codename: Operation Sea Lion) had been successful, Hitler had planned to form a new government along the lines of that in occupied Norway. Top of the list of those trusted to form the government was Oswald Mosley. Hitler had decreed that Blenheim Palace, the ancestral home of Winston Churchill, was to serve as the overall headquarters of the German occupation military government. During the rapid invasion of France, the Duke and Duchess of Windsor, who'd been in France, fled by road into Spain and then Portugal to escape capture. Hitler believed the duke was sympathetic to the Third Reich and planned to reinstate him as Edward VIII in occupied Britain as a puppet king; there was serious effort put into trying to entice the duke into a position where he could be kidnapped from Spain (Operation Willi). In the end, the duke and his duchess were plucked from Portugal by the British to be installed out of harm's way as Governor of the Bahamas for the remainder of the war.

While Henry was in London, he contacted Nigel, hoping they could meet to get more information on members of the Right Club who might be candidates in the frame for investigation. Surprisingly, Nigel was cagey about meeting in London and said he'd prefer to come up to Leeds, where it would be more discreet; next Tuesday at the Mill was agreed upon. Henry managed to get Gerry Engel on the phone and brought him up to date on the Helmut kidnapping situation. At the institute's meeting with James, both Gerry and Hamish Finlay had been shocked by the revelation of Helmut's kidnapping; they'd observed James was agitated. While Hamish was still in Bradford, he was keen to see James in the next couple of days; Henry said he would tell James to contact him tomorrow. When asked when he thought James might start at the wool institute, Gerry said it was up to Hamish but obviously finding the two Germans was a top priority at the moment. Henry didn't get the impression that Gerry was having cold feet about James, and with that they agreed to keep in touch if anything materialised.

***

Lord Sketchley was in a very good mood. Things seemed to be falling nicely into place. The German scientists were cooperating well; and the plan he had hatched for so long was taking shape.

In 1935, the Prince of Wales, the future King Edward VIII and later Duke of Windsor, made a speech calling for a closer understanding of Germany in order to safeguard peace in Europe. From this idea the Anglo-German Fellowship (AGF) was established in September 1935, and Sketchley was one of the first to join. It had a sister organisation in Berlin called the Deutsch-Englische Gesellschaft. Some of its members were fascists and the organisation, which was decidedly pro-Nazi in bias, was aimed at the influential in society. Its membership was dominated by businessmen keen to promote commercial links. However, on the outbreak of war, the AGF ceased to exist.

As a last-ditch attempt at averting war, the Parliamentary Peace Aims Group was formed to '*urge the government, while still there might be some hope of a settlement before war with all its horrors broke over Europe, to explore possibilities for the calling of a Conference prior to a negotiated peace*'. Sketchley supported this and was in favour of appeasement towards Hitler and Nazi Germany, arguing that Neville Chamberlain and his government should concentrate on the threat posed by Joseph Stalin and the Soviet Union. Sketchley had even gone to Germany with other likeminded British aristocrats in April 1939 to celebrate Hitler's fiftieth birthday, giving the Führer great satisfaction and valuable propaganda material.

As a result of Sketchley's overt support of the Nazi regime, even after the Blitz had started, and his outspoken criticism of Churchill as a warmonger, King George VI sacked him from his position as a Steward of the Royal Household. This was humiliating to Sketchley and still cut deeply to this day. Since then he'd adopted a low profile. The long-held fear that a Labour government would ultimately lead to a communist state was now a distinct possibility. It was, in his view, as plain as the nose on your face, but some people just couldn't see it. As a former MP he still had the ear of like-minded politicians and peers and some considerable influence. By chance he'd not joined the Right Club and was glad he hadn't, since leading members had been interned during the war, and he was conscious that the security services still monitored right-wing groups. The major hiccup encountered while picking Stein up at Leeds University confirmed they'd stirred up a hornets' nest, so he was relieved that another one had been removed recently.

Tom Hardy. Sketchley knew his family, but never realised until now that he was an informer. Apparently, he'd been talking to a woman called Angela Jones from MI5, so they'd have to keep an eye out for her. Another one to find urgently was the man who'd removed Helmut Schultz from the hotel in Leeds. Helmut called him James, and he seemed to know more than he should. Stein had said he was working for The Wool Research Institute.

The latest opinion poll Sketchley had seen confirmed his worst fears. Labour was probably heading for an election victory. It was, to all intents and purposes, a three-horse race, with the Liberals trailing far behind the Conservatives and Labour. There were only twenty-two days left until polling day on the fifteenth of October, and he'd just learned that the State Opening of Parliament was fixed for the third of November, so he needed the practical details for the tabun administration to be finalised in the next two weeks. He also needed to find out, during the eighteen days between Election Day and the State Opening of Parliament, when the BBC would be setting up its lights and cabling in the Lords' Chamber, so that the tabun release positions could be organised.

The election campaigning was now in full swing, and he had to admit that the current Prime Minister, Sir Alec Douglas-Home, despite his suitable background, experience and undoubted talents, didn't come across as well as Harold Wilson in television interviews and debates. Douglas-Home was stereotypical of the aristocratic Conservative, stiff and unbending, whereas the younger Wilson was more in-tune with modern day culture. He regarded himself as 'a man of the people' and was successful at promoting this image. Wilson was constantly ramming home the message that the UK urgently needed to modernise after 'thirteen years of Tory misrule'. Perhaps because Wilson was a Yorkshireman, he reminded Sketchley of J. B. Priestley, with his cosy fireside chats during the war, smoking his pipe, which used to go down so well.

Sketchley had decided that whatever the outcome of the election, it was time for a change of politicians and ruling aristocracy. His star was about to rise again, and a powerful new Anglo-German alliance would be the ultimate bulwark against communism and the Jews. Naturally he expected to be at the centre of this.

***

Back at Angela's flat, our discussions hadn't moved much further, but over a nice bottle of German Mosel wine she gave me a thorough examination befitting her MI5 rank and pronounced that I'd come through the first practical test with flying colours and would satisfy the standards required for working undercover. When I queried if the test was also applicable for MI6 work, she said, if I put on a German accent in the morning, we could go through it all again and find out.

'*Sehr gut. Wunderbar!*' we both exclaimed after a serious workout at eight o'clock the following morning.

Then the phone rang.

'Hello, Dad,' she said, somewhat breathless. 'No, I'm fine, just dashed downstairs,' she lied, with a broad grin on her face. 'Oh, I see. Yes, fine, I'll make sure I tell him as soon as I see him this morning. Bye.'

'What's that all about?' I said while putting a couple of slices of Hovis bread in the toaster.

'Henry's spoken to Gerry and he wants you to ring Dr Finlay. He'd like to see you today before he goes back to London tomorrow, so you'd better get on the phone after breakfast. He also said Nigel wants to come up to the Mill again next Tuesday, sounded hush-hush.'

'Damn it, Angela—time's ticking rapidly away, we haven't got a clue where the Germans are and haven't got a plan yet. Is Henry coming back to Leeds for the meeting?' I said, my frustration showing when I realised we were on the back foot again.

Angela nodded, and with that we both ate our breakfasts in silence, pre-occupied with our thoughts, the euphoria of the undercover training sessions put out of mind.

I rang Hamish Finlay as soon as I'd finished my breakfast. His secretary told me he was available all day up until three p.m., so I said I'd be there around ten o'clock, which was fine. It was drizzling again as I rode over to Bradford on the Lambretta, reminding me that I must see about getting some all-weather protection soon. It had somehow gone completely out of my mind, on account of Helmut's kidnapping and the undercover examinations.

I dashed into the institute's building at the bottom of Church Bank and announced myself to the receptionist. Apparently Dr Finlay's office was located in another building at Bradford University, which required a ten-minute walk across town.

'Hello again, James,' said Dr Finlay, putting me at ease immediately. 'I suppose it's too early to know what's happened to Helmut Schultz?'

'Yes, I'm afraid so; the police have nothing to report as yet,' I said politely.

I filled him in on Helmut's background and our worries that he might be used to synthesise a nerve agent, working with Dr Stein. Hamish, as he said I should call him, confirmed to my relief that he was very willing for me to start whenever I wanted. He said with my background I would fit into the organisation very well, as they planned to take on more graduates—chemists, physicists and engineers—when they moved to their new building in Ilkley, which would be in two to three years' time. They couldn't do it yet since they didn't have the space or facilities, but they were on the lookout for suitable people. Hamish confirmed, as Gerry Engel had previously mentioned, that my dual role was to be kept secret. He suggested I'd need a cover story in the short term to account for my absences until the Germans were found. Hamish didn't know the target for the nerve gas attack, which was top-secret, and he didn't ask.

The interview, if it *was* an interview, was a piece of cake, and I began to relax and look forward to finding out the work and processes I would be involved with.

'I'll introduce you to Tony Pickard, who will be your manager in charge of training for your technical service role. He's in the next office, if you'd like to follow me.'

Tony Pickard was a middle aged, decidedly overweight, no-nonsense, bluff Yorkshireman, reminiscent in speech to the cricketer Fred Trueman. When Hamish had left the room, Tony eyed me somewhat suspiciously before remarking, 'What do you know about wool? Owt or nowt?'

'Well, wool socks keep my feet warmer than cotton ones do, and if you wash them in hot water they shrink,' I volunteered, taken aback by the line of questioning. I'd not expected this—was it the beginning of the Spanish Inquisition?

'Bugger all then,' was Tony's put-down, meant to make me feel inadequate. It worked. 'I see you're a chemist, Leeds University. I suppose there's a few grey cells which we could fan into flames,' he said, attempting a form of humour, with the faintest smirk. 'Where you been working since leaving university?' he asked, picking up that I'd graduated a few years ago.

'I've had a change of career,' I said awkwardly, realising I now needed my cover story immediately. 'I was trained as a priest, but I've changed my mind,' I said honestly.

'I've not 'eard that one afore,' said Tony, struggling to contain his amusement. 'It could be appropriate, I suppose, since we work with fabrics, to have a man-of-the-cloth on board.' He sniggered, fumbling on his desk for his pipe and tobacco pouch and lighting up, pleased as punch to have come up with a good aside. Under normal circumstances, I would have appreciated this witticism but not this time, with the snide way in which it was delivered.

I decided to try to gain back some initiative by informing him that for a few weeks I wasn't going to be available full time. 'I'm still attached to a parish and need to help out on a part-time basis for six to eight weeks until my replacement arrives.'

'Does this mean we could look forward to early morning Mass services in the future, then, eh?' said Tony sarcastically from behind his smokescreen.

I ignored this comment since it was not worthy of a reply.

Tony thought it would be a good idea to visit the labs, which were situated in the building at the bottom of Church Bank. We walked across town, mainly in silence to concentrate on not being knocked down by buses and cars as we crossed a number of busy roads. Tony led me into a lab on the ground floor of the building.

'This is Brian Drake; he runs the chemical treatments department for me. Take note of what he says—you'll learn summat,' said Tony, staring directly at me.

I shook hands with Brian, a pleasant-looking man probably a bit older than me who smiled with some embarrassment at Tony's introduction.

'Have you done any more work on setting treatments, Brian?' said Tony, turning his attention away from me and glaring at Brian.

'Yes, we've tested some, but we're still waiting delivery of certain chemicals. They've been on order nearly three weeks now, but we're not getting any sense out of the supplier,' said Brian apologetically.

'You'd better try ordering it from somebody else then,' said Tony. 'You can show Jim here what we're doing with setting treatments. It'll be good if he could start on it straight away, as we're a bit short-staffed since Joyce left.' Tony nodded at me, as if to say, '*Listen carefully—you'll learn summat!*' and then walked off and left us to it.

'Don't worry—his bark's worse than his bite,' said Brian once Tony had left. 'Anyway, we don't see him too often since his office is across town. It'll be different when we move to Ilkley.'

Brian and I were on the same wavelength. He was obviously a good wool chemist and told me they were working on making wool trousers fully washable in response to the new synthetic fibres which were inherently washable. This involved not only preventing wool shrinkage but also imparting a durable crease which withstood multiple washes in a domestic Bendix machine. Another section was working on different kinds of fabric shrink-resist treatments whilst Brian's department was involved in looking at different chemical setting agents to give a good, wash-resistant crease.

Brian explained that chemically, for wool, it was the same mechanism that applied to human hair: ladies go to the hairdresser and have their hair washed and set using a chemical reducing agent and then dried so the hair remains in the new configuration. All hair—human, sheep's wool and other animal fibres—are proteins called keratin and contain a sulphur-based protein which unzips in water and reducing agents, and reforms by zipping-up again in a new configuration when dried. Different chemicals have varied effects, and they were partway through examining a range of setting agents. Brian showed me some impressive fabric samples that had been washed at least ten times without shrinking, and the crease was still pretty sharp—not as sharp as Gerry Engel's trousers, I thought, but still acceptable to me. Brian explained that the hydrogen sulphide smell often noticed in hairdressers was a product of the setting treatment.

I mentioned that for the next six to eight weeks I could only work part-time, depending on finishing the work in the parish. Brian was happy with that, and I said I could come in on Monday next week if that was OK. It was.

On my ride back to Leeds, I went over my eventful morning's experiences at the institute. On the one hand I was delighted that I'd been accepted by Hamish and had no doubt the work would be absorbing. On the other hand, Tony Pickard was going to be difficult to work with. Brian had told me he'd been deputising as head of the institute until Hamish had been appointed, and the general feeling was that Tony's nose had been put seriously out of joint when Hamish was put in over his head. It would appear it was not just me he'd singled out for a hard time; I was just going to have to live with it for now.

Brian told me the really good news that Tony was going to be away for the next three to four weeks. He was heading to Australia and New Zealand with Hamish; apparently everybody in the lab was looking forward to this.

CHAPTER 10
'BIRDS OF A FEATHER...'

'I think using a hairdryer is a good idea to vaporise the tabun,' said Stein as soon as they arrived back at the laboratory.

'We might need more than one, especially for a large building,' responded Helmut, pleased he had contributed to the sheep trial at the hall.

'We'll ask Thompson to go and get some as soon as possible. In the meantime, you could prepare the remainder of the samples; we'll need to do another trial at the hall to test the hairdryer method too,' said Stein, indicating to the minder that they needed to speak to Thompson.

Stein and Helmut had been single-mindedly focused on keeping Lord Sketchley satisfied. They were both, in their own ways, terrified of what he might do to them and with Teutonic efficiency had done what they were good at: synthesising tabun. Thompson, Stein thought, was beginning to become nervous too, probably because he'd picked up their body language and had realised he was participating in something very dangerous, although he had readily agreed to source three hairdryers without asking any difficult questions.

Stein knew, and had discussed with Sketchley, that tabun acted primarily as an inhalation hazard and tended to disperse rapidly due to its volatility, but he'd told Sketchley to keep the chapel locked until he made another visit in a couple of days' time. Nevertheless, decontamination of the chapel was important before they carried out the next trial. Thompson had been instructed to get some bleaching powder (calcium hypochlorite) which had now arrived at the laboratory. It would inactivate tabun by releasing hydrogen cyanide gas. From Stein's experience, he was sure the tabun would almost certainly have fully dispersed by now, but he would still sprinkle bleaching powder around the floor and over the dead sheep, just to make sure. Another good indication of its dispersion would be the absence of an almond-type smell from the chlorobenzene solvent which was present in the tabun from its synthesis.

Stein knew from his work during the war that an 80/20 tabun/chlorobenzene combination, which was used to fill shells, was the best for maximum dispersion. His plan was for Helmut to prepare all the tabun they needed over the next few days and then see if the hairdryer dispersion method was likely to work, using chlorobenzene on its own since it had a similar volatility to the tabun/chlorobenzene mixture. After this they could go back to the hall and finalise the sheep trials. Hopefully, more comfortable accommodation—which he thought they deserved—could be found for them at the hall.

***

Sketchley had just received a call from the minder at the laboratory, informing him that the Germans had suggested visiting again the following Monday or Tuesday. That would be good, he thought, since he wanted to be able to clear up the chapel. The dead sheep were still in there and possibly contaminated, and the farmer couldn't understand why they wouldn't allow him to fetch them out and dispose of them. Mind you, he was in no real hurry to test if it was safe to enter, so had little choice but to take Stein's advice.

Since the Germans were being very cooperative, he did wonder if there was a place for them in the new order, but hadn't totally decided yet. He'd wait until they'd finished the job. For the laboratory people, it was more clear-cut, as they'd been offered a deal to compensate them for loss of earnings while the tabun was being synthesised. They'd jumped at the chance to make easy money, but the minders were reporting that Thompson's customers were constantly ringing up for their orders and being fobbed off. Sketchley would need to tie up loose ends to avoid embarrassing questions later on. An early laboratory closure due to a tragic accident might be the ideal solution. If things went well in the next week, the laboratory phase could be terminated—in more ways than one!

***

Angela and I spent the weekend catching-up on old times, interspersed with soul-searching discussions on the best way forward before our meeting with Nigel on Tuesday, but she thought it was a good idea for me to start work on Monday morning—to get my feet under the table, so to speak. I still had a smile on my face as I entered the institute's building just as the cathedral clock started to chime nine o'clock. I asked for Brian Drake at reception and he soon appeared, wearing his white lab coat.

'Morning, James. Let's get you registered and kitted out,' he said, leading me into the account department. 'Come into the lab across the corridor when you're through here, OK?' he added.

The registration was straightforward, mainly filling in forms and giving bank details, etc.; they did ask for exam certificates, which I didn't have on me but said I would bring in later this week. I could feel that I was under scrutiny, which is probably normal when a new person starts in an organisation; everybody takes notice and you're assessed. I was conscious that I should try to appear fairly normal, so I just smiled and said very little.

Brian got me fitted out with a white cotton lab coat in which I felt quite at home, and then gave me a quick tour of the building to point out the different departments and facilities before leading me back to his lab and introducing me to Janet, his second-in-command. Janet showed me how to put creases in wool fabric samples by making up solutions of setting agents in water and then spraying the fabric evenly all over, followed by folding the fabric in half and steaming on a Hoffman press set for a steam/bake/vacuum cycle. Being used to working in a chemical laboratory environment, I must admit that it seemed a bit strange to find a Hoffman press, washing machine and a large drying cabinet attached to the normal laboratory equipment such as analytical weighing balances and a fume cupboard. Janet showed me how to carry out the procedure with a dosage range of the setting agent, done in triplicate on the fabric samples. She thought that this would take most of the morning, and she would then show me how to measure the crease angles in the afternoon. She left me to it, and I began to find my way around the laboratory. I thought to myself, tongue-in-cheek, *She's obviously got other, more pressing work to do.*

I'd just about finished steaming the last batch of samples when Brian came back into the lab and said, 'It's lunchtime, James. We normally go out for a sandwich—want to join me?'

I readily agreed, took off my lab coat and followed Brian out of the building. I was keen to get his views on the institute and the staff's opinion of Hamish in particular.

We made our way swiftly across the bottom of Church Bank, past the post office, Forster Square Station and the Midland Hotel, which brought back unpleasant memories of Helmut's abduction. Without any prompting from me, Brian chatted enthusiastically non-stop about the institute and how he thought Hamish Finlay was going to be a dynamic leader. He wasn't certain how he would find the move to the new building in Ilkley since it would mean a longer journey for him to and from work, but he relished the prospect of working in modern laboratory facilities with an on-site pilot plant to scale up promising treatments.

After walking across the bottom of Cheapside, Brian led me into Kirkgate and immediately into the Shoulder of Mutton pub.

'Is it the usual, Brian?' said the barman as we entered, and started to pull a pint of Sam Smith's bitter.

I indicated that I would have the same. There was a small selection of sandwiches on offer behind the bar, and I opted for a cheese one which was generous enough to satisfy a navvy. Brian chose corned beef and pickle of similar size. He paid for it and waved away any contribution from me as, for a new employee, he was allowed to charge it to expenses. We sat down in the small snug and simultaneously sampled the bitter, which was good.

The Shoulder, as Brian called it, was a typical no-nonsense city centre pub—probably not one you'd take a girl to on your first date, but a serious drinking establishment ideal for an evening pub-crawl or a stag night. Brian was obviously a regular, and I could see he was well-practised at imbibing beer as two-thirds of a pint disappeared rapidly without him batting an eyelid. The barman appeared as if by magic with another pint and placed in front of him; I declined a second as I was keen to tackle my sandwich and concentrate on quizzing Brian for more information.

'What's your background, Brian?' I ventured, as it was about the first time I'd been able to get a word in edgeways.

'After doing science A-levels at school, I went to Bradford Tech, the Institute of Technology, chemical technology department, before joining the current wool textile institute,' he said between massive bites of his corned beef sandwich and gulps of his second pint. 'It was very good training, since we were taught by guys doing cutting-edge wool research. You did chemistry at Leeds, didn't you?' he said to my surprise. The bush telegraph had obviously been very active since my visit last week.

I nodded but conceded that I knew very little about wool technology, backing-up the 'bugger-all' opinion of what Tony Pickard thought I knew.

'Don't worry. A lot of it's chemistry anyway; you'll pick it up easily,' he said, finishing his second pint in one final flourish.

'The setting agents Janet gave me a list of, I couldn't find all of them in the lab,' I said, thinking aloud about the work I'd been doing that morning.

'Right. We're waiting for some to be delivered, as I told Tony last week. We still can't get a response from the supplier, which is odd, since I was at Bradford Tech with one of the partners, Steve Mitchell. He must be away, since he hasn't rung me back.'

'Interesting—what can you tell me about this firm? Are they nearby?' I probed. I had a strange feeling that there might be a connection with the abduction of the Germans.

'Well, they're called Thompson Laboratories, and they're based in an old mill complex in Burley in Wharfedale. Steve set up the business about five years back with his friend Julian Thompson, who is also a trained chemist. Because we knew Steve well, we gave them all our business, and up to now they've been very good and reliable.'

The hairs on the back of my neck started to stand on end with excitement.

'Do they have any laboratory facilities?'

'Yes. Julian is experienced at synthesising organic chemicals. He can carry out small bespoke syntheses of out-of-the-ordinary chemicals, although I understand the bulk of their business is now standard reagents for schools, universities and the like.'

Bingo! I thought to myself. *I must look over their premises.* It seemed too much of a coincidence that they appeared to not be contactable at this time.

'Do you want me to call in there and see if I can get some sense out of them on the way home?' I volunteered. 'I'm actually going to Otley this evening, so if I could leave a bit earlier this afternoon, maybe I could find out what the problem is?'

'Great idea, James, I'll give you their catalogue when we get back.' Brian stood up to go, which prompted me to finish the remains of my pint.

I was impressed with Brian; he was totally committed to his job, and Tony Pickard was very fortunate to have him running his department. Brian had previously alluded to a likely personality clash with Tony when they moved to the new building in Ilkley as they would all be together and Tony could be highly irritating at close quarters.

Brian quickly found the Thompson Laboratories catalogue and a list of the outstanding orders. He had not visited the premises but thought it wouldn't be too difficult to find since Burley in Wharfedale was a village. I said it would be Wednesday before I was in next and could continue the fabric crease measurements. He said he would tell Janet.

I set off on the Lambretta. It was cold but dry, which was good since I still hadn't sourced any all-weather protective clothing. I guess it had slipped from my memory, thanks to the additional thorough MI5 examination tests Angela had put me through over the weekend. I found myself smiling again at the thought. The journey from Bradford to Burley was uneventful, and it was approaching half past three as I passed the church and then the Malt Shovel Hotel at the start of the village. I stopped briefly opposite the hotel to ask a couple of men stood talking outside if I was close to the old mill. They told me to take the road further on the right—if I reached the Red Lion, I'd gone too far. They were correct; there was a small lane, which I took to be the one they had mentioned and turned into it, past a terrace of fifteen to twenty stone cottages on the left. In the distance, I could see the outline of some large buildings, which I took to be the mill.

The entrance to the mill complex was through two once-very-impressive large stone gateposts. The road then forked, and I carried straight on towards the large main building. It appeared eerily deserted. There was no immediate indication as to where Thompson Laboratories was, but I was acutely aware that I could be in some danger if Stein's and Helmut's abductors were in residence. I decided to park the Lambretta out of sight behind an adjacent hut opposite the main buildings and approach carefully on foot. Once I'd switched off the Lambretta's engine, it was very quiet apart from the light breeze and the swishing water of the River Wharfe, which I realised was just behind the mill. Obviously at one time it had been used as the main source of power for the mill.

I was better off on foot, as the rough, cobbled road would have been difficult for the Lambretta's small tyres. The large mill clock high up on the wall showed five o' clock—going home time, I thought—but the place was deserted, which sent a shiver up my spine. I carried on towards the end of the buildings, past some large warehouse doors, and then at last I saw a small white sign announcing 'Thompson Laboratories'. There was no light on in the office, which was disappointing, so I decided to look round the back of the building to see if there was another entrance. I stumbled over a dead crow, which added to my apprehension.

A low hum, over the noise of the river, became audible on turning the corner. This seemed to come from a fan coupled into an extraction pipe leading through the building wall, probably to a fume cupboard system for Thompson Laboratories. My heart began to beat faster—I knew I was on to something—then I noticed about six or seven more dead birds of different kinds on the ground underneath the vertical exhaust pipe. A live bird, startled by my presence, flew from its perch on a stay bracket, indicating that the fumes from the exhaust system were poisonous, and I knew what that was from! I turned to return to the Lambretta as fast as I could, since this was definitely a job for the police. I was also aware of a faint chemical smell of almonds, which spooked me even more—was it cyanide? Anyway, I felt alright and was stumbling back along the way I'd come when there was a noise from the opening of the large warehouse doors behind me. A big black car drove out and stopped.

I didn't think I'd been seen, as I'd dodged behind the hut. There was a further noise, presumably from the closing of the warehouse doors. I looked carefully round the hut and saw the black car drive past; in the back seat were Stein and Helmut. Hastily, I started up the Lambretta and set off in pursuit. The mill clock still said five o'clock—time obviously goes more slowly in villages than towns.

In the haste of trying to catch up with the black car, I forgot to note its number. It had stopped at the end of the row of cottages, which allowed me to close in on it as it turned right towards Ilkley. I chanced that there was nothing coming on the main Burley road and rode straight out without stopping so I could get closer to try and read its number. Suddenly, the front passenger window opened and a couple of shots rang out, one hitting my headlight, the other my rear tyre. I lost control, and fell off as I hit the curb with my front tyre, landing on my left shoulder with a loud thump. My left side was numb, but everything seemed to work. It was probably fortunate I was only doing about ten to fifteen miles an hour.

The couple of men I'd taken directions from fifteen minutes earlier picked me up, enquiring, 'Has tha passed tha test, lad?'

They soon realised it was no accident on my part as I picked up the spent bullet from the gutter and held it up under their noses.

'Where's the nearest telephone? I need to ring the police,' I said abruptly.

By then a number of people had appeared, having heard the commotion, and one lady said, 'You can use ours. My house is just here.'

'Inspector Broadley, I've found where the Germans were taken. It's in Burley in Wharfedale. I've been shot at and I'm injured,' I blurted out as soon as he came on the phone.

'Great, where are they now?' said the inspector calmly, apparently more concerned about their whereabouts than my wellbeing.

'They drove off after I found them,' I said weakly.

'You mean, tha's lost 'em?'

I agreed, and then collapsed in a dead faint.

Chapter 11
It's Not Only Wool That Can Get Creased!

Sketchley was incensed when Stein and Helmut arrived at the hall with the two minders and informed him that the lab had been discovered, almost certainly by Helmut's previous minder, James, from the wool institute. While Stein and Helmut got to work decontaminating the chapel and the sheep, Sketchley interrogated Colin, his chief strong-arm man. Colin Fraser was an ex-army captain, not old enough to have served in the war, but fanatically anti-Semitic and pre-war would have easily slotted into the Hitler Youth movement in Germany. Since leaving the army he'd been very active in the National Socialist Movement and had trained active members in combat tactics and weapons' use on one of Lord Sketchley's estates, which was where he first came to Sketchley's attention. He had fallen under Sketchley's spell as to the need to change the current democratic way of government in order to avoid, at all costs, the possibility of introducing communism to the UK. He firmly believed that the ends justified the means and had no qualms at all in eliminating people who opposed this view. In fact, he had demonstrated this admirably by getting rid of David Lithgow, whom he knew very well, and others. It hurt him deeply that Sketchley was now about to accuse him of being trigger-happy since he, in his own mind, had only been carrying out orders.

'Why did you have to shoot at him when he was only on a scooter? You could have easily outrun him in the car,' fumed Sketchley.

'Well, I think I hit him, since he fell off the scooter,' said Colin defensively. It had been a split-second decision to fire. He'd first caught sight of James peering from behind a shed, and the fact that James had then followed them had confirmed Colin's suspicion that he was on to them.

'But you don't know for sure, do you? And you've stirred up another bloody hornet's nest now.'

Colin had to admit he wasn't certain he'd hit James and there had been a few people about on the road who might be able to assist the police in their enquiries. He didn't mention the latter, as he knew Sketchley could easily replace him—with deadly implications for himself—and things had been going so well up to now.

'What about the lab's owners?' probed Sketchley.

'Well, we disposed of Thompson just before we left, since Stein said they'd made enough of the chemical to do the whole job. You said we didn't need him anymore.'

'And what about his partner?'

Colin had been dreading having to answer this one. Thompson's partner, Steve Mitchell, was away on holiday and due back later in the week; he'd planned to return and tie up loose ends then. He hadn't known that they'd been rumbled when he'd dealt with Thompson.

'It's not been your finest hour, has it Colin?' Sketchley said icily, weighing things up carefully. Unfortunately, Colin wasn't the brightest button in the box, but Sketchley had to be careful how he handled him. They were at a crucial stage, and there was nobody else who could replace him at such short notice. Sketchley had found him good at following orders if they were simple, but his impulsiveness in situations where forward planning was required was his Achilles heel. How he'd managed to make captain in the army defeated him, but it probably said a lot about the standards of army officers nowadays.

'Do we know where this Steve Mitchell lives?'

Colin nodded, and slowly the pennies began to drop as to how he might intercept Mitchell before the police got to him.

'Better organise dealing with Steve Mitchell, then,' said Sketchley to a much-relieved Colin, who took an inward sigh of relief before both of them left the room to see how the chapel clean-up was progressing.

***

Both Stein and Helmut had witnessed their minder, Colin, fire a couple of shots from the car window as they turned onto the main road in Burley after leaving the lab. They had instinctively turned round to see a man on a scooter crash, apparently hit by the fire. The man had been wearing a crash helmet, but Helmut was almost certain it was James as there was no other logical explanation. Helmut was extremely worried, for James and himself and Dr Stein. The look on Stein's face mirrored his own before they were ordered to cover themselves up in blankets, which had been overlooked by their minders on setting out. Helmut had the chilling feeling that they were very much on their own now.

At the hall, Stein was pleased that the chapel seemed safe to start cleaning up. There was very little trace of the chlorobenzene's almond smell, but they still sprinkled some of the bleaching powder around, especially over the dead sheep. Then, wearing protective gloves, they pulled the sheep out of the chapel by their legs and assembled the carcasses at the side of the steps to the hall entrance, ready for collection by the farmer. It was clear to both Stein and Helmut that they were not going to have enough time to carry out the hairdryer trial that day since they needed to set things up, and the farmer with the replacement sheep was absent.

Just then, Sketchley and the minder who gave the orders came out and looked at the dead sheep, keeping a good distance from them.

'Are they safe now?' asked Sketchley.

'Yes, no problems,' replied Stein, somewhat out of breath from the exertion of moving the sheep and adding, 'We can't do the next trial until tomorrow.'

'Right, I'll get the farmer organised to remove the carcasses and provide the animals for tomorrow. Any special instructions for disposing of these?' said Sketchley, pointing at the carcasses.

'Not eat, put in ground best,' said Stein, temporarily losing control of English, as he was thinking about setting up the hairdryers for tomorrow's trial.

Sketchley nodded and went inside the hall to look at his calendar in his study. It was now just seventeen days to the general election and thirty-six to the State Opening of Parliament. Keeping his fingers crossed, he was optimistic that the hairdryer trial would be successful and he could report to his co-conspirator that things were on schedule. He'd kept a very low profile for the last few years; he knew the security services were keeping an eye on the NSM—in particular at his other estate, where Colin had run the instruction courses for the NSM. As far as the authorities were concerned he was still in Kenya, where he had a farm in the Happy Valley region. Over a year ago he had returned to the UK on a false passport under an assumed name, Ronald Shaw, and lived in a cottage close by, ostensibly as an estate worker. He'd been temporarily spooked that Tom Hardy and his colleague David Lithgow were in the security services but they'd now been silenced. Only Colin Mitchell knew of the idea behind the abduction of the Germans—that was why Sketchley needed to keep him on side for the present. He was certainly not in on the whole plan, though, nor the identities of the cabal.

Sketchley, for once, allowed himself the luxury of visualising the power and rewards he expected to come his way once the rotten wood of democracy was cut away. One thing he was good at was forward thinking and planning, as well as implementing the required changes, however severe they might seem at the time. He'd seen first-hand how it had almost worked for the Third Reich but for the intervention of the Americans during the war.

The stakes were very high this time. He almost wished that the socialists would win the general election—it would make it easier to justify the actions they were about to take to the hoi polloi, who in his eyes were mainly ignorant peasants, only interested in football and having a good time—but it was now or never, and he was the one who was about to cast the die.

He quickly came out of his trance-like state, picked up the phone and instructed the farmer in the disposal of the sheep carcasses and the need for replacement animals tomorrow.

***

The first thing I was conscious of after passing out was the pungent odour of smelling salts, which made me vomit all over the newly scrubbed floor of the kind lady who had let me use her telephone. I felt terrible and must have been close to fainting again when a man firmly took hold of my wrist, found my pulse and shone a bright light into my eyes.

'He could be concussed,' I heard him say.

It turned out he was a local off-duty doctor who lived about three doors away. He decided to take me in his car to the local hospital where he worked in Otley. During the short journey, I gradually became more aware of my surroundings and the sickly feeling subsided. I felt like sleeping, as the inside of the car was cosy and warm.

After being helped into the waiting room in the minor injuries clinic, I sat in a chair until a nurse called me about five minutes later and led me into the treatment room, where there was a doctor in a white coat and also the off-duty doctor who had delivered me to the hospital.

'I'm Doctor Ellis and this is Doctor Newton, who brought you here. I understand you fell off your scooter. How are you feeling now?' the white-coated doctor said with a quizzical, almost disbelieving look on his face.

I had recovered most of my senses and was now intensely concerned that Inspector Broadley wouldn't know where I was, and I had lost the best lead we'd had on the Germans in days. Instead of any of that, I said, 'Much better thanks, but very sore.'

Dr Ellis indicated that he wanted to inspect my injuries, so I took my coat, jacket and shirt off to reveal extensive bruising and swelling down my left arm and side, as well as superficial grazing which had bled onto my shirtsleeve. A nurse quickly dabbed surgical spirit over the area, resulting in sharp pain.

'Sorry,' she said unconvincingly, as I exclaimed, 'Ouch!'

'He seems a lot better,' said Dr Newton.

Dr Ellis prodded and moved my limbs about, which was uncomfortable, but he announced authoritatively that I hadn't broken anything. 'I don't think we need to keep you in, but it would perhaps be wise to rest up for a couple of days just to be on the safe side.'

The attitude of the two doctors was professional and polite, but there was a certain degree of snootiness, which I attributed to a lack of understanding of how the accident had actually happened. They were implying some recklessness or lack of skill on my part, which I thought I ought to put right, since they could easily have been looking at a more serious injury from a gunshot wound if I'd been less fortunate. I pointed out that I had been following—nay, chasing—a car on behalf of the police as I was a member of the security services. It was difficult for me to say which one, MI5 or MI6, as I wasn't totally sure myself who I was working for at the moment. OK, I'd pulled out into the main road dangerously because I didn't want to lose sight of the car, but the reason I'd fallen off the scooter and crashed was because I was being shot at, one bullet smashing my headlight and the other puncturing my rear tyre.

The expression on the two doctors' faces changed in an instant. I'd obviously enlivened a rather drab, routine day for them. I completed the coup-de-grace by magically producing from my trouser pocket, Houdini-like, the spent, deformed bullet I'd picked up from the gutter. Both their mouths hit the floor, and they couldn't do enough for me. By the end, I had them both eating out of my hand. They were almost pleading for more details but totally accepted that I couldn't tell them any more, obviously, for *official security reasons*.

Dr Ellis insisted that I use his office to contact the police and arrange for somebody to collect me; he then organised for the nurse to get some painkillers for me to take away, and said if I needed anything else I'd just to ring. I thanked Dr Newton for his assistance and care, and he then left with a spring in his step.

I sat down in Dr Ellis's comfortable chair and proceeded to try and contact Inspector Broadley. No joy. The sergeant at the station said he had already left. I explained where I was and said I would ring again when I knew where I was going. The nurse, equally amenable now, brought me a bottle of tablets and a very strong cup of NHS tea, which worked wonders, just as well as a Double Diamond would. Neither Angela nor Henry were at the Mill, so Mavis took the details, saying they might be back at Henry's house in Otley, which would be convenient for me if it were true.

I was beginning to feel much better now and toyed with the idea of trying one of my old jokes out on an unsuspecting medic who might be willing to listen: "*What do you give a man who's got everything?*" "*Penicillin.*" Or even a Tommy Cooper joke: "*Doctor, Doctor, it hurts when I nod my head!*" "*Well, don't do it then.*"

I got up and nearly seized up, creased with intense stiffness and ache from my injuries. I sat down again, quickly taking a couple of the painkillers with the remains of my tea, having completely forgotten about the jokes.

I first rang Angela's flat, as I didn't remember her saying she was going anywhere else apart from the Mill. She answered.

'Ah, James—have they made you work overtime on your first day at work?' she said breezily.

'No—can you come and pick me up from Otley hospital? I've had a crash on my Lambretta,' I said weakly.

'How bad?'

'Bruises to both my body and ego. I found the Germans, but they got away!' I said apologetically.

'You let them get away?' This was the second time today I'd detected implied criticism from someone who didn't know all the facts.

'Well, they did take a couple of shots at me,' I said defiantly.

'I'm on my way!' she said abruptly, putting the phone down.

Angela and Henry turned up at the hospital about forty-five minutes later. The tablets were working and I was now able to shuffle around with a little more freedom. It did occur to me that my pasodoble was going to be less energetic for quite some time.

'What's the story, James?' said Henry as he was admitted into Dr Ellis' office, where I was still in residence, followed closely by Angela.

I quickly related the fortunate discovery that Thompson Laboratories in Burley in Wharfedale was the site to which Stein and Helmut had been abducted, and purely by chance, it was linked to the wool institute and the work I'd been taught to do this morning. I'd thought it was a long shot, but the excessive delay in Thompson supplying chemicals to the institute and the difficulty in contacting them was worth a trip to their premises to get some answers. Call it a hunch, if you like, but this time I'd hit the bullseye.

'Yes, James, but why didn't you let us or the inspector know what you were doing?' said Angela, back into her critical mood again.

'You're right, Angela, as usual. With hindsight, I should have done that. I'd been careful in inspecting the outside of the Thompson building, but when I found evidence of poisonous vapours being emitted from the lab, I was on my way to contact the inspector. How was I to know that they were about to drive off just then?'

'OK, very unlucky, I agree—but you'd still no backup in place,' she quibbled.

'At least, James, you've found out something very useful, and they now know that their laboratory has been found, which might have seriously interrupted or foiled further preparation of the nerve agent,' said Henry, putting an experienced and positive spin on things.

'Have you now spoken to Broadley, and does he know where you are?' said Angela, a little calmer now.

I mentioned that I'd left word with his desk sergeant as to my whereabouts and was expecting him to ring. Just then, the office door opened and in walked Dr Ellis, followed by Inspector Broadley and one of his detectives.

'Quite a full house, now. Perhaps you'd like to use a larger office down the corridor?' said Dr Ellis diplomatically. I could see we'd probably overstayed our welcome.

'Perhaps we should meet up somewhere outside,' I said. 'I think the good doctor is keen to reoccupy his office.'

'We could go to my place—it's only five minutes away,' said Henry. 'And we think, James, you'd better stay over for a night or two until you're on your feet again.'

From the look on Inspector Broadley's face, I could see he wanted to fire off a number of questions, but he'd been primed by Dr Ellis that I was OK but needed a couple of days to get over things.

'Aye, awright then,' said the inspector, leading us all out of the office.

I gingerly followed and shook hands with the relieved-looking doctor. We were the centre of attention for many of the staff on the way out. Obviously word had spread about my story.

Mrs Jones lived up to her nickname, Amazin' Grace. She'd only had a few minutes to gather herself together before we descended on her, but she fussed around, with some help from Angela, pouring mugs of tea or coffee—and in the case of Henry and myself, generous tots of Glenfiddich single malt whisky.

'You'll be no-minding a bite to eat?' she announced as she sped off to the kitchen, reminiscent of Janet in *Dr Finlay's Casebook*.

I appreciated this as the whisky would give me a short-term boost but I realised I needed something to eat as I'd only had a sandwich and a pint at lunchtime.

'Nah then, lad—tha's not goin' to be doin' a quick-step for a while, eh!' chuckled the inspector, his reaction reminding me of how injuries to cricketers hit by the ball in the box region always seem to inspire mirth in their teammates and spectators. I don't know why people react this way, unless it's that they're just relieved that it's not them experiencing excruciating pain.

I rapidly updated the inspector on my experiences and was interested in his comments. He'd turned up at the scene after I'd been taken to hospital and had pieced together the likely events from my brief explanation on the phone and the eyewitnesses. The two men from whom I'd asked directions and who had picked me up out of the gutter backed up my story of the big black car and my crash due to being shot at. Another lady witness said there only looked to be two people in the car, the driver and the front seat passenger who had done the shooting, which was interesting since I'd definitely seen Stein and Helmut in the back. Nobody, including me, had managed to get the number of the car, but it could very likely have been very similar to the one used to kidnap Stein from the university. The police were unable to determine in which direction the car had been heading, as it could have turned off the main Ilkley road towards the moor, but they would do a door-to-door investigation tomorrow. They'd visited the Thompson Laboratories office, which was all closed up, just as I'd found it, but it was dark, so the inspector had decided to talk to me first before they forced entry and possibly spoiled any useful evidence. He wondered if I'd be up for it tomorrow morning if he sent a car for me. I said I would make sure I was.

Henry did reiterate his earlier comments that my actions had spoiled their laboratory base and could seriously have interfered with their production of the nerve agent, so it was significant progress. The inspector grudgingly agreed and added the comment, 'Tha's goin' to need another scooter, lad—that Italian job's a write-off!'

Shit, I thought. I'd forgotten to insure it—fortunately, nobody had asked me about this, yet.

The inspector and his detective left us to have a nice meal served by the now very chatty Amazin' Grace.

After the meal we were all sitting in the lounge, Henry and I each with another tot of whisky, when the phone rang.

'It's the inspector for you, James,' said Henry.

I took the phone. 'Hello, Inspector. What can I do for you?'

'We've just fished a body out of the Wharfe. His wallet says he's Julian Thompson—is he anything to do with the laboratory, does tha know?'

'Yes, he's one of the owners. Was he drowned?'

'No, shot in t' head. Twice.'

CHAPTER 12
THE SWEET SMELL OF SUCCESS?

Henry and Angela had travelled to the Mill together early on Tuesday morning. Nigel was expected around eleven a.m. for the meeting, and Henry had decided to see him alone. Angela had seemed a bit disappointed when he'd told her, but she'd be available in the building if she was required. James wasn't up when they'd set off, he was waiting for the painkillers to take effect before he attempted to 'trip downstairs'. In James's case he was booked to go back to Thompson's premises with the inspector, which was his top priority.

Henry was keen for Nigel to bring him up to speed on any surviving members of the Right Club who might be capable of masterminding treason on the scale they were looking at today. His main worry was that he, and possibly Nigel too for that matter, were seriously limited in manpower, and if they were right, the person or people pulling the strings might be in positions of power, so secrecy was paramount. Nigel had basically confirmed this by wanting to meet at the Mill.

Nigel had caught the early train from King's Cross, so he arrived at the Mill around ten-thirty a.m., shuffling a little faster than normal into the meeting room, where they shook hands and Mavis rapidly conjured up a cup of coffee with a selection of biscuits.

'There's been a major development, Nigel,' Henry said as soon as they were seated.

Nigel listened intently as Henry described in detail yesterday's events. He shuffled uncomfortably, especially when he learned that the two German scientists and their abductors had evaded capture again.

'I thought Brittain understood that he hasn't got the authority to work for MI5 now?' said Nigel tetchily, glaring at Henry.

'Yes, he knew. Angela had told him he'd been taken off the case, but on his first morning working at the wool institute, he realised there might be a possible connection to the breakdown in communication with the chemical supplier and the institute, so he followed it up on his way home,' said Henry, bending the truth slightly for James' benefit.

'Where's James now?' Nigel said, still irritated.

'Well, as I mentioned, he's supposed to be resting up for a day or two to recover from his bruises, but he's agreed to help the police with their enquiries.' Henry omitted to mention that James was revisiting the Thompson Laboratories site again this morning.

Henry, normally a diplomatic man, was beginning to get irritated with Nigel's attitude and decided to take the initiative by focusing the discussion on the important facts. 'You didn't come all the way out of your comfort zone to quibble about James' bending of the rules, did you? In the army I think they call it using your initiative, don't they?' he said sharply, fixing Nigel with a stare that put him in his place.

'No, you're right, Henry. I just didn't want to rock the boat at MI5 any more than it is at the moment, you understand?' Nigel gulped, realising he'd overstepped the mark.

'Anyway, Nigel, you could always explain it away by saying I'd asked him to keep an eye on things, so he could be working for MI6 at the moment, OK?'

Nigel gulped again—he hadn't thought of that. He'd not seen Henry in this guise before, and he desperately wanted to keep on the right side of him, for obvious reasons.

'Look, Nigel, like it or not, we're on our own right now and our DGs are not going to be supporting us, as I proved last week in London with mine. I thought the object of this meeting was to flush out any potential villains from the Right Club who could be capable of masterminding this plot. You have intimate knowledge of this since you were involved. I wasn't,' said Henry, getting down to brass tacks.

'Yes, Henry, since we last talked, I've been frantically making discreet enquiries. The main source of information I've been trying to get my hands on is the *Red Book*, which lists all the Right Club members' names.'

'The *Red Book*?'

'Yes. In 1944, after a tip-off, we—MI5 that is, and Special Branch—found it in the flat of an American embassy cypher clerk, Tyler Kent. Also found were numerous copies of classified documents, including secret correspondence between Churchill and Roosevelt.'

Henry knew about Kent's arrest and that, having been charged under the Official Secrets Act at a secret trial, he was convicted and received seven years. Henry was also up to speed regarding the aims of the Right Club, since he'd just finished reading Archibald Ramsey's autobiography, *The Nameless War,* which was written post-war in an attempt to justify his actions.

'Great! Did you find it?'

'No, it's disappeared. It's all a bit hazy now, but the best guess is that it was returned to Ramsey after the war, but we can't ask him since he died in 1955!' Nigel added ruefully.

'Shit! It would have been incredibly helpful. Why was the book found in Kent's possession?'

'Ramsey had given it to Kent for safe-keeping since Kent was covered by diplomatic immunity, but the US Ambassador, Joseph Kennedy, waived his immunity, which led to his arrest, trial and conviction.'

'You must have some records at MI5 of people you were keeping tabs on, haven't you?' persevered Henry.

'The obvious one who lent his estate for NSM's training activities is Lord Sketchley, but he's abroad at the moment, and has been for the last few years.'

Henry nodded his head, remembering the unfortunate David Lithgow who'd been shot after recognising the mysterious Colin outside Leeds University.

Apparently, Sketchley, after his fall from grace in court circles, had spent increasing amounts of time at his Kenyan farm avoiding post-war rationing, licking his wounds and indulging in the excesses of the 'Happy Valley set'.

'A lot of the high-profile Right Club members we know about can be discarded since, like Ramsey, they died off or don't have the resources or knowhow to be seriously considered,' Nigel added. 'We don't think Sketchley was a Right Club member, but he fits the profile to a T: filthy rich, politically ultra-right wing, anti-Semitic, pro-Nazi and decidedly anti-communist. Perhaps the hedonistic lifestyle has overridden his political ambitions?'

Henry nodded again. Nigel made a good point; maybe Sketchley had left word that in his absence the NSM could use his estate for their purposes, but they had to get a fix on this Colin, and it would seem that James had probably come closest to that yesterday. They were both coming round to the same conclusion, that they ought to have had James in on the meeting. Nigel was the first to suggest it. Henry went into Angela's office and asked her to see if James had left to visit the laboratory scene with Inspector Broadley.

'It seems James feels well enough to accompany the inspector back to the laboratory,' he reported when he re-joined Nigel. 'It would be interesting to find out if they dig up any clues as to where the abductors may have gone when James gets back.'

***

The painkillers had worked well enough for me to consider getting dressed and going downstairs for breakfast. I found Grace in the kitchen listening to the chatty, cultured tones of Jack de Manio on *The Today Programme*. I eased slowly onto one of the Habitat kitchen chairs, indicated to me by an unusually silent Amazin' Grace, who was absorbed in the discussion on the radio. Just then, the telephone rang in the hall, which necessitated Grace going to answer it, muttering to herself on the way out that 'He's no got the time wrong today.' I smiled to myself, as I'd heard about de Manio's occasional on-air difficulty in telling the time and his well-publicised embarrassing gaffes, such as announcing a documentary on Nigeria titled *The Land of the Niger* with a double g.

I helped myself to a slice of toast, buttered it and cut it into five soldiers to dip into a still-warm boiled egg. My mind tuned in to the radio, where there was an election interview with George Brown, Labour's main frontman, who was enthusiastically laying into the government's pathetic performance in deterring British scientists from emigrating to the USA in particular. He cited the eminent physicist Fred Hoyle's recent letter to *The Times*, which had called it 'The Brain Drain', trotting out damaging statistics to illustrate the extent of the problem. The main cause was the government's woeful underinvestment in science research funding which, of course, would be redressed under a Labour government. Jack de Manio chipped in provocatively with a quote from an address by the Duke of Edinburgh to the Association of Technical Institutes, commenting that 'the Brain Drain was a very nice compliment to our educational system.' I couldn't hear the spluttering response from George Brown since Grace put her head round the door and interrupted, 'James, the inspector wonders if you'll no be well enough to go to the laboratory in the next thirty minutes?'

'Yes, tell him I'll be ready,' I replied, sinking the last soldier into the yolk of my boiled egg and swiftly draining a cup of tea.

After getting ready and donning my jacket and coat, I waited in the kitchen and looked out of the window onto the gravelled hard surface which acted both as a parking area and a turning circle. The long stretch of back garden led down to the River Wharfe. I could see about halfway across the river, which was running pretty high and swiftly round a curve before passing through Otley, and I realised that Julian Thompson must have floated past here yesterday before getting caught up on the weir in the centre of the town.

The inspector's car appeared, making a crunching sound on the gravel which broke my train of thought. I bade farewell to Grace and took a deep breath as I set off to inspect the laboratory.

Henry's house was only about ten minutes' drive from the laboratory in Burley in Wharfedale. We quickly arrived at the disused mill complex and parked in front of the large warehouse doors from which I'd seen the big car drive out yesterday afternoon.

'Nah then, James, we've touched nowt. Maybe you'd like to go through what you did and saw afore we break in,' said Inspector Broadley calmly.

'Well, I parked my Lambretta behind that hut there, and then since there weren't any lights on in the offices, I decided to have a look round the back,' I said, leading the inspector and his driver to where I'd been yesterday. I pointed out the suspicious dead birds scattered under the extraction from the building. There was still the swishing sound of the river, but the hum of the extraction fan was absent. 'There's still a faint sweetish almond smell; it was stronger yesterday. I was worried that it could be toxic—cyanide, for example—so I retreated quickly, as I was sure it was where Stein, at least, was holed up. I was going to ring you when they drove out of the warehouse, and you know what happened then,' I said to the nodding inspector.

'Reight, lads, get these doors open,' Inspector Broadley instructed a couple of burly policemen who'd arrived whilst we were inspecting the rear of the building, one with a large jemmy and the other with a sledgehammer.

The doors were no match for the jemmy and soon slid back to reveal a dimly lit warehouse occupied by two caravans and a Thompson Laboratories van. Our attention was focused on the side door which presumably gave access into an office and laboratory. It was not locked, and we walked through into a simple office with one desk and filing systems. There was another door, which I assumed led into the laboratory.

'Before anybody goes charging in, be careful. There may be very toxic chemicals inside, and it might be better if I went in first, OK?' I said, looking at a worried Inspector Broadley.

'Aye, lad, tha's right. It's one of the reasons we waited on thee.'

The first thing I noticed when entering the lab was the sweet almond smell, stronger than outside, which was disconcerting. I heard Inspector Broadley's voice from the office telling me he could smell the chemical and asking if I was alright.

'Thought cyanide smelt of bitter almonds?' said the inspector perceptively.

He was right; all the textbooks tell you it's a bitter almond smell. I had to admit I had not actually experienced it before, but the smell in the laboratory was definitely sweet.

On walking further into the tidily kept laboratory, I noticed an empty Winchester bottle stored with some other empties labelled 'chlorobenzene'. This was not going to kill me if I sniffed it, so I unscrewed the cap and put my nose to it. Relief—it was the sweet almond smell, it was obviously being used as a solvent, panic over.

'Come in, Inspector. The smell's not cyanide, it's chlorobenzene. Well spotted—you ought to have been a chemist,' I said. The inspector had gone up a further three points in my estimation.

'Aye, I once smelt breath of a suicide victim who'd took cyanide. It were bitter,' confided the inspector, very helpfully. I wished he'd mentioned this earlier!

I turned my attention to the laboratory, where there were clear signs that the fume cupboard had been used recently as there was some still wet, dirty glassware present. In a small office partitioned off from the laboratory I found protective clothing and high-quality face masks hung up behind the door, indicating that some dangerous preparations had been taking place. In a box stored separately in a ventilated area used for filling Winchester bottles was a bottle of phosphoryl chloride and sodium cyanide, both chemicals which I knew from memory were typical of those needed in the synthesis of organophosphorus compounds such as pesticides and nerve agents. I was now more than ninety-five percent sure this was the laboratory used to prepare the nerve agent and that our worst fears were being realised.

'Any clues that Germans were here?' inquired the inspector.

'You mean you don't take my word for seeing them in the back of the car when it left the warehouse?' I said, irritated.

The inspector backed down somewhat but couldn't understand why other eyewitnesses had said they'd only seen two people in the car as it escaped. I couldn't explain it either. There were no other useful papers or notebooks present in the laboratory or offices which could be linked to Stein and Helmut. The only thing that struck me was that the laboratory was tidier and better organised than any lab I'd seen or worked in.

We turned our attention to the warehouse, where the two police officers had been looking around. There was a back door to which they had found the key and opened. It backed on to the river and was about ten yards further on from the extract duct we'd viewed previously. There was a well-trampled area just outside the door where there was evidence of people smoking, tab-ends trodden into the dirt. On a ledge just inside the door was a neatly arranged pile of cigarette stubs, almost identical to the one I'd seen when Helmut was being questioned at the police station, clear evidence Helmut had been here. A search of the caravans clearly showed that people had been sleeping there, but there were no clothes or belongings remaining, tending to suggest that they were not coming back. Perhaps they had completed the nerve gas synthesis?

'Awe right, I'll get fingerprint team in to see if we come up with owt,' said the inspector, satisfied that we'd found something useful. 'One thing, James—if you work for security services, why did you start work at this wool research place?'

This was a particularly good question which I wasn't prepared for. Instead of answering, I just tapped the side of my nose with my finger, and the good inspector nodded understandingly. The mention of the wool institute reminded me that I didn't think I'd told the inspector about the bullet I'd picked up from the gutter last night.

'Is this any good to you?' I produced the spent slug from my trouser pocket and handed it over.

'Right. Post-mortem's being carried out today; maybe we can get a match with those that shot Thompson.' The inspector pocketed the bullet. 'What else do you know about Thompson Labs?'

'Well, according to the lab manager at the wool institute, Julian Thompson's co-owner is called Steve Mitchell,' I said.

Despite feeling physically creaky again, my brain seemed to be back to normal and I realised I should tell Brian Drake that I'd been injured and might not be in for a day or two.

'What's his name?' probed the inspector.

'Brian Drake. He's a friend of Steve's; they were at college together, and Brian had been trying unsuccessfully to speak to him about the outstanding chemicals the institute had ordered, which was my excuse for visiting Thompson's premises yesterday.' I thought I had mentioned this to the inspector before, but things were a bit hazy about what I'd reported and to whom.

'Owt else you haven't told us?' said the inspector tetchily.

'I'm sorry, Inspector, I'm not fully recovered yet. I'm not totally sure what I told you last night as it's still a bit hazy. In fact, I could do with sitting down for a minute—I'm feeling a bit faint,' I said rather lamely, although it was true.

'OK, James. Maybe we've got enough to be goin' on with for now; take yer time,' he said apologetically.

I sat down on a chair in the office and decided I ought to ring the Mill and speak to Angela. 'Is it OK to use the phone, Inspector?'

'Better not James, till we've done fingerprinting. Want to go back?'

I nodded. It would be a good idea—I could speak to Angela or Henry and update them on our findings at the laboratory.

On the way back in the car, as we approached the junction where I'd had the accident, I thought it would be a good gesture to buy a large box of chocolates or flowers for the lady who'd let me use her telephone last night. I suggested this to the inspector, and he agreed. There was a newsagent's nearby, so I bought a large box of Black Magic chocolates. I knocked on her door and she opened it looking rather startled.

'Hello again,' I said. 'I've just brought you these as an apology for throwing up all over your kitchen floor yesterday.'

She was delighted.

'Come in, lad. How are you? Want a cup of tea?' she said generously.

I declined since I'd got the inspector waiting for me in the car outside, but I wondered if I could make another quick local call to tell Angela I was on my way back to Henry's. I promised not to do a repeat performance, and she readily agreed. I told Angela I wasn't up to coming into the Mill but would give her some useful information later.

***

'I think we should go back to my place now, Nigel, and hear what James has found out. It's only twenty-five minutes away, and you'll have plenty of time to catch your return train this evening, OK?' Henry said after Angela reported to them what she'd heard from James.

'Didn't he say anything else?' Nigel said disappointedly before Angela could leave the room to get her coat.

She shook her head. The three of them set off in Henry's car to hear the latest from James.

***

By the time the inspector had dropped me off at Henry's, I was feeling rough. After a quick 'hello' to Grace, I swallowed a couple of the painkillers which I had left in my room—an oversight I was determined not to repeat in the future. I sat in the lounge, looking forward to a quiet half hour. Grace had sensed my condition and, apart from bringing me a cup of tea, left me to it.

It barely seemed like five minutes before Henry, Nigel and Angela burst into the room, full of anticipation.

'Right, James, what have you found out?' said Henry brightly.

'I've only got a limited amount of time before I catch the London train, so we need to press on, OK?' said Nigel in his usual insensitive manner.

'Can you no see the poor bairn's under the weather?' barked Amazin' Grace from the doorway.

Henry, back in diplomatic mode, diffused the situation nicely by suggesting, 'I think a restorative is in order, don't you?' then opening a new bottle of Glenfiddich single malt and pouring me the equivalent of a triple measure you'd get in the Black Bull up the road.

I wasn't sure if I should be taking it on top of the painkillers, but sod it, the temptation got the better of me. Henry was not as generous with the measures for Nigel and himself, and Angela preferred a cup of tea, since she predicted she'd have to ferry

Nigel back to Leeds to catch his train and she was determined to make sure he caught it!

I can report that the restorative powers of a good single malt work very quickly. It went straight to the spot. Maybe it was a combination of the painkillers and the whisky, but the grey mist and tiredness lifted quickly. Even though Henry had primed Nigel on my adventures up until last night, I went over them again, stressing that I thought it was too much of a coincidence that Thompson Laboratories' chemical supply service had suddenly dried up—and crucially, they also had the laboratory facilities capable of synthesising the nerve agent. The other important factor was that the lab was relatively close to Leeds and Bradford.

Nigel uncharacteristically praised my initiative, but true to form, he couldn't resist pointing out that I should have kept the police, Angela and Henry in the loop. I conceded that, with hindsight, he was probably right.

Inspector Broadley's scepticism as to whether I'd imagined seeing Stein and Helmut in the back of the fleeing car due to concussion still rankled, so I spelt out the evidence to dispel this notion. There was strong evidence that toxic fumes were being emitted from the laboratory's fume cupboard exhaust pipe, in the form of dead birds nearby. Some of the chemicals found were typical of those needed to synthesise pesticides and nerve agents—namely phosphoryl chloride, sodium cyanide and the solvent chlorobenzene. This must have been happening very recently, since I detected the sweet almond smell of chlorobenzene yesterday and to a lesser extent this morning. Although we found no documentation to identify Stein and Helmut being there, Helmut's arrangement of cigarette butts in the warehouse was a signature trait of his I'd noticed previously. There were also strong indications that people had been sleeping in the two caravans in the warehouse. Henry, Angela and Nigel totally accepted this.

The fact that Julian Thompson had been murdered and I'd been shot at was evidence that these people were prepared to risk everything for their cause. There was one loose end—what had happened to Steve Mitchell, co-owner of Thompson's business?

Would his body be turning up in the River Wharfe shortly? Inspector Broadley was following this up as a matter of urgency.

I'd left the really bad news until last. I believed that Stein and Helmut had fulfilled all the required nerve agent synthesis, and the laboratory phase of the plot had been completed. They'd removed any incriminating documentary evidence, eliminated Thompson and tidied up the lab. I'd just been a few hours too late to catch them red-handed, which probably saved my life.

Henry summed things up succinctly. 'The key to this is the Colin character. He's the direct link to the mastermind.'

'There's one way to prove this,' I said. 'Inspector Broadley's going to check if the bullet I picked up was from the same gun that killed Julian Thompson.'

'And probably killed David Lithgow and Tom Hardy,' added an excited Nigel.

Chapter 13
'What Did I Do, to Be So Black and Blue?'

Despite the close call nearly being discovered when driving away from the laboratory, Sketchley was in excellent spirits. The second sheep trial had worked perfectly—just as well as the first, in fact, if not better.

Four days had passed since the Germans had left the lab for good, having prepared all the tabun necessary to complete the job, and as the police had not been near the estate, he was fairly sure they were in the clear. He could now concentrate on phase two: how to gain access to the Lords' Chamber in order to set up the equipment ready for the big day. It was just under two weeks to the general election on the fifteenth October, and the State Opening of Parliament would be on the third of November. It was going to be tight, but he had completed his part on schedule. He picked up the phone to report his success to his co-conspirator.

'Hello, Jock. We're all set at this end. Are you ready to put our plan into gear for the next step?' he said confidently.

'Right, excellent. I'll inform the duke and make sure he's not booked a trip away on the third of November,' said Jock to a rather confused Sketchley.

'I thought he'd agreed in principle to be available from the middle of October to early November. What haven't you told me?' he said, puzzled and a bit worried.

'I've told you before how the duke blabs when he's entertaining, especially after a few too many snifters—which is every night nowadays—so I thought it wise to keep the timing under wraps until we'd got things organised. He doesn't need to know the fine detail anyway,' said Jock.

Jock was Sir John Montgomery de Fife Murray, a second-generation baronet with estates in England and Scotland. He was also very rich, his family having originally made its money growing tobacco in Rhodesia, and in shipping. His friends joked that he was the original chain smoker. He was one of a select group of friends who regularly dined with the Duke of Windsor and his wife in Paris, where he kept them up to date with the latest court gossip. The duke was still bitter about the way he had been treated over his abdication and still hankered after playing a major role in Britain again. He believed he still had a significant following in the country who would support him if he got the chance.

In fact, a few chances to get the duke back into Britain had been lost. One, through no fault of his own, was that Germany had lost the war. Hitler had earmarked the duke as the pro-German puppet king to replace his brother King George VI. The duke had made no secret of his admiration for Hitler and Nazi Germany and he had carried on secret communications with the regime during the war, to the despair of Winston Churchill, his cabinet and the Americans. At the end of the war, the duke and the duchess returned to France with the fading hope that they would be invited back into the royal circle in Britain.

Another opportunity arose as a result of the failing health of King George VI, who in 1949 was not expected to sufficiently recover from an operation to be able to carry out his royal duties. Traditionalists within the royal court were terrified about the influence the Mountbatten family (Lord Louis and Prince Phillip) would have on Princess Elizabeth, the natural successor and heir apparent. She had married Prince Phillip in 1947, and they feared the House of Windsor would become the House of Mountbatten. The idea of a possible regent to step in and cover for the young, inexperienced Princess Elizabeth was rife and widely discussed. There was a limited number of suitable candidates capable of performing this role, and Kenneth de Courcy, a long-term confidant of the duke, was the prime mover in suggesting a plausible course of action to innocently position the Duke of Windsor as the best possible choice; the duke was optimistic and thought his chances were fifty-fifty. De Courcy suggested buying a working agricultural estate within an easy drive of London to gain favour with the British public, where he would be available if the King were to be permanently incapacitated. The duke, to the despair of de Courcy, dithered too long, the King recovered from his surgery, and the opportunity was missed.

When the King died in 1952, de Courcy wrote to Winston Churchill suggesting Elizabeth II develop a closer relationship with the Duke of Windsor, but to no avail.

De Courcy was well known to Jock and Sketchley and they had supported his efforts in the past, but with the looming possibility of a socialist government, they believed a more radical solution was necessary to safeguard Britain from communism. Since the war, Jock and Sketchley had kept relatively low profiles, unlike de Courcy, who in 1934 had founded Courcy's Intelligence Service, which continued to provide early warning anti-communist intelligence to businesses and government. They knew, because de Courcy had told them, that he was being watched by the security services, so they had steered clear of involving him directly. They had adapted his plan to reinstate the Duke of Windsor as the titular head, believing it would help stabilise the country and avoid anarchy after removing the ruling classes and leading politicians.

'Yes, Jock,' said Sketchley, 'I know all that, but we've a limited time now to get access to the Lords' Chamber when the BBC are setting up their equipment for the outside broadcast, so what's the plan?'

'Don't panic. They're starting week commencing nineteenth October. I suggest you send your man down to have a look and

I'll organise my tame BBC contact to show him the ropes, how's that?' said Jock.

Sketchley breathed a sigh of relief. He thought he'd drawn the short straw in organising the Germans, but Jock was as committed as he was to the scheme.

As he put down the phone, Sketchley did wonder, not for the first time, how the Duke of Windsor would react to the sudden shock of being thrust back onto the hot throne. He viewed the duke as a basically weak, indecisive man. Jock knew him well and said he would do exactly what Wallis told him to do; apparently, he couldn't even choose which tie to wear without consulting her. As Jock put it, the duke was putty in her hands. It was common knowledge that the duchess' feminine wiles extended to other influential men willing to be moulded by her. Jock had said that the right strategy was for the duke to be told that he had no option but to do it for the good of the country; his ego was such that he would fall into line. Sketchley hoped he was right.

***

Four days had gone by since I'd visited the laboratory with the inspector and met with Nigel, Henry and Angela in Otley. The accident had knocked the stuffing out of me, good and proper! I'd obviously suffered a delayed reaction after falling off the Lambretta. I'd developed incredible bruising all down my left side, and I couldn't get Louis Armstrong's rendition of Fats Waller's old hit tune 'What Did I Do to be So *Black and Blue*?' out of my head. I'd even suggested to Angela that *Ain't Misbehavin'* was appropriate for my condition at present, but it didn't amuse her. No change there then. Nevertheless, in between renditions, I'd managed to contact Brian Drake in Bradford to inform him of the situation and that the inspector would be talking to him about Julian Thompson's demise and the whereabouts of Steve Mitchell. Brian was shocked at my news and promised to cooperate as best he could. He promised to look up Steve's address, which he thought he had at home. The only good news was that Tony Pickard had gone on his business trip, so it was going to be all quiet on the home front for at least a month. It was necessary to tell Brian that I'd been shot at, as it might be reported in the local papers and the inspector would no doubt mention something. Brian must have wondered what I was really up to but diplomatically didn't ask any awkward questions.

A follow-up call with the inspector resulted in no new leads as to where the big black car might have gone. Nobody the police had spoken to could tell them which route out of Burley in Wharfedale it had taken. The inspector, true to form, left the best until last. The bullet I'd picked up out of the gutter was from the same gun that killed both Julian Thompson and David Lithgow. He was still waiting to find out if it matched the one that had shot Tom Hardy. So, the kidnapper David Lithgow had identified as Colin was key to finding out who was behind this, and I was pretty sure that we were on the right track.

I was getting used to the excellent attention from Angela's mother, Amazin' Grace. She was in her element making sure I wanted for nothing. It seemed to have given her a new purpose in life, and I interpreted this as an excuse to find something useful to do, since moving into the Otley area must have been a big change for her. I'd picked up that she'd joined the Mothers' Union and was on a monthly rota as flower arranger at the local parish church as well as becoming an enthusiastic new member of the Otley Women's Institute, so she was not exactly twiddling her thumbs. She'd confided in me that she wished Henry would accelerate his plans for retirement. Up until now, all that he'd done was organise the move, since which something had always seemed to crop up at work to take priority—the current situation was a case in point. She was making inquiries for him about a greenhouse. He'd always said he wanted to grow tomatoes, and now would be the right time of year to get one in time for next year's growing season. In fact, she'd rung up a builder to come and give her a quote for installing one, but she needed Henry's input on size and best position at the bottom of the garden. I thought it was an excellent idea and had even looked over the garden and decided where I would position it. Naturally I shared my thoughts with her.

My attention was taken away from Henry and Grace's domestic affairs when the telephone rang and Grace put her head round the door, saying, 'There's a lady asking about you, will you no speak to her?'

I shuffled into the hall and picked up the receiver.

'Is that James Brittain?' said a voice that sounded friendly and vaguely familiar, but I didn't recognise it.

Caught off guard, I answered in the affirmative.

'Ah, good. I'm Jane of *The Yorkshire Post*. I understand you were injured in an accident in Burley in Wharfedale and wondered if you could fill me in on some of the details?' she said, getting straight to the point.

Bells started ringing in my head, drowning out Louis Armstrong, and I was irritated with myself for being drawn into this. The last thing I wanted was for my story to be plastered over the broadsheets.

'How did you get my name?' I said, thinking out loud.

'Well, it was from the lady who was at the scene and let you use her phone. You left her your name and some chocolates as a thank you, which was thoughtful. Also, two men who helped pick you up gave me interesting information. I thought it would make a good human-interest story,' she added.

Damn, I now remembered saying to the lady after giving her the chocolates that if she remembered anything else to give me a ring, so I'd left her Henry's number. Listening to Jane speak jogged my memory, and I could visualise Margaret Rutherford's Miss Marple character at the other end.

'What specifically did you want to ask me?' I said, hoping it was something simple which I could finalise quickly.

'I understand you were following a car and somebody in the car took a shot at you—is that right?' Jane persevered.

I was beginning to think she should consider auditioning as an understudy for Miss Marple.

'What gave you that idea?' I inquired lamely.

'Well, you showed the bullet to the two men who picked you up,' she said rather cockily.

I was getting into deep waters now and decided to steer clear of incriminating myself any further. I might have already said too much, but I decided the inspector could sort it out—after all, he was more used to handling the press in this type of situation than I was—so all I said before putting the receiver down was, 'You'll have to ask the police. It's in their hands now,' much to the annoyance of Jane, who was left spluttering on the other end of the line.

I walked back into the relative peace of the lounge to the faint strains of Louis Armstrong again humming in my head. I definitely felt less sore and more comfortable this morning once I got myself moving, which helped me put Miss Jane Marple to the back of my mind.

***

Although it was Saturday, Henry and Angela had travelled to Leeds for a pre-arranged meeting with Inspector Broadley. They wondered if there was any further news about the bullet that killed Tom Hardy—did it match with the one James had provided? They'd asked Nigel to see if he could pull a few strings to speed things up, since he was based in London where the tests were being done, and he was also making discreet enquiries about the estate where the NSM had been running firearms training courses, with a view to seeing if they could link this Colin character to it. It was a pity James was still indisposed, as his inside knowledge of the wool institute and relevant people would have been useful, so it was mainly left to the inspector to come up with something. Top of the list was finding Steve Mitchell, to see if he'd been disposed of like his partner Julian at Thompson Laboratories.

The inspector greeted them at the police station and led them into his office, where a half-eaten pork pie was still on his desk. He quickly placed it in a drawer out of sight as Angela and Henry sat down.

'Young James 'as taken a turn for t' worse, I understand?' he said sympathetically.

Both Angela and Henry nodded.

'Strange, cos he seemed OK on Tuesday. 'appen he'll perk up by Monday,' said the inspector, forever the optimist. 'T' bullet

James found matches one that shot Special Branch officer in London.' He wasted no time getting down to the nitty gritty.

'Excellent,' said Henry. 'That confirms what we thought: this mysterious Colin laddie is their hitman. Any joy in finding the missing laboratory owner?'

'No. Man at wool institute James works with thinks he an t' wife are still away on 'oliday, according to his mother.'

There then followed a discussion where the inspector voiced his doubts that Henry, Angela and James were being fully cooperative with the police and were, in fact, telling them only what they thought they needed to know. He cited James' unsatisfactory explanation as to why he had just started work at the wool institute while apparently still working for the security services, and that they hadn't spelt out how serious the threat to the nation was, or what/who was the intended target. The inspector realised there were certain things that had to be kept secret—if it was to do with national security, for example—but every time he came in contact with his chief constable, he was asked these questions and he didn't have satisfactory answers. The other factor was that the case had now escalated into a major investigation and was costing a fortune, and he needed something more substantial to present to his chief when he asked for more resources.

Henry totally understood. 'You're quite right to bring this up, Inspector. I'm sorry if we've given you the wrong impression— it was unintentional—but I think I can satisfy most of your concerns without infringing national security.'

Henry then went on to expand on James' involvement. 'As you probably know, James helped MI5 foil a serious attempt on President Kennedy's life last year. He was temporarily attached to MI5 and worked closely with Angela. He was shot in the leg whilst thwarting the assassination attempt but has just about fully recovered from that now and was looking for another job.'

'Yer mean, he doesn't work for thee now then?' snorted the inspector.

'Well, I'd got to know James during his convalescence and arranged an interview for him with the main director of the wool institute at the pesticide conference at Leeds University. It was purely by chance that he got involved in this latest case,' said Henry.

Most of it was true, apart from the long-term undercover plans which the inspector didn't need to know, or the fact that Henry worked for MI6 and not MI5.

'Trouble seems ter follow him around, doesn't it?' chipped in the inspector with a grin. Henry could see that he was getting through to him.

'Now, since we knew James, he is temporarily working with us again to try and sort this mess out; it's nothing sinister,' he said. 'The question is who or what's the target—we don't know. We're pretty sure it's political and connected with the upcoming election, which makes it a high priority. I hope that helps?'

'Yer mean, tha don't know what this toxic chemical's going to be used for? Bloody hell!' said the inspector incredulously. 'And I thought I'd got problems!'

'I'm afraid that's about the sum of it. We're grateful to James for getting this latest lead, but it's worrying that it looks as if they've made enough of this nerve agent for their intended target,' said Henry honestly.

'Let's hope he picks hisself up quick-sharp like now,' said the inspector with feeling.

'Nevertheless, we should try and pin down this Steve Mitchell. Did his mother say when they were due back off their holiday?'

'No, that message only came from t' fella at wool institute— his mother wasn't in when we called; I've a man calling back again this afternoon,' said the inspector.

Henry and Angela agreed to catch up with James in the meantime to see if he could remember anything more about Steve Mitchell since he knew more about the ins and outs of Thompson Laboratories than they did, and with that they agreed the meeting was finished. As soon as Henry and Angela had left the office, the inspector opened his drawer, took out the pork pie and sank his teeth into it before he attempted to continue with his next job.

***

'I can't find Thompson's partner,' said Colin Fraser to Sketchley.

'Why?' said an irritated Sketchley. Colin was beginning to get on his nerves, did he have to organise everything for him?

'Well, he was not at his home address in Bradford. One of his neighbours said they thought he and his wife were still on holiday, but they didn't know when they were back. Thompson told us he was due back on Thursday but must have got it wrong. The neighbour thought his mother might know but didn't know her address, and we can't go back to the lab now since the police will probably be still crawling all over it.'

Sketchley calmed down a bit; obviously what Colin said made sense. They would have to have patience. The problem now was that Sketchley wanted Colin to accompany one of the Germans down to London to meet up with Jock's tame BBC sound engineer to look over the Lords' Chamber. Colin's sidekick, Charlie, would have to deal with tidying up the Bradford matter; Sketchley would have preferred Colin to do it as he had an outstanding aptitude and relish for disposing of unwanted problems. Charlie, whose nickname was 'Rickets', was a little on the slow side but had proved to be reliable and loyal. Unfortunately, he stood out from the crowd on account of his bandy legs and gait so was best kept for low-profile jobs.

Just then there was a knock on the door and Charlie ambled in, saying, 'Sorry to interrupt, but I think you ought to see this.'

He handed the latest edition of *The Yorkshire Post* to Colin, who read out the lead article's headline: '*Wool Institute's Scientist in Thrilling Chase of Laboratory Owner's Murderers!*'

Sketchley snatched the paper from Colin and hastily scanned the article, which described the brutal killing of Julian Thompson and the brave chase by Mr James Brittain, of the wool institute in Bradford, in pursuit of a high-powered car. As a result, Mr Brittain was involved in an accident after his scooter was hit by bullets fired from the fleeing car. He sustained severe bruising and was now recovering at home in Otley. A quote by Inspector Broadley linked the murder of the chemical laboratory's owner to the occupants of the fleeing vehicle. The motive behind the murder was unclear and further enquiries were ongoing. The police requested any eyewitnesses to the incident in Burley in Wharfedale to come forward as soon as possible.

The writing style of the article wouldn't have been out of place in a Raymond Chandler or Dashiell Hammett novel, with James portrayed as a dashing Phillip Marlowe or a Sam Spade type character. Sketchley wasn't remotely interested in the style. On the one hand, he was concerned about the publicity the article would generate, but he'd half expected that anyway; on the other, it gave him valuable information about who was pursuing Colin. Most importantly, it identified James Brittain, who unfortunately hadn't been seriously injured. It also confirmed where he was located and that he worked for the wool institute in Bradford. Sketchley decided he might learn more from the younger German, since he'd admitted he knew James.

All this made up Sketchley's mind to send Stein with Colin to London to recce the Lords' Chamber, and to keep the younger German as backup on the estate to ensure Stein continued to play ball.

CHAPTER 14
THERE'S NOTHING COMMON
ABOUT THIS BLACK ROD

By Monday, my recovery from aches and pains was definitely well on the way. After the initial stiffness on getting up in the morning had faded, apart from tenderness where the bruising was the worst, I was almost back to normal. Henry and Angela had given me the inspector's news that the bullet I'd picked up was from the same gun that had killed David Lithgow, Tom Hardy and Julian Thompson. I felt very lucky that I had managed to escape being number four on the list. The enforced rest had allowed me to ponder my situation and review exactly where we were at the moment. I was pleased to note that Louis Armstrong was no longer playing constantly in my head—perhaps the stylus needle had worn out. I was sick of hearing it by now, anyway. It had been decided that I was probably the best placed to find out more details about Steve Mitchell from Brian at the institute. Maybe another lunchtime session at the Shoulder of Mutton would be the best way to tackle it.

On Monday I got up in time to catch Henry over breakfast and inform him that I was fit enough to go into Bradford. I'd planned to take a bus since my Lambretta was scrap, but he offered to run me to Guiseley Station so I could catch the train to Bradford's Forster Square Station, which would be more convenient.

I walked the short distance from Forster Square Station, past the post office to the institute's entrance at the bottom of Church Bank. Under normal circumstances I would have been late as it was twenty past nine, but I didn't expect any comments as I hadn't told them I'd be starting again, and I hoped they would appreciate the effort I'd made to return to work. I was right. Brian Drake dashed out of the downstairs lab as soon as he saw me and shook my hand vigorously. He saw me wince a little in pain and apologised. After arranging to bring him up to speed at lunchtime over a sandwich and a pint, I continued my setting and creasing experiments with the help of Janet, who had sourced some additional chemicals from another supplier.

'Right, James, tell me all about last Monday. Give me all the lurid details,' said Brian expectantly after making serious inroads into a pint of Sam Smith's bitter in the Shoulder of Mutton.

I filled him in on the main details, some of which he knew already, and told him what Henry had told the inspector—that I was helping the police with their enquiries, since by chance I'd witnessed the abduction of Stein at Leeds University and as Helmut was going to work for the institute, I'd agreed with Gerry Engel to take him over to Bradford to meet Dr Finlay. Brian seemed satisfied with that, but I omitted to mention any involvement of security services or evidence of the nerve gas synthesis at Thompson Laboratories. I just said I'd seen a car driving away with Helmut and Stein in the back seats.

'Why were they interested enough in the Germans to shoot at you when you followed them?' said Brian.

'Well, I don't know, maybe they thought I knew more about them than I did. I didn't know they'd murdered Thompson then. As to why they targeted Dr Stein and Helmut, I can only guess they needed them for their chemical knowledge. The police haven't shared any information about that with me. They are extremely concerned for the safety of Steve Mitchell though, and asked me to pass on anything else you may remember about him,' I said, getting round to the main object of the meeting.

'Helmut's trained as a pesticide chemist, isn't he?' said Brian astutely, ignoring my comment and starting on his second pint, which had just been placed in front of him by the landlord. Brian was well and truly on the ball and I could see where his reasoning was leading, but before I could answer, he continued, 'Nerve agents are very similar to pesticides. Perhaps they've been synthesising these at Thompson's?'

'Look, Brian, I'd tell you if I knew what they're up to, but the police are playing their cards very close to their chests,' I said, hoping he would drop it. 'What did the inspector tell you?'

'Not a lot more than you have,' he said, looking somewhat disappointed, before concentrating temporarily on demolishing his bacon and sausage sandwich.

There was a momentary silence while we both ate and I tried manfully and unsuccessfully to catch up in the pint-quaffing department. I was about a third of the way down my pint when Brian said, 'Steve's been delayed coming back from his holidays due to his wife going down with a severe case of the trots, his mother said. It's bad timing, since his mother's gone away to visit her sister in Scarborough. She'd promised to get some shopping in for them coming back but she's not sure of their movements now.'

'Well, his wife's inconvenient movements might have saved Steve's—and possibly his wife's—life,' I said dramatically, with an unintentional pun. I then explained that the police thought Steve was at high risk too and needed to get to him before the killers did. I was also thinking to myself that I might be in the same boat as Steve, since by now Helmut would almost certainly have told the killers that he was going to work for the wool institute—and possibly my connection to it too.

'Right, James, that wasn't made clear to me by the inspector. I was still in shock at the time at what had happened to Julian and you,' said Brian, initially grimacing at my inappropriate pun.

'Do you know which airport Steve will be flying into, and his and his mother's addresses?' I asked, finally beginning to make headway with Brian but not with my pint.

'Steve's mother said they were visiting some friends in Germany near Munich and originally would be coming back into Manchester, but of course it might be different now it's been rearranged. I've got the addresses back in the office and his mother's contact phone number in Scarborough.' Brian glanced at his watch and stood up. It was time to return to the institute.

I nodded as usual to the security man on the reception desk.

He looked up and said, 'Nah then, 'ave you seen this?' laying out the front page of *The Yorkshire Post* in front of us on the counter.

The headline read, '*Wool Institute's Scientist in Thrilling Chase of Laboratory Owner's Murderers!*'

'I didna know we'd taken on a James Bond impersonator at institute. Mind yer, tha'll have to get summat better than a scooter to chase 'em with next time!' said the receptionist, chuckling away to himself.

***

Stein was not a happy man. Sketchley had given him a good talking to, telling him that for the good of them both he had better do exactly as Colin said. They were going down to London to examine the Lords' Chamber minutely and decide where they were going to install their equipment. It had been arranged for them to be shown round by a BBC engineer who mustn't get wind of what they were planning; Colin would try to distract him if necessary. It had been made crystal clear to Stein that he and Helmut would end up like Julian Thompson if things didn't go to plan or if either of them tried to escape. Until then, Stein had only guessed that Thompson had met an untimely end, but Sketchley chillingly confirmed it by showing him the report in *The Yorkshire Post*. Once again, Stein was struck by Sketchley's uncanny similarity to an SS officer he'd once had the misfortune to rub up the wrong way. Stein's strong self-preservation instincts were on high alert, and the nightmares he'd experienced during the war were ever present.

They had travelled down to London partway by car—not the high-powered black car which seemed to have disappeared from the estate but a smaller, less conspicuous Ford Anglia. Stein could guess why.

They were now heading towards Westminster on the tube line train they'd boarded after parking the car at the Stanmore terminus. He had not been too impressed with the road journey; a lot of it was stop and start on crowded single-lane roads, apart from a new section of M1 motorway. By comparison, Germany had built autobahns between major cities pre-war which he'd become used to, and the difference was black and white. On the other hand, he was impressed with the tube, which he could see from the station plan on the carriage compartment wall was taking them directly to Westminster.

Colin Fraser had said very little to Stein on the journey so far, no conversational chat at all, which made Stein decidedly uncomfortable. He wasn't aware that Colin was on trial with Sketchley as well but could see he was preoccupied with his own thoughts. Stein ticked off the stations they stopped at, and when the line went underground, he waited expectantly for the next station's platform lights to illuminate the sign. He counted down: Baker Street, Bond Street, Green Park and finally Westminster where they alighted. While they were riding up on the escalator Colin told him to keep quiet and that he would do all the talking. Stein assumed he didn't want the BBC man to know he was a foreigner, and he was happy in this case to play second fiddle.

As soon as they emerged at street level into the bright outside world, he saw a man with a BBC sign on a board waiting nearby. He introduced himself as Justin, Colin shook his hand and they all headed for the Palace of Westminster, Colin explaining that Stein was his engineer without mentioning his name. It didn't matter anyway, as Justin was full of waffle and out to impress them with his knowledge of Parliament. He led them directly to the visitors' entrance of the Palace of Westminster, where he'd arranged beforehand to supervise the delivery of some scaffolding which was being carried through into the Lords' Chamber. Stein was surprised that there appeared to be little security on view, but he picked up from Justin's explanation that Parliament was in recess, and no MPs were around since they were all campaigning for next week's election.

Justin led them through St Stephen's Hall into a large open area, the Central Lobby, where he paused and pointed to the left, explaining that was the way to the House of Commons' Chamber. On the day of the State Opening of Parliament, an official of the House of Lords called Black Rod would be sent from the Lords' Chamber to the Commons' Chamber to summon MPs to hear the Queen's speech. Traditionally, the door of the Commons is slammed in Black Rod's face to symbolise the Commons' independence; Black Rod then bangs on the door three times, after which it is opened, allowing admittance. All the MPs, talking loudly, then follow Black Rod back to the Lords' to hear the Queen's speech. Initially, Stein was not really interested in this detail, but he soon pricked his ears up when Justin said the newly elected MPs trooped out of the Commons' Chamber, through the Central Lobby to stand in the Peers' Corridor and Lobby to hear the Queen's speech to the assembled lords and ladies. Justin was in his element explaining this as he led them in the opposite direction to the Commons' Chamber along the Peers' Corridor into the Peers' Lobby, which opened out into the House of Lords' Chamber.

Stein had to admit that the whole of the parliament building was built to impress. The Lords' Chamber was truly magnificent, larger and higher than he'd expected, with a viewing gallery above. Two workmen erecting scaffolding to the side of the throne area caught his eye. Justin explained they were going to install some special lights for the live broadcast. While Colin was chatting to Justin, Stein took the opportunity to detach himself and examine the throne area, looking specifically for plug sockets. He could now see that Sketchley's original plan, with their modifications to disperse the nerve agent, could work if the timing of the release was organised carefully from the right positions. He was right in his original views that for maximum effect the tabun should be emitted into the atmosphere at a low level; any higher would risk it drifting towards the roof, making it less effective. It was becoming even more obvious to him that they would need an additional hairdryer, since he judged the optimum release points to be close to the thrones and the opposite end of the Lords' Chamber as well as in the Peers' Lobby and Corridor, where all the MPs would be congregated, and thus ideal positions to create panic. Stein had already seen the speed with which tabun immobilised the sheep, and he could imagine there would be adequate time for it to take effect before the victims realised they were feeling ill, by which time it would be too late. Ideally, he would have liked to have synthesised another batch to be on the safe side, but providing they got the timing right, he believed they had a sufficient amount to complete the job.

Stein walked back to the Peers' Lobby and Corridor area and noticed there were some toilets in the corner of the lobby; this would be an excellent place to secrete the equipment before they set it up. One thing that was critical was the time switches. They'd devised a simple delayed action on/off system, but they had to be sure of the exact timing of the speech for maximum effect. Stein was worried about this and needed to discuss it with Sketchley, but he thought it could be used to his and Helmut's advantage, as he was going to argue that they needed to be on site a couple of hours before the speech to set things up and switch on the timer. The confusion afterwards could be their only chance to try and make good their escape. Stein had seen enough to finalise their plans back at the estate, where Sketchley, with his inside knowledge of the ceremony, would be able to provide the optimum timing details and arrange for the next visit to set things up.

Stein re-joined Colin and Justin and nodded to Colin that he'd seen enough, so they thanked Justin, who looked disappointed as he'd just been getting into his stride, going into vast detail about the history of Parliament.

They retraced their steps out of the Palace of Westminster and headed for the tube station. Stein's mind was racing again, and he took note of the map on the station wall, since he realised this could be a quick exit route to potentially all the railway stations in London. On the rather boring journey back to Stanmore to pick up the car, the enormity of what he and Helmut were involved in struck home. Up until now, it had seemed just an intellectual exercise—the killings were not of his doing and out of his hands. It was clear that he was safe from being disposed of until the deed was done; after that, assuming it went to plan, the odds were completely reversed. He tried to put himself in Sketchley's shoes. It was obvious he and Helmut would be an embarrassment to a new ruling class—they knew too much. What he would do in Sketchley's position would be to permanently remove them in order to avoid future complications. This was why they needed an escape plan. Better to be shot attempting to get away than in a sordid, deserted back-alley. He would discuss it with Helmut when they returned, and with that, they started back on the long journey to Yorkshire.

***

Rickets had been primed by Colin, before he'd set off to London, as to what was known about Steve Mitchell's whereabouts. Thompson had shown Colin Steve's Bradford address on a card file in the laboratory's office. He'd written it down but noticed there was another address alongside it, which unfortunately, he hadn't made a note of. He'd made one visit to the Bradford address a couple of days ago and found no one in. A neighbour who'd seen him had told him that Steve and his wife were on holiday and she didn't know exactly when they were due back. His mother might know, but she didn't know her details. He guessed that the other address was his mother's. They couldn't go back to the laboratory as the police were probably still present; however, he figured it might be possible to go back at night as they still had the keys. This was a job for Rickets.

Rickets normally handled the running-around jobs which didn't require him to make decisions. He relished the chance to carry out a job like this with an element of danger to it; he didn't doubt that he could handle it. Colin had told him exactly what he wanted him to do. Rickets was very familiar with Thompson Laboratories' layout and knew exactly where the card file box was located, so he couldn't see any problems. As a backup, he could take a gun with him to scare anybody off if he was challenged, but Colin thought this was most unlikely, as the laboratory was in an old, almost empty mill complex with nobody living in the near vicinity.

These were Rickets' immediate thoughts as he parked just past the Red Lion in Burley in Wharfedale soon after midnight. It was well after the pub's closing time and the road was totally deserted; there wasn't even anybody walking a dog before bedtime. He soon found the lane down to the mill complex and saw a light in only one of the terrace houses as he walked silently past them. He felt calmer as he walked down the empty lane. It was a dark night, cloudy with only occasional glimpses of the moon to show him the way. He was surprised how far it seemed; previously he'd only driven down this way. On reaching the large door leading directly into the laboratory office, he turned the key in the padlock and walked inside. He switched on his torch to find the office door, so far so good. It was going to be easy; there was still a faint almond smell lingering from when the Germans had been working in the laboratory. He hadn't a clue what any of this was all about, but he didn't care as he was well fed, the work was exciting at times and he could follow his passion for bird-watching on the estate in his free time. Previously, he'd been sad to see so many dead birds near the laboratory, which he couldn't understand, and thought since it was quiet, once he was done inside, he'd have a look around the back of the laboratory to see if they were still there.

After sitting down in the office chair, he quickly located the box file on a nearby shelf. He put the torch down and methodically thumbed his way through the card index until he reached 'M'. Under 'Mitchell, Steve', he found what he was looking for and pocketed the card to give to Colin on his return. There were two addresses on it, so he was sure Colin would be pleased.

His mind was on the birds as he got up, left the office and went out of the warehouse. He decided he'd lock up after he'd been round the back of the building. Sure enough, the dead birds were still there, but it seemed to be just as he'd remembered, so things hadn't got any worse. He thought it was time to get back. He was very pleased with himself and retraced his steps to lock the warehouse door.

'Nah then, what're you up to?' said a voice from in front of the warehouse door. It was a policeman who had been examining the open door and spotted Rickets' torch beam as he came round the corner.

The policeman shone his bright torch on Rickets, blinding him. Rickets panicked, pulled out his gun and fired at the light. There was a groan from the policeman and a thud as his body fell to the ground. Rickets didn't wait, he ran as fast as his bandy legs would carry him back towards his car on the main road. What a pity—things had gone so well until now.

On the way back, he decided that since he'd got the information he'd been sent for, he wouldn't mention having been disturbed.

Chapter 15
'What Manner of Man Is This...?'

I was deep in thought, going over and over my encounter with the ravishing Miss Havisham in the Brotherton Library at Leeds University when I'd returned the books we'd borrowed about the Palace of Westminster. She had enquired pleasantly as to whether they had been of any use, and I'd got a knowing look when I replied that since they were supplied by herself, Miss Havisham, we'd had 'Great Expectations' and were not disappointed. I followed it up by saying in our line of work it was very rare that we got such helpful and accurate information. She'd politely asked what line of business it was, and I, throwing caution to the wind, volunteered, 'Security services,' which seemed to flick a switch in her, resulting in a radiant smile and, leaning over the counter with a come-hither look, she'd said, 'Tell me more!'

Just then, somebody from behind rudely and irritatingly started shaking my sore shoulder, saying, 'Get up, James. There's been a major development; we're needed at the Otley hospital, ASAP.'

It was Henry.

Why is it that I could never seem to find out how interesting dreams turn out? I'd had this dream before and never remembered the outcome after I'd woken up, but now was not the time to dwell on it as I quickly dressed and hurried downstairs to jump into Henry's car. It was four thirty by my watch. Apparently, Angela was on her way, but it would be later when she arrived from her flat in Leeds. All Henry could tell me was that a policeman on routine patrol duty had been shot outside the Thompson Laboratories premises and was being treated at the Otley hospital where I'd been taken last week.

'We've come about the policeman who's been shot,' said Henry to the first person we met as we entered the hospital, who turned out to be the night sister. She asked us to wait and went to find the doctor on duty that night.

'Oh, it's you again,' said a surprised Dr Ellis, who had treated me last week.

'Inspector Broadley asked us to come as soon as possible since we live in Otley,' said Henry. 'It'll take him some time to get here. How serious is it?'

'Well, he's been very lucky. It's just a flesh wound, and we've been able to patch him up without putting him out. Do you want to see him?'

'Yes please; that's a relief,' I blurted out.

We followed the good doctor along the corridor and into the same treatment room I'd occupied. On the way he asked me how I was doing. I said I was improving but it was taking longer than I'd expected. He thought I was doing fine.

'Now then, Constable, these gentlemen are working with your Inspector Broadley. They've arrived ahead of him and would like a word, if you're up to it,' said Dr Ellis, introducing us nicely.

The constable nodded. He had his left arm in a sling and was quite pale faced, even after drinking a strong cup of regulation hospital tea.

'What can you tell us, Constable?' asked Henry, not beating about the bush.

'I'm Constable Braithwaite, sir,' said the constable, speaking quickly. 'I was on normal night shift but I'd been asked to look in on Thompson Laboratories. I found the warehouse door ajar, and as I was plucking up courage to go inside, this man appeared from round the end of the building. I saw his light first and then I challenged him, shining my torch on him. He just pulled a gun and fired at me.' It was obvious the constable wanted to get this off his chest; he was still somewhat in shock.

'Did you get a look at him? I queried.

'Well, he looked like a fairly normal-looking bloke, thirty-forty-ish, he'd got dark clothing on and a flat cap. Unfortunately, I stumbled just as he fired, and fell over, and all I saw then was him running away from me with a funny gait. I'm sure he'd got bow-legs, bandy-like, very distinctive.'

'Did they dig a bullet out of you?' said Henry, just before I was about to ask the same question.

'I don't think so; you'd better check with Dr Ellis. I wasn't that interested in watching them sew me up. In fact, the pain-killing injection is wearing off now, and it's bloody sore.'

I commiserated with him and decided to go and tell Dr Ellis that his patient probably needed some painkillers. I wanted to be sure we could get as much information as possible out of him before he got fed up with us or keeled over. As I was walking down the corridor towards Dr Ellis' office, I was reminded of the old Shakespearean chestnut about bow-legged men: '*What manner of man is this who wears his balls in parentheses?*' I was pleased I'd kept it to myself, as on previous occasions when I'd trotted it out it hadn't been well received and I'd been Bard from telling similar jokes for the foreseeable future. Joking aside, Constable Braithwaite had noticed something very useful which might prove decisive in the future. I was also keen to revisit the lab and see what the object of the break-in had been.

On finding Dr Ellis in his office, I took the opportunity of asking him if he'd found a bullet, but he assured me that it had passed straight through the flesh.

The same nurse who had brought tears to my eyes by dabbing my injuries with surgical spirit quickly provided the magic tablets which would alleviate the constable's pain.

'Did the man only fire one shot? What did you do then?' asked Henry as I re-joined them.

The constable nodded and added, 'Well, apart from bleeding, I managed to go into the Thompson's office and ring the station and ambulance.'

'Did you notice anything out of the ordinary in the office?'

'No, not really. All that was on the office desk was a card index box. I wasn't really in a fit state to take everything in; I was waiting for help to arrive.'

'Yes, I can imagine,' said Henry, just as Inspector Broadley dashed into the room followed by Angela.

'Nah then, lad, understand tha's 'ad an interestin' shift?' said the inspector with his usual tact.

'Yes, sir, you could put it that way if you like. I've had quieter nights.'

We brought the inspector and Angela quickly up to speed with the salient facts, which were confirmed by a nodding constable, and then Dr Ellis reappeared and suggested we let the constable have a rest as they needed to check him over again. We thanked the constable, wished him a speedy recovery and readily accepted Dr Ellis' offer of the use of his office to talk things over.

'I suggest that James and Angela go and inspect the scene as soon as it's light; it would be very useful if we could find the bullet. Is that OK by you, Inspector?' said Henry as soon as the office door closed.

'We've 'ad van parked aside door, wi' two armed officers guardin' it at moment. Don't worry, I want to 'ave a butcher's missen,' said the inspector seriously.

'I've not had chance to mention this to you yet since I only just found out yesterday from Brian at the Institute, but Steve Mitchell's return home was delayed due to his wife's illness,' I said. 'Brian found out from Steve's mother, who lives close by. She was going to get some shopping in for their return, but she's now gone to Scarborough to visit a relative. I've got her telephone number in Scarborough. It could be very relevant to the break in, couldn't it?'

'Yes indeed. Something else to follow up later on today,' said Henry, voicing the view of the majority.

'Agreed,' said Angela. 'I'd be interested to see the lab setup since it looks like I'm going to be spending more time up in Yorkshire, and a fresh pair of eyes could be useful.'

***

Sketchley was beginning to wind himself up for the final push. Colin had reported a successful visit to London and was complimentary about Stein, who had acquitted himself well and identified the key areas in which to place the equipment. Apparently, he wanted another hairdryer for maximum effect. Charlie had also found the addresses of Thompson's partner at the laboratory last night.

Sketchley still hadn't decided what to do with Stein and Helmut afterwards. Logic told him to tie up loose ends and eliminate them, but they had valuable knowledge which might be useful in the future. They were needed in the run up to the State Opening, so he had to keep them sweet until the deed was done, after which two extra unknown bodies would go unnoticed amongst the elite who had perished, if it came to that. Stein had been to see him and impressed on him that it was critical to time the tabun release for when the MPs were summoned into the Lords' Chamber and the speech was being read by the Queen. He wanted to set the time clocks in the morning to go off at this moment, so it was best if he and Helmut could be present in the morning to deal with it. He had agreed, as he had always anticipated that this would be the case, since the danger of mistakes by anyone unsure of how to handle the equipment was too great. He needed to confirm that the itinerary was still the same, and to this end he picked up the phone.

'Jock, just thought I'd update you on the successful visit to London this week. Thanks for laying on the BBC contact. He was very useful, and we managed to get the information we needed.'

'All systems go then. What else do you need?'

'Ideally, we need to have access on the morning of the State Opening to set the apparatus up, so do you now have confirmation on the time of the Queen's speech?' queried Sketchley.

'I was wondering about that. Security gets a bit twitchy just before the event, but this time they've got the BBC crews to worry about, so I'll see what's possible. Any chance you could arrange for the devices to be planted a few days or a week earlier?'

'Our experts need to set the time clocks to go off while the speech is in progress, so any last-minute change of plans could be a disaster for us, understand?' said Sketchley forcefully.

'Understood. Leave it with me and I'll have a chat with my BBC man,' said Jock, sounding a little less confident now. 'Oh, and by the way, I've just come back from Paris after having a quiet word with the duke and duchess. They will be around and available for the third of November; they pressed me relentlessly for more details, but I said it was best they didn't know, which didn't go down too well.'

'Right, I was wondering about that too. All we've got to make sure of is that the time clocks are correctly set, OK?' said Sketchley, reinforcing what he thought was the main obstacle to a successful coup d'état.

***

Angela had turned up at the hospital in the minivan. She said it was probably relatively safe to use again now, and anyway there wasn't any real alternative without incurring extra expense and awkward questions from London.

Since it was still dark, we all, including the inspector, went back to Henry's house for an early breakfast. Amazin' Grace was already up, having anticipated that her services would be required, and she was intensely inquisitive as to what had happened. She got to work quickly and supplied us with freshly brewed coffee and toast, and I, being closest to the toaster in the kitchen, volunteered to keep it loaded and supply us all, leaving Grace to concentrate on frying bacon and eggs, in which the inspector had been keenest to indulge.

As you have probably guessed, I am no slouch in the kitchen, having picked up a number of tips from my mother, who could rustle up a tasty meal from next to nothing. Truth be told, I had more inclination in that department than Angela, who always readily allowed me to take the initiative whenever we shared a meal at her flat. She definitely didn't take after her mother, but I had to admit she had other talents.

We were all surprisingly quiet whilst eating breakfast. I was particularly taken with Robertson's Silver Shred marmalade, which had just the right kind of bite to act as an appetising hors d'oeuvre to the bacon and eggs. The inspector obviously thought so too, as he managed three slices before I managed to get a look in after my toaster duties.

I got the impression that Grace was growing impatient with waiting for any feedback when she said, 'Will you no be back for lunch, Henry? Are you going back to the hospital, or did the poor policeman no survive?'

'No dear, the constable's going to be fine—just a flesh wound. I think I'll be going to the Mill to meet Angela and James after they've visited the scene of the crime. It's becoming lighter outside now so we ought to be moving, don't you think?' said Henry with a broad hint as I swallowed the last piece of crispy bacon and drained my coffee cup.

Angela suggested I might drive as I knew the way to the laboratory. On the way she voiced her concerns that we didn't seem to be making fast enough progress with the investigation and were running out of time. The election was imminent and the State Opening of Parliament not long after.

'Well, we wouldn't know what we know now but for me,' I said defensively.

'Yes, I know, James. It's not you I'm getting at. Is the inspector pulling his weight?'

'Like us, he's got budget and manpower constraints. He's not just looking at investigating one murder—it's two now, and two attempted ones if you count the attack last night. Every day, something else crops up. I don't think anybody else would have done any better.'

The debate ceased as we arrived on the outskirts of Burley in Wharfedale and drove the short distance into the old mill complex where we came upon the police van and the inspector's unmarked car parked in front of the Thompson warehouse. We parked and got out of the minivan and walked over to the inspector, who was chatting to two constables in the police van. It was one of those mid-October days when you are finally sure that autumn has departed and winter is chomping at the bit to remind you of hard times still to come. There was a nitheringly stiff easterly wind cold enough to freeze the balls off a brass monkey, as I'm sure the inspector was about to point out.

'Right. We've touched nowt; where do you want to start?' said the inspector, apparently indifferent to the cold. Mind you, he had the advantage of being sensible enough to be wearing a smart Gannex overcoat which I hadn't seen before. I hadn't initially put him down as a dedicated follower of fashion up with the likes of Harold Wilson. Perhaps he was a fan. I must ask him sometime.

I walked to the corner and looked back towards the warehouse door. 'Well, from what Constable Braithwaite said, his attacker came from round the end of the building here, which leads to the river—in fact, where I'd investigated last week. Maybe we should first see if we can find the bullet which went through the constable,' I said, trying to visualise what the constable had described.

'Look—here's some blood on the cobbles. This must be where he fell,' said Angela excitedly.

I dashed over to take a look and scanned the area nearby for evidence of the stray bullet. It wasn't there, but the day was dismal and made any fine detail difficult to make out clearly.

'Anybody got a torch?' I looked hopefully at the two constables.

'Yes sir, just a minute,' said one of them, dashing back to the police van and retrieving a heavy duty torch, which made all the difference.

We all walked in a line towards the warehouse door, searching the ground for anything out of the ordinary. The only thing we found was a 1951 sixpence, which the inspector took charge of. We reached the warehouse door and, as Constable Braithwaite had said, it was slightly ajar, sufficient to walk inside. I entered with the torch, and the beam immediately picked up the spent bullet on the floor in front of me.

'Got it!' I exclaimed in triumph. 'He must have kicked it inside as he stumbled towards the office.'

I found the light switch and turned on the lights in the warehouse. Everything seemed the same as I remembered it: two caravans and the Thompson Laboratories van. We followed an intermittent trail of blood across the floor into the office.

'Don't touch nowt. We need to check for fingerprints; we can compare any with others we found afore,' said the inspector.

There was evidence of the constable's blood on the chair, desk and particularly the phone, which he'd said he'd used to summon help. He was spot on with his observation of the open box file on the desk and its alphabetically listed names of clients, suppliers and personnel. The contents of the box file were fanned out on the table like a pack of cards. Interestingly there was a gap in them under the letter 'M', as if some records had been removed.

'M could be for Steve Mitchell, Julian Thompson's partner. We need to go through these now, Inspector, to see if it's right.'

The inspector and Angela nodded in unison, seeing the relevance of my remarks.

''Ere, put these on afore you touch 'em,' said the inspector, handing me a pair of kid gloves from his Gannex pocket.

'While you're doing that, James, I'll have look in the lab, as I haven't seen it before,' said Angela.

'Good idea, but be careful—don't touch owt,' I said, lapsing easily into dialect but avoiding the double negative the inspector was fond of using.

Angela smirked as she left the room; I wasn't sure if it was because of my poor impression of the inspector or that I was treating her as if she was incapable of assessing the risks in the laboratory, even though she was as well qualified a chemist as myself. The inspector decided to join her, leaving me and one of the constables in the office.

Examining the card system was not going to be a big job; there were only forty to fifty cards in the system since the company hadn't been established for long. Most of the entries, written in neat blue ink, were of clients, followed by suppliers, and less than half a dozen were just individual names. Sure enough, Julian Thompson was listed as 'Thompson, J.', followed by the address and telephone number, so the absence of any entries in the 'M' category confirmed to me that the intruder had been after the contact details of Steve Mitchell.

'Owt or nowt?' inquired the inspector as he and Angela came back into the office after a quick look-see into the laboratory.

'Yes, it's as we thought—the bandy-legged intruder was interested in Steve Mitchell's address. We've got to intercept him before he becomes your third murder victim, Inspector.'

'Reight, I'll get fingerprint man on t' job and bullet checked,' said the inspector decisively, indicating to us that it was time to leave, so we left the police to lock up and headed back to the Mill.

Henry was on the phone when we arrived. He motioned to us that we should sit down, and we helped ourselves to cups of coffee provided by the ever-efficient Mavis.

'Yes, Nigel, I'll get back to you, Angela and James have just walked in. Cheerio,' Henry said, hanging up.

'Find anything useful?'

'Yes, the spent bullet. And we're pretty sure he's got the address of Steve Mitchell, Thompson's partner,' Angela answered.

'Excellent. Who's doing what now?' said Henry with a sigh of relief.

'I suggest we ring Steve's mother in Scarborough to try and find out when she's coming back home,' I said. 'I also need to speak to Brian at the institute, since I intended to go in today but with what's happened it's not possible now.'

'Right, James. I'll ring Steve's mother and find out as much as I can while you deal with the institute, OK?' said Angela.

'Oh, and by the way, Nigel's come up with some interesting information,' said Henry.

CHAPTER 16
'MISS MARPLE'S INFLUENCE EXTENDS TO YORKSHIRE?'

Rickets was pleased to have been given responsibility for the disposal of Steve Mitchell. Colin had praised him, which was unusual, but it might have been influenced by Colin's equally successful trip to London with the older German. He didn't understand what was going on but he realised it was important and was keen to keep Colin in his good books. He'd already forgotten the police shooting incident; it was water under the bridge as far as he was concerned, and he was determined to do a good job with his latest assignment. Colin had stressed that he should travel over to Bradford after dark and visit the two addresses he'd picked up from the laboratory. There was a complication Rickets was worried about: he didn't know Bradford, and even though he'd been given a detailed street map, he was unsure he could find the addresses first time, at night, on his own. He was very sensitive about admitting he was a slow reader and some long words baffled him, so he needed a practice run to identify the right street and house numbers. Once he'd found the right place, he was good at remembering the roads and buildings.

Colin was going to be busy and had gone shopping in the small white Ford Anglia, so Rickets took the big black Rover, which he'd been told to park in an out-of-the-way stable after their hasty departure from the laboratory. He liked driving the big Rover; it made him feel important, and it was fast. He didn't see the need to mention it to Colin.

Rickets had no problems finding his way past Burley in Wharfedale and the road to Leeds. He took a right turn at a roundabout with a big fish and chip restaurant nearby he'd always fancied trying and then followed the sign for Bradford. He was now in unknown territory, and according to his reckoning, he needed to turn left at some major traffic lights in a place called Shipley. The two addresses on the file card he'd taken from Thompson Laboratories were 32 and 46 Plumpton Road. Colin had identified them on the street map for him and he was heading roughly towards them, so he thought. The day was overcast and rainy but not as bitterly cold as when he'd been at the lab. The good thing was that both addresses were close to one another, so that should make things easier. After the left turn he knew he should take a right shortly afterwards; he did so at the next set of traffic lights and then ascended a steep hill. It didn't seem right, but he was in a line of traffic slowly following a bus. At the top, the road levelled off and he went past a large pub called the Wrose Bull, and he quickly regretted not stopping there to ask for directions. Shortly after, he saw a post-box and a post office close by, so he pulled in, went inside and asked for directions. He didn't know how to pronounce or read 'Plumpton', so he showed the file card with the two addresses to the post office man and was told to carry on about half a mile, turn left and take the second turning on the right, which was Plumpton Road. He followed the instructions and parked just after he'd turned right.

He got out of the Rover, crossed over the road and began walking along Plumpton Road. It was a long road and he passed a few people out walking who eyed him curiously. It never occurred to him that his gait made him stand out as something out of the ordinary.

He easily located the two addresses. The houses were semi-detached, lower half brick, upper half pebbledash, with good-sized front gardens. These were not deprived people who lived here; he'd never lived in anything as good as this. He would get great pleasure taking them down. Satisfied that he'd identified the target houses, he noticed that many of the houses had red election stickers in the windows and some orange-yellow too. He now remembered there was a general election coming up shortly, but he wouldn't be voting as he had no interest in politics.

He hastily retraced his steps back to the Rover and returned home, ready to make the real excursion that evening, or the following one—whichever Colin decided.

***

Angela, at the third attempt, had managed to speak to Mrs Mitchell, Steve's mother. Mrs Mitchell was staying at her sister's boarding house on Albemarle Crescent in Scarborough, which she ran with her husband, Ralph. It was the off season, and they normally met up at that time of the year when things were quieter. Angela, with as much tact as possible, informed her that her son, and possibly her daughter-in-law, were in considerable danger, since his business partner, Julian Thompson, had been murdered. Mrs Mitchell, audibly upset, told Angela the reason for their late return from Germany, but the latest information she'd had from Steve was that his wife was now on the mend and they hoped to be back in the UK by next Tuesday, in time for them to vote in the general election. She didn't know any flight details, but she gave Angela the telephone number of the friends they were staying with.

Angela thought it might be best if James rang Steve, as he had more of the background details from working at the institute. She felt a little easier now as to how things were going. At least they were getting somewhere with finding Steve Mitchell, who might be able to supply important information about who he had rented/loaned laboratory facilities to. It was clear that Steve and his wife couldn't stay at their own house for the foreseeable future since this would be watched from now on.

She went into her own office, which was being used by Henry and James at the moment, to tell them the good news.

***

'Come in, Angela,' said Henry. 'Let me fill you in on what Nigel's just told me.'

'First thing, Henry, James—I've spoken to Mrs Mitchell, and Steve and his wife are coming back next week. I've got their phone contact in Germany,' said Angela, enthusiastically.

'Great!' I said. 'Do you want me to ring him, since I work for Brian and Steve knows him very well?'

'Just what I was about to suggest, James,' said Angela.

We both then gave Henry our full attention as he was keen to tell us Nigel's news.

'As you know,' said Henry, 'Nigel's top priority was looking into the possible link between the elusive Colin character and the Sketchley estate where the National Socialist Movement had been running firearms training courses. This was the place that Tom Hardy had been keeping an eye on before he was murdered. Apparently, one of the gardeners had seen Lord Sketchley about a month ago and heard he was now somewhere in the north of England.'

'How did Nigel find this out?' I said, impressed.

'By chance, Nigel found out that the estate had reported a major leak from the mains water and the water board was called in to fix it, so Nigel arranged for one of his men to tag along and ask a few questions. A gardener was earmarked to liaise with them and never twigged that he was being pumped for information,' said Henry, not realising he'd inadvertently strayed into James' pun territory.

'Good for Nigel. He's always been good at twigging and pumping people—was the man he seconded a drain on his resources?' I quipped, pleased at the stroke of luck. Perhaps things were beginning to go our way for a change.

There was the predictable groan from Angela.

'Nice one, James. The gardener's inadvertent leak might indicate Lord Sketchley is involved,' said Henry with a twinkle in his eye, entering into the spirit of things, 'but the north of England is a big place and we've still got to find him.'

'Did Nigel's plant find anything out about Colin from the gardener?' I asked innocently.

'Only that they all seemed to leave at the same time. The work isn't finished, so he might still find out more information, but he didn't want to arouse suspicions.'

Despite the fact that we'd obviously entered onto fertile ground where we could easily cultivate numerous asides, I judged correctly that Angela was not in the mood for levity right now.

'OK, since we've got Steve Mitchell's number in Germany, I'll see if can contact him,' I said, getting up and taking the details from Angela before walking into the other room to use the phone.

'Oh, hello,' I said to the female English voice that answered. 'Could I speak to Steve Mitchell, please? Yes, my name is James Brittain; I work at the wool institute with a friend of his, Brian Drake.'

'Steve Mitchell here,' said a male voice. 'What can I do for you, Mr Brittain?'

'I was given your contact details by your mother. I understand you are coming back to the UK next Tuesday? …Good, have you been in contact with Thompson Laboratories since you left? … No, right. Unfortunately, I've got some bad news for you. Julian Thompson was murdered last week, and we think you are in extreme danger when you return, from the same people who murdered him,' I said to an extremely distraught Steve Mitchell.

I managed to get out of him that he and his wife were booked on a Lufthansa flight into Manchester Airport on Tuesday 13th October, arriving at midday. I told him somebody would meet them, and as they needed to stay in a safe house, I wondered if the Scarborough Hotel where his mother was staying might be a possibility? He said it would be for his wife, but he'd need to be close to the business so he could try and pick up the pieces. He volunteered the particularly useful information that they had been approached some time ago for the hire of their laboratory facilities for two to three weeks and were offered a sum of money too good to turn down. Julian had dealt with it; it was all arranged over the phone, and they'd even got a two-thousand-pound cheque deposit. Julian had received a list of chemicals to get in just before Steve went on holiday. I asked him for names, but he couldn't remember any details—except that the man Julian had dealt with was called Colin!

***

Rickets was still in Colin's good books. He was dispatched in the white Ford Anglia to dispose of Steve Mitchell and told it was very important that he use this car from now on since it was less conspicuous than the Rover. He hadn't, of course, told Colin he'd used the big Rover earlier to find 32 and 46 Plumpton Road; after all, Colin didn't need to know. He was instructed to make it appear that it was a disturbed robbery—and be sure to use a silencer to avoid alerting neighbours. Two shots to the head was the standard procedure with which he was familiar. He'd assisted with the firearms training Colin ran at Lord Sketchley's estate down south, so he was a capable assassin when required. In fact, he got a kick out of it, if truth be told.

This was all very well, but it was the third night in a row he'd drawn a blank. There was still nobody in at either 32 or 46 Plumpton Road, and Colin hadn't told him what to do in this case. Each time, he kept getting psyched up and was getting decidedly edgy as time went on. It was now Monday 12th October. Out of desperation he decided to break into number forty-six to see if he could find anything useful.

It was a dark night and the wind was blowing, so he didn't have to be ultra-careful at keeping quiet. The side door, which was in shadow from the street lamp, was easy to force and he stepped into the kitchen. He walked through into the hall and opened a door into the lounge, pulling the curtains on before he switched on his torch to inspect the interior. A small table next to an armchair held a telephone and an open address book, showing Mary and Ralph's Scarborough address and telephone number. Rickets was astute enough to realise this could be important, so he folded the corner of the page over and put the book into his pocket to show to Colin when he returned.

He glanced at the sideboard, which had a small tin box on it with 'Gas, Electric, Rates – money' written on the lid. He recognised the word 'money' and opened the box. Inside he found a five-pound note, two ten-shilling notes and three half crowns. He swiftly pocketed the lot, since Colin had impressed on him that he should give the impression robbery was the main motive for breaking in, and he might as well get something out of it.

Rickets was correct in his assumption that Colin would be supportive of his efforts. Initially, Colin was irritated that Steve Mitchell hadn't been dealt with yet, but realised it wasn't Charlie's fault that he wasn't in and the address in Scarborough was useful—perhaps explaining why Steve's mother was also not at home. Still, it was an inconvenience he could have done without at the moment. He instructed Charlie to keep going back for the next couple of nights to see if Mitchell returned, telling him to park his car out of the way and lie in wait round the back of the house if necessary. Above all, he should make sure he wasn't recognised. Rickets agreed, and although he was not finding it as easy as he'd first anticipated, he didn't have any option but to agree.

***

Stein had updated Helmut on the successful trip to London and told him Colin couldn't wait to report back to Sketchley with the good news. This had taken the pressure off them both, and because of their cooperation, they were not as closely watched now as when they'd been at Thompson Laboratories. Colin had sourced an additional hairdryer for them to take to London, since they didn't have access to as many tools at the estate as in the laboratory, and he'd had to do quite a lot of running around to buy some of the items which Stein had requested. In the meantime, Stein had told Helmut that their best chance of escaping Sketchley's clutches would be in London, in the midst of chaos after the tabun was released. He had seen there was a tube station very close to Parliament, where they could lose themselves before heading, perhaps, for a Channel ferry.

Helmut agreed and said he'd caught a glimpse of his or Stein's passport in the top drawer of Sketchley's desk. They should try and recover these as soon as possible, then all they needed was some money. They were both in agreement that to survive they had to make a run for it at the opportune time. Helmut did wonder if they should have tried to make contact with James, or leave clues as to their whereabouts, but quite frankly they didn't know where they were and had been too closely watched to attempt anything. Stein had already negotiated with Sketchley for Helmut to assist him in setting up the equipment in the Lords' Chamber, since he needed the expert help that only Helmut could provide.

Over their time together at the laboratory and estate, Stein had formed a good opinion of Helmut's knowledge and practical abilities. Yes, he had some eccentric habits, but he could work with him and he would make a satisfactory assistant. He had promised him, should they manage to escape back to Germany, that he would find him a research fellowship to compensate for the one at the wool institute, and this seemed to be acceptable to Helmut. Stein wasn't sure if he could actually come up with this, but he had to keep him on side and words were cheap, so he would worry about this if and when they escaped. His top priority was self-preservation.

Stein had been granted an audience with Sketchley in his office. He was well received, and the only purpose of the meeting was to confirm that everything was prepared and for Sketchley to listen to Stein's explanation of the setup to make sure he understood that the timing of the tabun release during the Queen's speech was the crucial part. It was, if Sketchley understood things correctly, just as he'd explained it all to Jock.

While they were talking, Stein was able to glance occasionally at the desk Helmut had mentioned. It was set at right angles to the door, so it was possible to view the contents of any drawer that was partially open. They needed to devise a strategy to draw Sketchley away from the office to get in and search the desk. He would discuss it with Helmut as soon as possible.

**

I was in the Mill when the phone rang.

'Nah then, James. I was hoping you were in t' office; I've got summat to tell thee,' said Inspector Broadley in a confidential manner.

'Oh good, I've got something to tell you as well,' I said. 'You first.'

'That *Yorkshire Post* reporter, Miss Whatshername, summat or other, you foisted off onto me t' other day has been pestrin' chief constable, and askin' awkward questions at press conference we were forced to have.'

'Miss Marple?' I said, tongue in cheek.

'Yer mean, *Murder on t' Orient Express* Miss Marple?'

'That's right. She said her name was Jane, and over the phone she sounded very much like Margaret Rutherford's Miss Marple,' I said jokingly. 'She was pretty sharp too.'

'She looks nowt like Margaret Rutherford in t' flesh—bit of a looker, if yer ask me,' Broadley said seriously. 'Anyhow, as a result, Chief's givin' me more resources. What does ter think about that?'

'Great—Miss Marple's influence extends into the wilds of Yorkshire, then? I'm sorry about lumbering you with her, but she caught me cold when I was recovering and she'd cleverly found out about me from the lady in Burley who helped me,' I said apologetically.

'No worries. Anyway, t' publicity you got prompted the chief constable to review the case since police didn't come out of it too well. What's tha got?'

'Well, I've spoken to Steve Mitchell in Germany and he's coming back to the UK next Tuesday into Manchester. I've told him he's in danger and shouldn't go home; he needs somewhere else to stay. Oh, and he said the person Julian Thompson dealt with was called Colin.'

'Well done—we can pick him up at t' airport. I need to speak to him too,' said the inspector, sounding very relieved.

'Yes, I was hoping you might suggest that. Can I sit in on the interview? I could be of some use as I work with Brian Drake, who's Steve's friend.'

'Sure, just give me t' details of flight Mitchell's arrivin' on.'

After giving the inspector all the information I had on Steve, I put the phone down and turned round to find Henry standing in the room with a concerned expression on his face. He'd obviously overheard my conversation and perhaps was going to take issue with me.

'James, I couldn't help hearing part of your conversation with the inspector. Your publicity in the press hasn't gone unnoticed in London with our DG either. He questioned whether you had the basic skills and aptitude for the role as an undercover agent and wondered if you were worth the long-term investment by the service.'

I gulped. I hadn't given too much thought to the *Yorkshire Post*'s article; it was not sought after, and I'd done nothing to encourage it. I hoped Henry would realise it was purely by chance.

'I'm sorry, Henry. It was unintentional and cropped up out of the blue. It was a clever piece of detective work by the reporter, but on the positive side the police have got more manpower to put on the case, which could be a great help to us since we're struggling in that department, aren't we?'

'That's more or less what I told the DG. He still doesn't think it's connected to extreme right-wing aristos or suspect MI5 operators, but he doesn't mind if the extra manpower is paid for out of the police budget. In any case, James, it might be worth trying to keep a low profile from now on.'

This was a mild rebuke from Henry, which was taken in the spirit in which it was given.

'Nigel's just given me an interesting nugget of information. Apparently, Harold Wilson has complained to the chairman of the BBC that putting on a repeat of *Steptoe and Son* in the last hour of polling next Thursday might influence Labour voters not to vote, so he's asked for it to be put on at a different time. The chairman is considering it.'

'Very interesting. It just goes to show how influential television is becoming in politics nowadays. Wilson's possibly right; it's well known that bad weather affects the turnout on polling day—more so for Labour supporters since fewer of them have cars than well-off Tories. Mind you, *Steptoe and Son* could always have used the horse and cart!' I said to an amused Henry.

CHAPTER 17
'TWO FALLS, TWO SUBMISSIONS OR…'

The return of Steve Mitchell and his wife, Elizabeth, turned out to be a bit of an anti-climax. We didn't learn a great deal more than he'd told me over the phone. His partner, Julian, had dealt with all the jobs that required hands-on practical chemical synthesis, whilst Steve handled the sales side, deliveries and invoicing. They had both thought that the deal was easy money; the worst they had to do was obtain the chemicals, some of which were a little uncommon, but they had no problems sourcing them. It was unfortunate that Steve's trip had cropped up just before the two German chemists arrived. The only thing which might be useful to us was tracing the cheque they had received as an advance. Steve was sure it had been paid into the bank by now, but it was probably traceable and there should also have been a covering letter with it.

Steve was very much as his friend Brian Drake had described him to me: a friendly, easy-to-talk-to man of similar age to Brian and probably an excellent salesman. As I had anticipated, he saw me as a useful link between himself and the inspector, and my involvement was easily explained by my connection with the institute. Elizabeth was much quieter than Steve, but she was quick to say that she'd prefer to stay with her mother in Ilkley rather than the Scarborough hotel I'd initially suggested. Steve thought this was probably the best solution for him too, as it was convenient for his business premises in Burley in Wharfedale. We emphasised yet again that they could be in serious danger from the people who had murdered Julian, and we could see from their expressions that they were taking this seriously. They needed to call in at their home to pick up extra clothing, as well as Steve's car. The inspector said the police would ferry them over and check that everything was in order at 32 Plumpton Road, and with that they departed.

'What does tha think, James?' said Broadley as soon as they had left the interview room.

'Disappointing. The best we can hope for is that there might be a lead when the bank comes up with the cashed cheque and Steve finds if there's a covering letter from whomever sent it. I suppose you'll follow up on that, Inspector?'

'Yes. We'll also keep eye on Steve and his missus, just in case. Does tha want to drop in at lab tomorrow, say, when Steve's in, case owt else jogs his memory?'

'Good idea. What time do you reckon?'

Ten thirty was agreed upon, and then I left. I was still staying at Henry's, so it would be very convenient to call in at the lab. Hopefully Henry would be good enough to drop me off there in the morning before he went to the Mill.

It was Tuesday evening. The Thursday general election was fast approaching, and I had to decide on who to vote for. I was still registered to vote in Bradford, so I thought it would be good to kill two birds with one stone by voting and then putting in another guest appearance at the institute to keep them happy. One advantage of staying at Henry's house was the television, by which I had kept up to date with election news on the BBC. The outcome still seemed poised on a knife edge. It had occurred to me on the way back that if the Tories managed to stay in power, would the ultra-right fanatics still go ahead with their attack on Parliament? I must make a point of asking Henry and Angela their opinion on this. It could be argued that it wouldn't be necessary if Labour lost, but a gut feeling told me they had already gone so far that they were hell-bent on creating anarchy regardless of the election result.

I got back to Henry's later than normal, since I'd been tied up at the police station. It was approaching seven o'clock, and there was nobody in. Then I remembered Henry had said he had to go out with Grace to a local church 'do'. I don't think Henry was too keen, but for appearances' sake he was obliged to do it. I was just about to consider going to the local chip shop for a fish and a penn'orth when I found a plated cold salad left for me on the table in the kitchen. Amazin' Grace had come up trumps again. I settled myself down in front of the television and gas fire to watch the latest developments in the election campaign. A roundup of prospective MPs haranguing sceptical voters was enlivened by the eye-catching actress Miss Honor Blackman, who was stealing the show using a megaphone. She was canvassing for the Liberals, and I seriously thought I could be persuaded to support Jo Grimond's party if she knocked on my door. Her role as the leather-clad judo expert Dr Cathy Gale in *The Avengers* was imprinted on my mind, and if the publicity was to be believed, she had a similar role as the provocatively named Pussy Galore in the newly released James Bond film, *Goldfinger*, a role in which I was sure she'd be *purr*fect.

This item was followed by another celebrity, Jimmy Edwards, who had actually been chosen to stand as Conservative candidate for Paddington North. The rumbustious, tuba-playing comedian, famous for the radio programme *Take it from Here* and *Whacko* on TV, was there sporting his trademark luxuriant handlebar moustache. In order to compare the brace of handlebar moustaches, the media couldn't resist the opportunity to pair him up with the equally loud Sir Gerald Nabarro, the sitting right-wing Conservative MP for Kidderminster. In my opinion it was a difficult choice—the difference, if any, would only be by a whisker.

Heckling was an occupational hazard encountered by most politicians in this election campaign. A lot of it was good humoured, and for those adept at parrying the jibes, it could often be turned to their advantage. Quintin Hogg, the leading spokesman for the Conservatives, was one of those who was good at this. Famously, when he was loudly targeted by a long-haired young man, Hogg leaned over the podium and retorted, 'Now, see here sir or madam, whichever the case might be, we have had enough of you!' The man was ejected to the applause of the crowd, and Hogg went on as if nothing had happened. He was also not averse to flamboyant gestures; he took exception to a Harold Wilson placard being waved in front of him by a Labour supporter and smacked it repeatedly with his walking stick.

I really ought to have made an effort to attend some meetings of my prospective parliamentary candidates in Bradford, but I'd put it off and now it was too late. I was going to have to make up my mind from what was in the newspapers and the limited news coverage on television. One thing that kept recurring was the immigration issue as larger numbers of dependents were joining immigrants already here. I'd already noted some weeks ago that there were ugly campaigns going on, particularly in Smethwick and other constituencies targeted by far-right groups.

I caught part of an interview with Harold Wilson, who rammed home again the message of 'thirteen years of Tory misrule' as well as Labour's more modern vision for the future based on meritocracy, with leaders selected for their ability not nepotism, rather than being dependent on people from the landed gentry who went to the right schools. This, of course, was aimed directly at Sir Alec Douglas-Home, who had been chosen by Harold McMillan as a man-in-his-own-image to lead the Conservative party when he'd resigned. There was of course an element of truth to all this, but it was pure politics, and I'd learned, even as a trained priest, never to take everything said by politicians as gospel.

Due to the very effective gas fire in the sitting room, I could feel myself drifting off into the arms of Morpheus—or, if memory serves, the arms of Dr Cathy Gale, who was gripping my arm in a vice-like half-Nelson and whispering in my ear, 'Vote Liberal and I'll show you a few more holds!' I don't remember whether I submitted or not, but it was another memory to replay on dark nights.

***

Colin was being pressured by Sketchley to tie up a few more loose ends. The one good lead they had on the man Colin had shot at when leaving the laboratory was from the *Yorkshire Post* article, which identified him as James Brittain of The Wool Research Institute in Bradford. It was reported that he had been severely bruised after crashing his scooter and was recovering in Otley. Colin now had some time to concentrate on finding this man, who was obviously dangerous. He had established that Brittain wasn't in at the institute at the moment by ringing up and posing as a reporter. He'd talked to a secretary who was very helpful, but she didn't know the Otley address where Brittain was supposedly still recuperating from his injuries. It might be worth a trip to the institute to familiarise himself with the layout.

The younger German knew Brittain, and Colin thought he should be able to make him divulge more information about him. Sketchley had warned Colin not to be too harsh with the German since they required his full cooperation, at least until the deed had been done in London.

'You know James Brittain of the wool institute, don't you, Herr Schultz?' Colin asked Helmut menacingly, ignoring Stein, who was also present.

'I met him at the conference, and he take me to hotel to meet institute boss,' said Helmut truthfully.

'Right. What else do you know about him?'

'*Gar nichts*—nothing. Just he work as technical service man for institute,' said Helmut, unusually fluent now as he was frightened he might be signing James's death warrant if he gave too much away.

'Helmut correct,' said Stein. 'We meet Herr Brittain and Dr Engel of the research institute at conference, Dr Engel told us he work at institute; he not research man so not of consequence to us.'

'So you don't know where he lives in Otley, then?' said Colin.

Helmut shook his head. Colin, mindful of what Sketchley had said, realised he wasn't going to get a lot more out of the two Germans. What they said made sense, but it didn't explain how Brittain had found Thompson Laboratories and why he was following them. Perhaps he was linked to the security services, or police, or both? In any case, he was as much a threat to their mission as Steve Mitchell.

Colin decided a discreet trip to the institute was in order. Unfortunately, he didn't know what Brittain looked like, so he needed somebody to point him out. Helmut Schultz was the obvious choice, but he would need to put the frighteners on to discourage him from trying to escape.

Colin drove into Bradford in the white Anglia and eventually found his way to what was locally called Little Germany. He managed to park on one of the side streets and walked down a fairly steep hill, appropriately called Church Bank since the cathedral dominated the right side of the road. The cathedral clock started striking eleven as he reached the outer door to the institute. On impulse, he entered and climbed up a winding spiral staircase to the reception desk, which was occupied by an elderly gentleman with a military bearing, sporting an incredibly short 'short back and sides' haircut.

'Which regiment were you in, sir?' said Colin with authority, standing to attention.

'9th Battalion of West Yorks, Green Howards, sir,' said the receptionist, now equally ramrod straight responding to an officer's question, just managing not to salute.

'Good man. Bradford Pal, eh. I'm Peter Asquith from the *Telegraph and Argus* and wondered when I could have word with James Brittain. I haven't time now but could make it later on this week.'

The ploy worked perfectly, distracting him from asking awkward questions.

'James Bond, we call 'im. He's not in reight now, but I'm telled 'e'll be in a Thursday, election day,' said the receptionist, delighted to be of assistance to a fellow soldier.

'Good, I'll call in again Thursday,' said Colin, extremely satisfied to have got this information. Then, without warning, he sneezed violently. Apologising, he blew his nose loudly into a handkerchief, which he rapidly took out of his trouser pocket. He was keen to get out of the building now.

As he hurried away, he glanced up at the cathedral above a high stone wall and wondered if there was a vantage point from where he could observe who came and went out of the institute's main door. Further up and across Church Bank, he noticed a big iron gate which was obviously a minor entrance into the cathedral grounds. He crossed over the road, pushed open the gate and climbed up some wide stone steps which led to the back of the cathedral. There was nobody around, so he was able to spend time inspecting the institute's five-storey building. The corner entrance was at an angle where he couldn't actually see the door, but it was possible to see clearly who was coming in and out. At the top of the steps a path led round the side of the cathedral that held part of an old graveyard, consisting mainly of flags with shrubs and trees, which gave good cover from the institute's windows across the road. It was as good a place as any to lay an ambush, providing he could get Helmut Schultz to identify Brittain. He also noticed there was another exit from the cathedral grounds via more steps, leading down to an elaborate iron gate facing Forster Square, which was obviously used for special occasions. On the way down these steps, he got a good view of the railway station entrance. This could be a good escape route, worth considering.

Highly satisfied with his visit to Bradford, he travelled back to the estate to deliver the good news to Sketchley, who he thought would be pleased. He was, and agreed to have a word with both Stein and Helmut to impress on them that their existence depended on full and willing cooperation.

***

Henry had a pleasant surprise for me on Wednesday morning. He'd organised a car for me, which would be delivered to his home address at eight thirty. It was rented, so it would be appreciated if I didn't write it off in a similar manner to the Lambretta.

A knock on the door at quarter past eight announced the delivery of a 105e light blue Ford Anglia. It wasn't brand new, but it was probably the newest car I'd driven, with a fully synchromesh gearbox. I thanked Henry and said I would use it immediately to go and meet Inspector Broadley at Thompson Laboratories to see if Steve Mitchell could give us any more information.

'Got some four-wheeled transport now, 'as ta?' sniped the inspector good-naturedly, when he spied me getting out of the Anglia at the laboratory.

'Yes, it's been loaned to me on condition I don't write it off like the scooter,' I countered before he could remind me of it.

Steve and Elizabeth Mitchell had been in earlier. He had carried out a thorough examination of the premises and given us his observations. Elizabeth normally helped out in the office three days a week, but Steve was going to need all the help he could get for the foreseeable future.

'Number forty-six Plumpton Road's bin broken into. Nowt much taken, some money, could be a coincidence,' said the inspector.

'That's your mother's address, isn't it, Steve?' I remembered.

Steve nodded.

The bank had confirmed that the cheque had been cashed and was trying to locate it for Steve to pick up. He couldn't find any covering letter, unfortunately, and Julian hadn't written down any contact details for Colin—or maybe he had, but it had been removed. He was desperately trying to catch up on orders that needed to be sent out. It turned out there had just been a delivery of chemicals from the supplier which included a substantial number of items for the wool institute as well as the outstanding setting agents I was interested in. I volunteered to deliver them for him, as I knew Brian Drake would be pleased to get them and I was going in to work tomorrow. Steve was grateful for this help, so I transferred cardboard boxes containing the institute's order into the boot of the Anglia. I thought it fortunate I had the use of a vehicle, because there was no way I could have carried them all on foot.

Steve and the inspector transferred their attention to the laboratory area. Steve pointed out a number of items of equipment that were new to him, a rotary evaporator in particular. They had planned on getting one themselves when cashflow permitted. He opened up a cardboard box containing two remaining sample bottles with secure stoppers. Steve had never seen these before and remarked that they were suitable for the transport of dangerous liquids. The inspector and I gave one another knowing glances without saying anything.

Elizabeth then came into the laboratory with a supplier invoice she thought we ought to look at. It was for a list of chemicals most certainly used by Stein and Helmut. Steve's immediate comment was that these were the sort of starting materials used for synthesising organophosphorus compounds such as pesticides. His eyes widened and he stared intensely at me, willing me to fill in the gaps for him. I looked away, declining to answer. The inspector defused the situation by declaring that we'd probably got all we needed to know for the present and would leave Steve and Elizabeth to pick up the pieces as best they could. He also said a police patrol would call in two or three times a day to make sure they were OK, which was appreciated.

I set off early the next morning to go to the institute. On the way, I called in at my local Bradford polling station to cast my vote in the church hall. Everything involved in the process of voting seemed antiquated, from the couple of presiding officials to the rickety wooden booths where you put your cross in a box with a pencil attached to a piece of string hanging in the booth. I even wondered if the pencils were the same ones used in the Lloyd George era. On the way out I shook my head with a smile at the two party workers, notepads in hand, keen to know who I'd voted for.

Yesterday, I'd spoken to Brian Drake to tell him I was bringing in the chemicals from Thompson's. He'd told me to unload the boxes by the warehouse door at the side of the institute and he would come down and let me in at half past eight. I was there early, so I banged on the shutter door, which eventually opened. After a delighted Brian had taken delivery of the chemicals, I drove to Little Germany, where at that time of day plenty of parking was available in the side streets. I walked quickly back to the institute and, using the normal entrance, climbed the spiral staircase, nodding at George, the security man who doubled up as stand-in receptionist when the two ladies normally in place were on comfort breaks or holidays.

Just as I was about to go in to report to Brian, George said, 'Tha's had a visitor, Jim. Man who said he were from T and A, said he'd come back today. Called hisself Peter Asquith.'

This was not welcome news. It was quite a few days since I'd had the accident on my Lambretta with its resultant report in the *Yorkshire Post*. It seemed a bit late for the *T and A* to pick up on it. I wondered what they wanted.

'Funny thing!' said George, producing a piece of paper. 'He sneezed and blew 'is nose, and when he'd gone, I found this on t' floor. I thought it might be summat special, so I telephoned T and A to speak to Mr Asquith. They told me they didn't have anybody o' that name workin' there!'

The hairs on the back of my neck started to rise. 'Let me have a look at the paper, George.' I was handed the paper and saw it wasn't just a piece of paper; it was a file card with two addresses on it. One read Steve Mitchell, 32 Plumpton Road and the other Mrs Mitchell, 46 Plumpton Road, Bradford!

CHAPTER 18
'IT'S BEEN A HARD DAY'S NIGHT...'

Henry had arranged earlier in the week for Angela and me to have a meal on Thursday evening with him and Grace, before following the election results as they came in on a special BBC TV programme after polling was finished. The bogus *T and A* reporter turning up at the institute plus George's good fortune in finding the file card taken from Thompson Laboratories had put a new perspective on our situation which needed urgent thought. I had to beg leave from the institute again, meaning that I had to take Brian partially into my confidence. He could see there was a major threat and was agreeable. It was a good job that Tony Pickard was still away, as I thought he would be less amenable to my demands and would want to know all the ins-and-outs of my affairs. Unfortunately, he was due back from his trip in just over a week's time.

I arranged with Inspector Broadley to have the institute watched in case the bogus reporter turned up. On quizzing George further, he was sure the man was ex-army, officer class from his bearing, and from his description he could very well be the 'Colin' character. To me, there seemed to be an air of desperation creeping in if they were trying to find me by turning up unannounced at the institute. What had been his plan if I'd been here—shoot me in the reception area? It confirmed that we were on the right track and we'd got them rattled.

These were my immediate thoughts as I drove back to Henry's house from the institute. Henry had suggested that rather than meeting at the Mill we might as well all go to his house in Otley for a council of war before the election results unfolded later in the evening.

'Nigel's been on the phone to report that there's no further useful news from the estate and the gardener who told him Lord Sketchley had been there recently has mysteriously disappeared,' said Henry.

'Percy Thrower vanishes,' I commented lamely, which was totally ignored by Henry and Angela.

'I'm not in my DG's good books either,' continued Henry, with a frown on his face. 'He thinks I'm spending far too much time here in Yorkshire and not concentrating on trying to unearth the source of leaks to the Soviets. I've told him I'm going to take some annual leave, which is long overdue.'

'About time too. You'll be able to organise the greenhouse delivery I sorted out for you, will you no?' said Amazin' Grace as she swept into the lounge with three pots of freshly made coffee and, you guessed it, a plate of mixed biscuits including Hobnobs. Grace's finely tuned hearing had picked up this snippet of conversation and immediately pounced on it. It's a gift I've often noticed women possess and frequently use very effectively to organise/manipulate the men in their lives.

'No dear, it's just a ploy to distract the DG,' said Henry smoothly to Grace, who was obviously disappointed with the response but, deciding not to pursue it further in front of us, left the room silently. Angela and I exchanged knowing glances, much amused.

'Nigel's still not been able to turn up any more information about members of the Right Club, or the elusive Lord Sketchley for that matter, so we're going to have to make do with what we already know,' said Henry. 'He's impressed that James seems to be getting somewhere in flushing them out by following up on Steve Mitchell. He suggests that we should issue you with a firearm, James. I understand you've been on a training course?'

Both Angela and I nodded, and I vividly remembered the police training course next to the golf course outside Leeds. Angela said she would organise the equipment when she got back to the Mill.

For the rest of the meeting, we concentrated on going over what we knew for sure and the possible next moves. One thing that we all agreed upon was that these people were determined to carry out their plan regardless of the result of the general election. Henry suggested it might be a good idea to use Sketchley's profile as a starting point to examine the occupants of large estates and stately homes in the north of England, taking Leeds as the centre and working outwards within a twenty-five-mile radius. I thought it was an excellent idea and fancied doing it myself, but Henry said he and Angela would start it and involve Inspector Broadley as needed.

***

Helmut was not happy. He'd been forced to accompany Colin on a mission to try and identify James Brittain. He didn't know James very well but had respect for him, as James had smoothed things over for him with the police in Leeds and they should have been working at the same wool institute. He and Stein had been placed in yet another impossible situation, and if he went along with Colin's wishes, he was almost certainly signing James' death warrant.

There were three of them in the car as they arrived in Bradford: himself, Colin and the one they called Rickets, whom they'd picked up in Ilkley. Colin told them to get out of the car and then led them along a number of side streets towards a big church across the road. The clock on the church tower was just striking half past eight as they went through an iron gate and up a flight of stone steps. At the top, Colin turned right onto a path which led towards the back and side of the church. There were a number of thick bushes which shielded them from prying eyes. Colin parted the branches to give them all a good view of the road and the building across it. He pointed to the corner of the building, where a woman was entering through a swing door. The intention was to wait and view the people entering the building, and Helmut would have to identify James Brittain if and when he saw him. The pfennig finally dropped—the building was the wool institute. Helmut concentrated on the increasing number of people approaching and entering the building. Most of them came from the centre of Bradford, none of them were James. The road was relatively busy, with a number of blue trolleybuses passing up and down. Fortunately, none of these obscured the entrance long enough to prevent them observing the entrants.

Time was passing, and Helmut saw Colin look up impatiently at the church clock. Just then, out of the corner of his left eye, he saw somebody walking down the road towards the institute. It was definitely James, but Helmut waited until James was ten to fifteen yards from the entrance before he pointed him out. Colin was annoyed that he hadn't mentioned it sooner, but Helmut countered that he'd been concentrating on the larger number of people coming from the other direction. Nevertheless, Colin had got a good look at James, and so had Rickets.

Colin nodded to Rickets and pointed towards the other side of the church. Rickets motioned to Helmut to follow him, and they passed the rear of the church and descended a large flight of stone steps to Forster Square, where there were numerous bus and trolleybus stops, and the entrance to the railway station. Rickets and Helmut took the train to Ilkley, where after coming out of the station, they crossed Brook Street and onto The Grove, where Rickets had left the big Rover, in which they travelled back to the estate.

***

Sketchley was not in a particularly good mood. He'd just learned that Rickets had had a run in with a policeman the other night when he'd revisited the laboratory. Sketchley had found out from the newspaper, and even Colin hadn't heard. Colin had just reported that Rickets was having difficulties finding Steve Mitchell, who didn't seem to have returned from holiday yet. Fortunately, Rickets hadn't shot anybody else—or, if he had, it hadn't made the newspapers.

The theory was that Steve Mitchell was being shielded, so there was only one solution—Colin would have to deal with

Mitchell, as Rickets was a liability and prone to gaffs. Helmut Schultz had identified Brittain as he was going into the institute, but he hadn't appeared again, so it looked as if he'd left by another door. Nevertheless, both Colin and Rickets now knew what he looked like, and it was just a matter of time before he could be dealt with. This was how Colin explained things to Lord Sketchley, putting the best spin on it that he could.

Sketchley was very much on edge. It was election day, and although they were committed to carrying out their Westminster plot, the result was still important to him.

He was well acquainted with Cecil King, chairman of the International Publishing Corporation (IPC), the biggest publishing empire in the world, including the *Daily Mirror* and some two hundred other papers and magazines. King had a high opinion of himself, genuinely believing that he was 'born to rule', and he certainly had enormous, undisputed influence in British public life. King himself believed that criticism of Churchill's government by the Labour-supporting *Daily Mirror* had caused that government's collapse after the war.

Even though their political views were diametrically opposed to one another, they occasionally swapped gossip, so Sketchley thought he would get King's view of the state of the election, since he had his finger on the political pulse of the nation. King was confident Labour would win, but that it might be closer than some of the opinion polls were predicting. Sketchley audibly winced over the phone, to the delight of King, who then offered an unexpected comment. He'd heard from certain sources that somebody was looking for The Right Club's *Red Book*, which had gone missing. Did Sketchley know anything about it? Sketchley knew King was close to some MI5 security people, and this revelation explained some of the recent events. It confirmed in his mind that James Brittain and Angela Jones were linked to the security services, and he would now have to be on his guard even more. He naturally feigned surprise and said if he heard anything, he would get back to King.

The call to King had proved to be very informative. Sketchley decided that a change to his plans might be advisable to reduce the risk of detection. He'd originally thought he might travel to London and stay with Jock in order to be close to the action, but the best place for him now was Yorkshire. Colin, Stein and Schultz could travel down to London the day before the opening of Parliament to finalise the equipment preparation and make sure the timers were correctly set to release the tabun at the optimum moment. Sketchley still hadn't totally decided what to do with Stein and Schultz. He was beginning to lean more in favour of eliminating them, which Colin could do as soon as the tabun had been released. God forbid that anything should go wrong but, if it did, they could be disposed of to avoid any chance of their giving embarrassing evidence against him.

Another thing that puzzled and worried him was, how had James Brittain found out about the laboratory? It was clear the premises were a no-go area for them now, as the police were obviously keeping an eye on it. Maybe Steve Mitchell had arrived back and was at work again, which was possible. The money Colin had paid Thompson Laboratories by cheque was from a bank account he had specifically set up for that purpose and wasn't going to be used again now. Sketchley was sure it wasn't traceable back to him, so he turned his attention to the search for Mitchell, Brittain and possibly Jones. He was keen to tie up loose ends.

***

After a good evening meal, prepared by Grace, we all settled down in front of the television in Henry's lounge. Henry poured me a large glass of the usual single malt whisky, and we waited for the BBC's election special to start. The black and white test card appeared on screen, and a cultured BBC voice announced, 'This is BBC One.'

The avuncular figure of Richard Dimbleby introduced things by saying, 'It is nine twenty-five on election day—the nation has voted, and the count is on!' This was followed by a fanfare of trumpets as the camera slowly panned across a busy studio with BBC backstage staff clearly visible and a large backdrop wall chart of the state of the parties—Conservative, Labour, Liberal and Others—which at the moment showed, '*results declared 0, results to come 630*'. We were obviously in for a long night.

Richard Dimbleby personified the ideal anchorman, with proven gravitas from having chaired the last five election nights. He introduced the panel of experts who would explain the significance of incoming results. These included Ian Trethowan; David Butler, an expert on elections; and Robert MacKenzie, a political analyst famous for his 'Swingometer', which attempted to predict the winning party's majority by comparing each parliamentary seat's percentage swing with its last election result as it came in. Robin Day and Cliff Mitchelmore were going to be on hand in another part of the studio to quiz candidates and people in the news, in their own inimitable styles.

Traditionally, probably to fill in time until the first results came in, what was described as a 'horserace' had been devised to see which constituency would declare its results first. This year it was a four-horse race between front-runner Billericay, Cheltenham, Exeter and Salford. Billericay had come first at the last election, so the BBC had stationed Raymond Baxter at the Billericay County Secondary School to report on the frantic counting of ballot papers. All the ballot boxes had been delivered, from as far afield as nine miles, in less than fifteen minutes. It was stressed that accuracy, not speed, was the most important thing, but there was an intense sporting rivalry to be the first to declare a result.

The general expectation of the experts was that from surveys carried out, there was a wish for change in the country and Labour was favourite to win, but by what majority was difficult to predict.

We were all taken aback by the sensational news which had just filtered out from the Soviet Union that Nikita Khrushchev had been 'relieved of his duties'. We turned the sound down on the television set to discuss this. Henry was half expecting a telephone call from his DG, since the uncertainty this created had major implications for MI6. I expressed my opinion that it might take our mind off our current project, which might prove fatal. Angela agreed. Henry said he would ring his DG in the morning, as everybody he knew would be focussed on our general election right now.

Disturbing news often doesn't come in single doses. In the early hours of Friday, the official New China News Agency announced that China had exploded its first atomic bomb. They then immediately proposed a world conference to ban the use of nuclear weapons. It was understood that the bomb was exploded in the 'Western Region of China' at 3 p.m. Peking time. The agency said that Red China had been forced to build a nuclear bomb because of a 'nuclear threat posed by the United States'. It boasted that the explosion was a 'major achievement for the Chinese people', that it strengthened Red China's national defence and was a 'major contribution to the cause of world peace'.

We almost missed the announcement that Cheltenham had won the race to declare the first result of the night at two minutes past ten; the result was a Conservative hold over Labour, followed shortly by Salford West, Billericay and Exeter. There were no major upsets in these results, with no changes of seats, but the flurry of results set the experts into a hive of activity with their slide rules and abacuses to calculate the percentage changes since last time.

A bit of much-needed light relief was introduced into the proceedings when it was announced that the comedian, Jimmy Edwards, had been defeated in Paddington North, and his failure was a second blow to the Parliamentary Handlebar Moustache Society, compounded by the retirement on grounds of ill health of Sir Gerald Nabarro.

It had been discussed by the experts that race could be an unknown factor in this year's election, and far-right factions had caused trouble during the lead up to the election. We were well aware of the racially fought campaigning in the Smethwick constituency by the Conservative candidate Peter Griffith against the Shadow Foreign Secretary, Patrick Gordon Walker, who was the sitting Labour MP. It was therefore a major shock of the evening when the Conservatives overturned the Labour majority by a swing of seven percent, prompting Lord Boothby, talking to Robin Day, to describe the Smethwick result as 'the most disgusting thing that's ever happened in politics—a racial fight in the worst American tradition.'

As the night wore on into the following morning, the prediction was that there would be a Labour government, but the majority was likely to be smaller than originally thought; as the broadcast was being wound up at eleven minutes past four, 426 seats had been declared, with 202 still to come. Despite the Labour lead being shown as sixty-eight, it was expected that the strong rural constituencies of the Conservatives would close the gap. In all, likely around twenty-six to twenty-seven million votes had been cast, with a turnout of approximately seventy-five percent, which was lower than the last election.

While the nation was voting, the Beatles were on their first full UK tour. They were playing at the Globe Cinema in Stockton-on-Tees, after breaking big in the United States earlier in the year. Robert Mackenzie noted that there was a low turnout in the Liverpool Exchange constituency and commented that the closeness of the result was becoming clearer—'It looks like being a hard day's night, or a hard day's day,' chipped in David Butler, since it was well and truly Friday morning.

A relieved, but still sprightly Dimbleby concluded: 'We hand over to four young men who somehow have managed to get in on this act like every other. Good morning,' as The Beatles' 'A Hard Day's Night' played out the programme at four thirteen.

CHAPTER 19
'IT'S ALL IN THE CAN'

Stein and Helmut had no idea that the general election had taken place and Labour had gained power, albeit by a wafer-thin majority of four seats. They had been totally shielded from the outside world, other than when Stein had been taken to London to view the Lords' Chamber and when Helmut had accompanied Colin to Bradford to identify James. They had eventually been given more comfortable accommodation than the caravan at the laboratory. They were now lodged in the Bothy, a detached cottage originally occupied by estate workers, which adjoined the estate's walled garden and the greenhouses, which had originally provided all the vegetables and fruit for the hall. It had all become run down to a large extent, mainly because there weren't enough gardeners to carry out the work. They had the run of the cottage and the walled garden, but the outside gates into the estate were locked, so it was effectively an open prison. The gate to the main buildings led to the chapel and kitchen facilities and was opened once a day, when they were allowed into the large kitchen-dining area where they ate their meals.

Stein and Helmut were largely bored since they had finished their tabun trials, and they talked over their escape options while they strolled round the garden, whose stone walls were at least twelve feet high and had, on the south-facing side, a number of large built-in chimneys, which had provided warmth for the protection of delicate soft fruit trees in previous times. These had long since disappeared, but there were still some hardier apple trees surviving, which provided windfalls to supplement their diet. They both agreed that they needed to retrieve their passports from Sketchley's desk, and the best time seemed to be on a Sunday, when Sketchley was not usually around. Stein suggested that he could perhaps create a diversion by asking to be shown round the hall. The cook, Mrs Whitaker, was the general dogsbody and had shown some sympathy towards the two Germans. He believed he could persuade her to act as a guide to escort him round the hall, whilst Helmut tried to enter Sketchley's office. On one occasion, Helmut had observed Sketchley fetch the office door key from a hook partially obscured from view just outside the kitchen door. He was fairly sure he could gain entrance to Sketchley's office, where hopefully the desk drawers would not be locked. They decided to try it on the coming Sunday, as time was short and they didn't know exactly when they would be required to go to London.

Stein knew they were fast approaching the critical stages when their lives hung in the balance. Deciding that he needed to try to tip things in their favour, he asked for a meeting with Sketchley in order to clear the air. The situation had escalated far beyond what he'd been told in Germany—mainly, he suspected, because of the unfortunate shooting outside the university. He had originally only agreed to prepare the tabun nerve agent since his wife had been kidnapped in Germany—but he was not too concerned for her as their relationship was on the rocks. From what Helmut had told him, James Brittain seemed to have some connection to the security services, since he had transported Helmut from Leeds to Bradford to avoid Sketchley's men picking him up. Stein was not too impressed by this, as Helmut had then been captured. Despite Brittain's amateurish actions, he had managed to locate Thompson laboratories, which resulted in his injury when he was shot at in their escape. It would seem that, in addition to the police, there was a low-key involvement of the security services to find them, but as Sketchley was sufficiently concerned to want Brittain out of the way, Stein was not too optimistic that he and Helmut were going to be found any time soon.

'What can I do for you, Dr Stein?' said Sketchley.

'I hope you are satisfied with tabun preparations? What happens after? I can help in future with other projects,' said Stein rather clumsily, but Sketchley knew exactly what he was getting at.

'Yes, you have been very ingenious. Colin was impressed by your expertise and cooperation in London, and I'm confident that it will work, providing we can get you into the Chamber to finalise the details at the right time. Is Mr Schultz of the same opinion as you?'

'I don't know. He good chemist but means nothing to me. I speak for me.' Stein was a pragmatist and survivor and thought there was nothing to lose by offering his services to Sketchley. He'd not mentioned it to Helmut since he couldn't entirely trust him to go along with it. In racing parlance, it's called backing your horse both ways. If one of them was going to die, he'd prefer it to be Helmut.

Sketchley was impressed with Stein; he was a man after his own heart. He was obviously intelligent, had weighed up the odds and wanted to come out on the winning side. Sketchley was tempted to take him further into his confidence but needed him to focus totally on making sure the tabun trial was successful. At this stage, Sketchley was prepared to offer him some crumbs of comfort to alleviate his fears, but he would reserve the option to keep the pressure on and dispose of him if things went badly.

'Look, Dr Stein, the world's your oyster if you pull this off, OK?'

Stein did not quite get the point of introducing shellfish into the conversation until it was explained to him. He visibly relaxed a little when he realised his survival was in his own hands.

Sketchley turned on the charm by going to a cabinet and pouring two glasses of Amontillado sherry and handing one to Stein. 'Let's drink to our success on the third of November.'

They clinked glasses and drank the sherry, Stein adopting the Teutonic custom of downing it in one, whilst Sketchley took his time over it.

While there was a momentary silence, Stein calculated they had just over two weeks to wait, so he asked, 'When do we go down to London?'

'Probably the day before so you can set things up for the following day. I'll confirm that in about a week's time. OK?'

Stein was pleased with himself. He'd got more details of when it was going to take place and an assurance that if it went well, he would benefit. He was tempted to ask if he could have it in writing but decided against it.

'So, Herr Schultz is likely to be unreliable. What do you think we should do with him?' Sketchley said unexpectedly, with a hint of menace in his voice.

'Helmut is nervous guy, wants quiet life, might be problem in future,' said Stein, equally coldly.

'OK, I'll talk to Colin about this later.' He indicated that the meeting was over.

Stein put his glass down on the desk, bowed in typical German fashion, and in doing so noticed the top drawer of Sketchley's desk was slightly open and therefore not locked.

***

A few days had passed since election day, and the plans we had for moving things forward had taken a setback. Henry had been summoned back to London by his DG, leave cancelled. As we'd discussed on election night, Khrushchev's removal from power had left worrying uncertainties for MI6 as to who was going to replace him. I voiced my opinion that MI5 wouldn't be too chuffed either, especially as the Labour party had gained power, which may put the service's survival in jeopardy, if and when Wilson found out about certain spies being let off the hook. Angela, true to form, took it in her stride and headed back to the Mill on the Monday following the election to try and pick up the pieces. She thought I ought to catch up with Inspector Broadley to see if there had been any further developments.

Amongst all the tension, I was amused by the news that the sprightly comedian, Ken Dodd, had popped up the day after the election result at Liverpool's Lime Street Station in full flow and congratulated Lloyd George on victory ('a wonderful woman'), and on being informed that Wilson was in No. 10, wittily pointed out, 'No, Miss Cilla Black's at No. 10 with "Old Man River".'

When I finally got hold of the inspector on the telephone, he was on his usual form, giving me the bad news first. 'Nowt 'appened. Bogus T and A reporter didn't turn up.'

'That doesn't surprise me,' I said.

'On Friday we 'ad a good look around surroundings to see if anybody had been watchin' institute. In t' cathedral grounds there were fresh footprints agin't wall overlookin' Church Bank. Guess what we found?' said the inspector tantalisingly.

'Well?'

'Rifle bullet, aside a bush. It were fresh!' he said triumphantly.

'So, somebody had been lying in wait for me on Thursday, is that what you're saying?'

'Aye, tha's reight.'

'I wouldn't mind having a look at the site. Can you show me?' I said.

'Get thissen down here double quick and we can go together now, OK?' he said obligingly.

We arrived within the hour at the cathedral's main gate, Inspector Broadley having taken the precaution of organising a couple of his men to meet us there in case of danger. I still hadn't picked up the gun Angela was supposed to be organising for me. We walked across the stone-flagged area past the cathedral's main door and headed towards the back of the building, approaching a path which led through another gateway and down to Church Bank. The inspector turned left off the path, brushing aside some bushes, making his way towards the perimeter wall. He then pointed out a set of footprints in the clay soil which showed at least two sets of heel prints close to a mature yew tree. The position gave an excellent elevated view of Church Bank and the wool institute's building. It was possible to see who came in and went out of the institute's entrance on the corner. A shiver ran down my spine as I remembered walking down Church Bank after parking my car in one of the side streets early on Thursday morning. I was mighty glad I'd left the institute by a back door.

The inspector showed me where they'd found the rifle bullet, close to the yew's trunk. I parted the branches to look across the road and immediately saw a neat pile of cigarette stubs arranged on the wall, which I pointed out to the inspector.

'Looks like Helmut was here; they probably used him to identify me.'

The inspector nodded and indicated that it had been well worth my coming if only to make such a good observation, but I should watch out for myself from now on.

***

Sunday lunchtime arrived and Helmut and Stein were let out of their walled garden prison to sample Mrs Whitaker's traditional Sunday lunch of roast lamb, roast potatoes, carrots, cabbage, Yorkshire pudding and gravy, followed by apple pie and custard. It was a step up on the food they'd endured at the laboratory facilities but not what they would have chosen at home. However, they were hungry, and nervous about the mission they were about to embark on—distracting Mrs Whitaker so Helmut could invade Sketchley's office.

Helmut was sceptical about the mint sauce he was expected to put on his meat. It smelt of vinegar and was a peculiar green colour. Nevertheless, the others, Dr Stein, Mrs Whitaker and Rickets, spooned it on enthusiastically, so he did the same. He survived the ordeal relatively unscathed and actually enjoyed the apple pie and custard, which was more to his liking.

The time had come for Stein to request a look round the hall. Mrs Whitaker seemed a little apprehensive, saying she had got the washing up to do, so Helmut offered to stand in for her, which she agreed to. Rickets was not interested in doing any menial tasks in the kitchen but said he'd be back shortly to open the gate and lock them back into the walled garden. Then he left the hall and went outside.

As soon as the others had left the room, Helmut started filling the sink with hot soapy water. He carefully placed the dirty crockery in the water and left it to soak whilst he retrieved Sketchley's office key from its hook just outside the kitchen door. Within seconds, he had opened the office door and silently closed it behind him. Heart pumping, he moved over to the desk. Just as Stein had told him, the top drawer was slightly ajar. When he slid it open their passports were clearly visible. He couldn't believe his luck; it was too easy. An added bonus was that on removing the two German passports, he found Stein's travellers' cheques underneath and quickly pocketed them.

Since everything had worked so quickly, he looked in the other drawers to see if he could find any more money, but there was none. The office was very tidy but there was very little of interest. A bottle of sherry stood on a silver-gilt tray, together with a few upturned glasses and a matching cut-glass decanter. Helmut took the stopper out. It smelt of alcohol, presumably whisky. He glanced through the window and caught sight of Rickets unlocking the entrance to the walled garden and turning to make his way back to the hall. Time to get out.

He carefully opened the office door, peering out to make sure the coast was clear, slipped out and quickly locked the door again, returning the key to its usual place as he went back into the kitchen to resume the washing up. For once, he felt a glimmer of hope, which had been in short supply for the past few weeks.

Stein, Mrs Whitaker and Rickets arrived back almost at once. Nobody noticed that he'd not got very far with the washing up, so he carried on slowly and methodically, placing each item in a rack to dry off. He was desperate for a cigarette but he wasn't allowed to smoke in the kitchen, so he started on the pans. His technique mustn't have been up to Mrs Whitaker's standards, so she politely but firmly elbowed him out of the way and took over, showing him how it should be done. Stein, anxious to know if Helmut had been successful, caught his eye, so Helmut nodded once and winked his left eye, which was on the blind side of both Rickets and Mrs Whitaker. Stein gave a little smile of acknowledgment as Rickets ushered them out of the kitchen towards their walled enclosure.

Both Helmut and Stein were in a good mood when they got back to the Bothy. They examined their passports and Stein inspected his travellers' cheques, which would have to be exchanged for money at some stage. They would have no chance at the estate, so it would have to be in London once they'd eluded their minders. Helmut suggested they should put the passports and money in a safe place until they were taken down to London. They decided to put them in one of the cupboards in the greenhouse, which housed some chemical fertilisers and insecticides, in case the Bothy was searched. They were satisfied with their day's work.

***

Sketchley was on his way back from his meeting with Jock at a Little Chef on the Great North Road, near Peterborough. Jock was keen on their full English breakfasts but Sketchley wasn't a fan of the American-style diner cafés, so he just opted for a standard coffee. They'd decided to avoid telephone calls in the short term in case the lines were being tapped. In an emergency they would use phone boxes. The main reason for the meeting was for Sketchley to pick up some cans of 35mm ciné film, which Jock had left in his car as they were bulky. It was known that *Pathé News* was going to shoot a movie of the State Opening of Parliament, in addition to the BBC television coverage. Stein and Colin had decided as a result of their visit to London that the best way of smuggling the tabun past security was by hiding the phials in film cans, figuring that the cans wouldn't be opened for fear of damaging unexposed film to light. Stein had previously arranged with Julian Thompson to get a range of spill-proof containers which would be suitable.

Sketchley was happy with the meeting. Jock had everything organised with his BBC engineer, Justin, who had been bribed to infiltrate Schultz and Stein into the Lords' Chamber early on the morning of the State Opening of Parliament, Tuesday 3rd November. The main ceremony started at five to eleven and finished at ten to twelve. Sketchley had worked out that there was a thirty-minute window of opportunity to release the tabun for maximum effect; he could pass on this information to Stein, who could then set his time clocks correctly. The other equipment had been sent ahead to the BBC contact, to be stored in one of the toilets in the Peers' Lobby. Jock had arranged for Schultz, Stein, Colin and probably Charlie to stay at his Mayfair residence the night before. Jock had joked that he wouldn't be there, in case they accidently spilt any tabun in the premises—he didn't want Sketchley to claim all the rewards.

As soon as Sketchley arrived back at the estate, he sought out Stein and Helmut. Rickets unlocked the gate into the walled garden, and he marched into the Bothy unannounced.

'There you are. This is what you asked for, isn't it? I don't know why you need so many of them though,' said Sketchley, depositing a bag of at least ten film cans on the table.

Stein picked one up to inspect it. It was about sixteen inches in diameter and contained unexposed film. The cans were sealed with an adhesive tape, which was easily removed.

'We can hide glass phials of tabun in box. Thirty-five-millimetre film is wide enough to fit,' said Stein.

Helmut went and fetched an empty sample bottle to demonstrate their idea.

'I see, very good. Will you take the film out? Can't you put them all in one can?' asked Sketchley, slowly beginning to understand.

Between them, Stein and Helmut demonstrated the principle of concealing the glass phials in the cans by cutting spaces in the film to make snug fits. The reason they wanted ten cans was to hide all the phials in one can and lessen the chance of them being discovered amongst the other cans if they were searched. Finally, Sketchley cottoned on. He hadn't appreciated how big 35mm was, since he only understood feet and inches. He declared it was a brilliant idea and left them to it.

**

I am sorry to say that there was no progress in finding large country estates where Stein and Helmut might be held; it wasn't for the lack of trying. A major irritation for me was that Tony Pickard was now back at the wool institute and hinting that I should be spending more time there. I was forced to contact Gerry Engel, who was back in London, to update him on the current situation. I told him I might have to transfer my attentions to London the closer it got to the 3rd of November. Henry had sensibly suggested that we should ask Gerry for help in trying to identify Stein and Helmut since, apart from me, he was the only other person who could easily do so. Gerry said he would certainly be around if needed. He also offered me the use of one of the vacant flats above the institute's offices, which were conveniently near Westminster in Carlton Gardens.

Henry told me he was currently tied up liaising with the CIA over the implications of Khrushchev's departure, so had not had any time to make the progress we needed. He had spoken to Nigel, who was similarly distracted by many worried MI5 officers who feared their house of cards was going to collapse under a Labour government. So no joy there.

The inspector's methodical investigations turned up more useful evidence. The break-in at 46 Plumpton Road was almost certainly related to the case. An address book was missing and a bowlegged man had asked directions for Plumpton Road at the nearby post office. The postmaster didn't remember the numbers, but the man was very distinctive and obviously not local.

One good thing was that Thompson Laboratories hadn't been revisited when I'd called in to see Steve Mitchell and his wife, who were valiantly trying to pick up the pieces of the business again. They were still staying with his wife's mother and would do so until the police told them it was safe to go home.

Angela and I were getting increasingly desperate with the lack of progress. We were pushing for more resources—at the least, extra security around the Palace of Westminster. It was of course out of the question that the State Opening of Parliament could be cancelled. It was obvious to me that this was going to go right down to the wire. Since things seemed to have gone very quiet recently, I considered transferring our efforts to London, but the thought of Nigel breathing down my neck didn't appeal.

Finally, it was agreed that if we were no further forward by the weekend, I would travel to London.

Chapter 20
'Remember Remember
the Third of November...'

Neither Angela nor I really enjoyed the meal we had together in her flat in Leeds the night before I travelled down to London. It could have easily doubled up as the Last Supper. We were still missing the final bits of the jigsaw to complete the picture.

Henry and Nigel were in London, where they had been working in the background, and I had agreed to meet them both on Saturday afternoon. Angela gave me a lift to Leeds station and fussed about whether I had everything I needed, especially the gun and ammunition she had procured for me. I had. Since it was on the way to the Houses of Parliament, I had arranged to call in at the wool institute's head office to see Gerry and leave a suitcase in the flat before meeting Henry and Nigel at the visitors' entrance of the Palace of Westminster.

From King's Cross Station I took the tube to St James Park on the Circle Line and walked from there to Carlton Gardens. I easily found the offices, which were in an upmarket area of London. *Typical of Gerry*, I thought. *He does everything with style.* I rang the outside bell, since the offices were closed for the weekend, and Gerry eventually appeared to let me in. We took the lift up to the fourth floor, where the flats were situated.

'It looks like we're going to need your services, Gerry. We haven't turned up any more information since I last to spoke to you. You and I are the only ones who have met Stein and Helmut, and we believe they'll be forced to assist in this potential attack.'

Gerry nodded, confirming he was keen to help. I got the impression that he was relishing the opportunity.

'I'm having a meeting with Henry and Nigel shortly and I'll fill you in when I get back, if that's OK?'

Gerry nodded again. I didn't realise he could be so quiet; the only thing he said was that he would give me a couple of keys, one for the office entrance and the other for the flat we were standing in. I thanked him profusely and made my way out to meet Henry and Nigel.

I found them in the visitors' entrance, talking to couple of suited men of military bearing. It turned out one was the commissioner of police for London and the other was a high-ranking special forces army officer. Nigel didn't introduce them by name, but indicated that I was assisting the security services and may be able to provide useful information which could enable their officers to identify the terrorists. Henry chipped in, telling them that I'd been instrumental in alerting the security forces guarding President Kennedy during his visit to Chatsworth House last year, thus foiling an assassination attack. This piece of information received minimal reaction, but at least they appeared to be listening to me. I was relieved Henry and Nigel had decided it was time to involve the police and army— we needed all the help we could get.

Since it was the first time I'd been to the Houses of Parliament, I suggested it would be useful if we could take a look at the Lords' Chamber and the area where the MPs would assemble to listen to the Queen's speech. On the way, with a nod of approval from Henry and Nigel, I outlined our thoughts as to what might be attempted. Both the commissioner and the army man were stunned at the implications and puzzled as to why we hadn't involved them sooner. Henry fielded this criticism by telling them that Special Branch and the Leeds police had been giving valuable assistance. He also pointed out that the masterminds behind the plot might be highly placed ultra-right-wing politicians or security people, so only a carefully selected number of people were privy to what we were about to tell them.

We'd reached the Lords' Lobby where the MPs were summoned to attend, and I immediately saw the potential for a dangerous mass-killing scenario.

'You're implying a modern-day gunpowder plot, aren't you?' said the commissioner.

'Yes, but this time it's the third of November—a couple of days earlier than the previous one,' I said seriously.

I decided to tell them what we knew and what to look out for when they were instructing their security officers.

'What we know for sure is that two German scientists have been kidnapped and threatened in order to make them prepare a nerve agent. We believe their intention is to introduce it into this chamber while the Queen delivers her speech. Having met them, Dr Gerry Engel of the wool institute and I can identify these scientists.'

Henry produced a photograph of the pesticide conference participants, with Stein and Helmut ringed for identification. I'd forgotten we'd had it taken, but apparently Gerry had remembered.

'It's possible that they might be forced into participating in the attack as the nerve agent is so toxic to handle safely,' I said.

'How would they use it?' asked the commissioner, who seemed a little slow at grasping the details.

'We don't know for sure. One possibility might be to throw it from the balcony, contained in glass flasks. On smashing, the fumes would be breathed in and kill the targets within minutes. Careful control of the balcony area seems to be a top priority,' I said. 'One of the main attackers who will almost certainly be involved is called Colin. He is military trained and has killed at least three people. I was lucky not to be the fourth,' I added.

Finally, after we had given them more details, especially of the laboratory where the nerve agent had probably been prepared, the commissioner said he would introduce me to his senior officer in charge of the police security arrangements. His name was Assistant Chief Constable Briggs, and he was outside.

I can't say I came away from the meeting totally satisfied that we'd left things in good hands. I didn't share my thoughts with Henry or Nigel, but agreed we'd meet up again on Monday to review things further.

***

The day arrived for Stein and Helmut to travel down to London. Early on Monday morning, they climbed into the white Ford Anglia as directed by Colin. They had packed the 35mm film cans in a cardboard box and carefully placed it in the boot. Stein muttered under his breath to Helmut that there being only three of them on the journey was to their advantage, although it was Colin who had the gun! It looked as if Rickets was out of favour, probably because his deformity made him stand out. They had gone over and over what they planned to do, and Stein had given Helmut a detailed description of the Lords' Chamber layout. They both realised that the odds of Colin eliminating them was high, once they'd served their purpose.

Colin couldn't be in two places at once, so their best chance of escape would be after they'd set everything up and were about to leave the building. They'd packed an iron bar in the equipment that had already been sent down to London, so at some time after leaving the building they would tackle Colin. Stein suggested Helmut should be the one to attack first, as he was the most strongly built, after which Stein would cosh him with the iron bar. If Helmut got shot in the attempt, so be it.

Colin drove directly into London this time and headed for what appeared to the Germans to be an affluent area. He drove to a cobbled street of converted mews cottages and parked outside one of the garage doors. The door was opened by one of Jock's men, who'd been waiting for them, and they drove inside. The Germans were ordered out and transferred the box of 35mm cans from the Anglia's boot onto an adjacent workbench. They realised the garage had been a stable in earlier times. They were fed, told to be ready to leave the house at six thirty the following morning, then locked up in a bedroom.

***

Monday morning arrived and I walked from the wool institute's flat past the Duke of York's Column and Horse Guards to the Houses of Parliament, where we'd arranged to meet. Henry was already there, so we compared notes while we waited for Nigel to arrive. Three quarters of an hour later, Nigel dashed up, out of breath and limping more than normal, apologising profusely for being late.

'Something's come up. We've got a lead on Colin Fraser, an ex-army captain who fits the bill,' said Nigel triumphantly. 'Apparently, the bank's traced the lab's cheque to him. The account has been closed now, but they've supplied an address. Angela just told me half an hour ago.'

'Great, but I bet he won't be at home. If it's a genuine address, he's probably in London now,' I said, excited, but annoyed with the bank for taking so long to respond.

'Angela's looking into Fraser's background history as we speak. I've told her we'll check in with her at regular intervals in case she finds anything useful,' said Nigel.

We'd purposely arranged to meet away from Henry's and Nigel's offices to keep a lid on things. In fact, Gerry had very kindly offered us the use of an office at the wool institute if we needed it. In light of the latest development, I suggested it would be sensible to take him up on it. It would be useful to involve Gerry since, as Henry had already flagged up, he was an extra pair of eyes who could identify Stein and Helmut. Henry, of course, knew Gerry, but Nigel didn't.

We made our way to the institute's offices and secured a vacant room, bringing Gerry up to speed with what we would like him to do. Then we phoned Angela to tell her of our whereabouts. It had occurred to me that it would be interesting to participate in the ceremonial search of the Parliament cellars to see if anything sinister, other than gunpowder, was hidden there. The special forces man had made a note to have some personnel kitted out with full protective equipment to go in first, just in case the nerve agent was being stored there. The commissioner had seemed a little too confident that their security measures would prevent anybody getting into the building who shouldn't be there. He wasn't against us being present to check if Stein and Helmut were around, but we had to keep out of sight as much as possible and report in first to ACC Briggs.

***

After Colin and the two Germans left to go to London, Sketchley was on edge until a phone call from Colin confirmed that they had arrived safely at Jock's townhouse. The two Germans had been no trouble, and they would leave early on Tuesday morning to set up the equipment in the Lords' Chamber. Colin had rung as instructed using a pre-arranged code in case the phone was being tapped.

Sketchley felt a little better and planned to have a double or triple scotch at eleven fifteen the following morning, to celebrate the beginning of a new era. He would get completely smashed when he watched on live television, in his office, the elimination of the rotten ruling classes. Ecstasy!

***

Helmut had slept fitfully, so he had no problem getting up early on Tuesday morning, and responded immediately when the bedroom door was unlocked and he was summoned down for breakfast. He judged that Dr Stein and Colin were in a similar mood, each preoccupied with his own thoughts. All he could manage for breakfast was a cup of coffee and a cigarette before Colin ushered them out of the house and into a different car from the one in which they had travelled to London. Jock's man drove them off for the Houses of Parliament. Helmut was designated by Stein to carry the box of 35mm film cans. He didn't mind as it gave him something to do with his hands. Colin had impressed on them both to keep quiet—if they were asked anything, he would do the talking.

They were dropped off close to the Parliament building where they were met by Justin, a fussy BBC engineer, who shook hands with Colin and Stein and provided each of them with a fawn-coloured coat, similar to a lab coat, with 'BBC' printed on the top pocket. They were led into the visitors' entrance where they were stopped and searched by a couple of armed policemen. It all seemed fairly friendly, as Justin was well known to the police, having been in and out of the building virtually every day recently. They were all thoroughly searched, before attention turned to the cardboard box of cans. These were carefully inspected, each one taken out and shaken gently. One policeman commented to the other that they all were of a similar weight and sealed, they need not open any as they contained unexposed film. So far so good. Helmut almost let out a sigh of relief, although it did occur to him that television cameras didn't use film, so why hadn't they been questioned about this? He stared at Stein to see what his reaction was, but he was as inscrutable as ever. His next thought was that as they'd all been searched, Colin must not have his gun with him! This made him more optimistic in thinking they might be able to escape.

Stein's detailed description of the Lords' Chamber was on the button; Helmut could visualise everything. As soon as they entered the Peers' Lobby, he identified the ladies' toilet where their main equipment was stored. They donned their BBC coats, and Justin said he would leave them to it. Colin indicated they should get cracking. Helmut was earmarked for transferring the nerve agent liquid into the dispensers, which he did out of sight in the ladies' toilets. Stein took on the responsibility of siting the equipment discreetly in suitable places and setting the time clocks to go off at ten past eleven.

Within twenty-five minutes, they'd completed everything and nodded to Colin, who'd been hovering around constantly. It had been ridiculously easy, as at that time of the morning, most of the security activity was outside with some movements in the galleries above, but that was all. Colin motioned that it was time to leave. They all took off their BBC coats, Helmut slipped the iron bar to Stein, who pocketed it without Colin noticing, and they all trooped along the corridors to depart the way they had entered.

***

There'd been no telephone calls Monday night or early Tuesday morning. Good news, you might think, as it would appear that nothing out of the ordinary had been found in the searches at the Houses of Parliament—but on the other hand Stein, Helmut and Colin Fraser were still at large.

In the institute's flat, I had set the alarm on the Teasmade to wake me at six thirty. It was not needed as I was already awake, but it served a useful purpose in providing me with a cuppa. I prepared to walk to the Houses of Parliament, making myself as presentable as possible and leaving the building at seven thirty. The walk did me good, settling my nerves a bit. I couldn't wait to go over the Lords' Chamber in minute detail just to make sure the police and army searches hadn't missed anything. It was still fairly dark as I approached the visitors' entrance we'd used yesterday, but a cordon of soldiers was already blocking the way, which was reassuring.

I said to a soldier, 'I've been told to ask for ACC Briggs. Can you let me through please?'

The soldier stood in front of me, blocking my way, and signalled to a uniformed officer closer to the entrance, for assistance.

'Now then, sir, no entrance without prior approval. It's my orders,' the officer said haughtily.

'I've got prior approval, yesterday. The commissioner told me to ask for ACC Briggs,' I repeated.

'They all say that. Move along please,' he said cockily.

I made to push past the soldier, dislodging the gun Angela had given me from its holster and causing it to fall with a clatter to the floor. The next thing I knew I was alongside it, face down with my hands cuffed behind my back. The butt of a soldier's rifle landed expertly on the back of my head, and I blacked out.

I awoke with a blinding headache in a locked cell, presumably in a police station. I heard the returning strains of Louis Armstrong croaking, '*What did I do to be so black and blue?*' in the background. I'd had a similar experience with overzealous police last year when I was accused of riding a stolen motorbike. This time might be more difficult since I'd been armed.

I looked at my watch. It was eight thirty, so there was still time if I could be released quickly. I banged loudly on the door until a voice from the other side said, 'Shut up. We're busy at the moment; we'll see to you later.'

This was no good. I was livid now and continued banging on the door in time with my throbbing headache.

'Get Wyatt Earp outa there and bring 'im to the interview room,' said an authoritative voice, which turned out to be the desk sergeant.

I gabbled my story out in a torrent of words obviously too fast for the sergeant to take down on his notepad.

'Hang on, you say you're James Brittain and attached to the security services, and you'd arranged to meet ACC Briggs to check over the Lords' Chamber for a potential attack. Is that right?'

I nodded.

'Well, there's a few things that don't add up, sir. ACC Briggs is not on duty, and we can't find any documents on you to confirm you're with the security services, and you're carrying a gun,' he said, trying to keep his temper which, like mine, I judged was close to boiling point.

I continued more slowly, telling him that I'd visited the building yesterday with MI5 and MI6 officers and discussed things with the commissioner of police and an army special forces officer. It had been agreed that I and Dr Gerry Engel would be present today to see if we could identify two German scientists who were possibly going to be involved, as we knew them by sight. It was vital that I should be allowed to return before the Queen arrived. I also pointed out sarcastically that it wouldn't be too difficult to check my story with the commissioner, as he would surely still remember meeting me yesterday.

The colour rapidly drained from the sergeant's face as he weighed up the prospects of dealing with the commissioner and the implications for him if what I was telling him was true. He quickly left the room, instructing a constable to keep an eye on me.

I was annoyed with the instructions I'd been given. Surely ACC Briggs must have known he wasn't going to be on duty this morning and should have told me who to ask for instead. Mind you, I had to admit that dropping my gun hadn't helped. I was probably lucky not to have been shot!

The time now was almost nine thirty—what the hell was he playing at? Still the sergeant didn't materialise and I was feeling decidedly ill, the percussive headache adding a new arrangement to Louis Armstrong's tune. Finally, the sergeant rushed back and apologetically confirmed my story. The commissioner had instructed him to provide an armed officer to accompany me back to the Lords' Chamber, where they would hang on to my gun for me.

We arrived back at the Palace of Westminster, where we were allowed through the crowds outside, this time entering the visitors' entrance without problem. Big Ben had started to chime eleven. Perhaps we still had time to get everybody out if things were not right.

Everything looked normal as we dashed along the corridors. As Big Ben finished chiming, the Peers' Corridor was blocked with MPs leading into the Peers' Lobby. It was quiet, though I could hear the Queen speaking and then my heart sank. I detected an increasingly strong smell of sweet almonds as we neared the lobby. We were too late. All I could think of was the dead birds round the back of the laboratory. Panic set in, and I blacked out!

***

The next thing I became aware of was the strong smell of smelling salts, which jolted me awake. There was no smell of sweet almonds, just ammonia. Had I been imagining things and having a nightmare? I wasn't sure what was real and what wasn't. I appeared to be in a small room, where the armed policeman who had accompanied me had stuck the pungent bottle under my nose and now seemed to be relieved that I'd come round.

A familiar voice behind said, 'Glad you're back with us now, James. You had us worried for a while.' It was Gerry, who then came into view.

'Where am I?' I spluttered, still trying to piece things together.

'You're in a room close to the Central Lobby. They thought you looked a bit untidy on the floor, getting under all the MPs' feet,' said Gerry smoothly.

'What time is it?' I said, still not quite with it.

'It's two thirty,' answered the policeman.

'I think we ought to get you back to the institute before we're thrown out,' said Gerry good-naturedly.

A couple of aspirins were given to me, and the headache lessened. Louis Armstrong still hadn't completely gone away—surely he must get sick of singing the same thing over and over again?

In a state of semi-confusion, I was taken the short distance from the Houses of Parliament to the institute by police car. There we got polite nods from the reception staff and went into a large meeting room, filled with the glorious aroma of freshly made coffee. I turned my attention to four men who were talking and drinking coffee. Facing me were Henry and Nigel. The other two turned round, smiling—Helmut and Dr Stein!

Gerry quickly gave me the good news that the Queen's speech had gone off without a hitch, apart from me collapsing among the MPs. Henry took up the story by announcing that we had been on the right track all along but had vastly underestimated the ingenuity and integrity of Helmut and Stein. They had successfully synthesised the tabun nerve agent and demonstrated its effectiveness on sheep to Lord Sketchley at some estate in Yorkshire, but had substituted the lethally toxic tabun/chlorobenzene mixture with the chlorobenzene solvent, which had just the same sweet almond smell. Only they knew this, so they had hoodwinked Colin Fraser into believing that everything had been set up properly. By chance, on the way out, Helmut, Stein and Colin had run into Gerry near the visitor's entrance, and Colin had bolted rather than fight with armed soldiers as well as Helmut and Stein. They had always planned to try to contact Gerry if they managed to escape Colin's clutches, since Stein had remembered the institute's Carlton Gardens address.

I was mightily relieved and had to admit I had misjudged Stein; I'd only met him briefly before he was kidnapped, so my first impressions were obviously wrong. Henry and Nigel were decidedly on a high now, and Gerry, judging the occasion to merit something stronger than coffee to celebrate with, produced a Glenmorangie single malt whisky to the delight of everybody. As Gerry poured generous tots for each of us, I got the chance to compare side by side the sartorial elegance of Nigel with Gerry. I was right—

Gerry won hands down. I was tempted to draw Nigel's attention to the merits of my working for a very smart wool institute but decided to save it for another time.

I was struck by the elegant symmetry of the way things had turned out, being introduced at the start to Gerry in the presence of Helmut and Stein and finishing in the same manner.

Obviously, there were still a lot of unanswered questions that needed following up, but that was for a future occasion, so we all enjoyed the moment. The combination of aspirin, whisky and adrenaline had put the headache on hold.

***

A week later, Henry, Nigel, Angela, Helmut, Stein and I were together in Inspector Broadley's meeting room in Leeds. There'd been some further developments. Colin Fraser still hadn't been found, but Sketchley was discovered dead in his office by his housekeeper, suspected of committing suicide while watching television. Broadley had visited the estate twice, once with Stein to confirm that this was where they'd been kept prisoner and once to identify Sketchley. According to Broadley, Sketchley's body was not a pretty sight—he could have chosen an easier method of topping himself. The exact cause of death was still being investigated. He had been drinking whisky, but the decanter was empty. Broadley said when he first went to examine the body, he'd thought he could detect a faint smell of sweet almonds, but not when he went with Stein. I asked Stein and Helmut bluntly— what they had done with the tabun nerve agent they didn't take to London? Stein was quick to answer, saying it was poured into the ground in the estate's walled garden. Helmut said nothing.

Back at the Mill, Nigel said he was drawing a line under further investigations, so my involvement was no longer needed. He was gracious, for once, in acknowledging my contribution in identifying the laboratory and wished me all success in my new career with the institute. It looked as if Helmut would also retain his position there, and Stein was lining himself up for a future contract with Gerry.

Angela, true to form, couldn't resist a dig at me for getting injured again, until I reminded her that but for the gun she'd insisted I carry, I wouldn't have been arrested. I tempered my remark to her by mentioning that I would start living in my new rented home now, and needed some expert advice on home improvements. Henry focused our attention by pointing out that we'd probably only discovered the tip of the iceberg and Sketchley's ultra-right-wing co-conspirators were still at large, and we should be ever vigilant for the future.

The one thing we all agreed upon was that we knew exactly what was wrong with the Right Club!

AUTHOR PROFILE

Keith is a born and bred Bradfordian and still lives there willingly. A degree in chemistry from Leeds University opened up a career in wool research at the IWS Technical Centre in Ilkley, where he obtained a PhD. Due to the decline of wool markets in the '80s he started working as a private health and safety consultant, trading as Envirocare, assisting companies with the new COSHH regulations. The endeavour was successful and Envirocare Technical Consultancy Ltd was formed in 1994, based in Bradford.

Since retiring, Keith started ticking off items from his bucket list:

- Investigating putting a bit of science into art on the theme of 'UV Light as an Alternative 3rd Dimension of Art?' Large collage portrait impressions of famous Bradfordians were created entirely from British stamps.
- *The Sixty-Three Steppes*, his first novel, was inspired by John Buchan's *The Thirty-Nine Steps*. A sequel, *From Czechoslovakia with Love*, was published in 2016.

Keith is also delighted to be participating with a colleague as EDPAL in The New Longitude Prize working with Lincoln University on a project investigating transferring wool science into the field of microbiology. The project was recognised by gaining a prestigious international Discovery Award to fund further research.

What's Wrong with the Right Club? is Keith's latest book in the James Brittain trilogy. It bridges the gap between the other two, showing James's introduction into becoming an undercover agent.

Website: www.stuckonstamps.co.uk
Twitter: @edmondson_g

***

A big thank you for purchasing this book. It means a lot that you chose this book specifically from such a wide range on offer. I do hope you enjoyed it.

Publisher Information

Rowanvale Books provides publishing services to independent authors, writers and poets all over the globe. We deliver a personal, honest and efficient service that allows authors to see their work published, while remaining in control of the process and retaining their creativity. By making publishing services available to authors in a cost-effective and ethical way, we at Rowanvale Books hope to ensure that the local, national and international community benefits from a steady stream of good quality literature.

For more information about us, our authors or our publications, please get in touch.

www.rowanvalebooks.com
info@rowanvalebooks.com

CPSIA information can be obtained
at www.ICGtesting.com
Printed in the USA
BVHW030839280521
608372BV00004B/18